Usborne
365 Illustrated Stories & Rhymes

Here is a wonderful collection of stories and rhymes from all over the world. Some are traditional and centuries old, and some were written just last week. What may surprise you is how many folk tales are so similar, even though they were told in very different times and places.

There is an index at the back listing the stories and poems, but you may simply want to read wherever the book falls open...

∾ 1 ∽
Little Red Riding Hood

There was once a girl who lived with her mother beside a forest. Everyone called her Little Red Riding Hood because of her hooded scarlet cloak.

"Will you take this cake to your grandma?" her mother asked one day. "Be sure to go straight there – and don't leave the forest path!"

Little Red Riding Hood set off, swinging her basket. Despite her mother's warning, she couldn't resist stopping to pick some flowers.

As she wandered from the path, a wolf leaped out from behind a tree. "Where are you off to, little girl?" he snarled.

"I'm-I'm taking some food to my grandma," replied Little Red Riding Hood, trembling. "She lives on the other side of the river, by the oak tree."

"Does she now?" said the wolf, his yellow teeth showing in an evil grin. He ran off, and was soon knocking at the door of the grandmother's cottage.

"Who is it?" called the old lady.

"It's me, your granddaughter," squeaked the wolf, trying to sound like a little girl.

Little Red Riding Hood's grandmother unlocked the door. The wolf leaped in, grabbed the frail old lady and swallowed her in one gulp. Then he put on one of her lacy night caps and jumped into bed, hiding under the covers.

A few minutes later, Little Red Riding Hood arrived at the cottage and knocked, *rat a tat tat*!

"Who is it?" called the wolf, trying to sound like an old lady.

"It's me, your granddaughter."

"Come in, my dear," cried the wolf.

Little Red Riding Hood ran to her grandmother's bedside. But somehow, she didn't look her usual self.

"My, Grandma," said Little Red Riding Hood, "what big eyes you have."

"All the better to see you with, my dear," croaked the wolf.

Little Red Riding
Hood looked closer. "My,
Grandma," she said, "what
big ears you have."

"All the better to hear you
with," said the wolf.

Little Red Riding Hood looked closer still. "My
Grandma," she said, "what big teeth you have."

"All the better to gobble you up," growled the
wolf, bounding from the bed.

"Help!" screamed Little Red Riding Hood, as the
slavering wolf swallowed her whole.

A passing woodcutter heard the commotion and
rushed in. There stood the wolf, licking his lips, a
satisfied smirk on his face. The woodcutter guessed
at once what had happened. Quickly, he slit open
the wolf's belly and Little Red Riding Hood and her
grandmother tumbled out with sighs of relief.

From that day on, Little Red Riding Hood never
stepped off the forest path... and, whenever it was
cold, the woodcutter wore a fine, wolfskin coat.

∽ 2 ∾

The Jumblies

They went to sea in a Sieve, they did,
In a Sieve they went to sea:
In spite of all their friends could say,
On a winter's morn, on a stormy day,
In a Sieve they went to sea!
And when the Sieve turned round and round,
And every one cried, "You'll all be drowned!"
They called aloud, "Our Sieve ain't big,
But we don't care a button! We don't care a fig!
In a Sieve we'll go to sea!"
Far and few, far and few,
Are the lands where the Jumblies live;
Their heads are green, and their hands are blue,
And they went to sea in a Sieve.

They sailed away in a Sieve, they did,
In a Sieve they sailed so fast,
With only a beautiful pea-green veil
Tied with a riband by way of a sail,
To a small tobacco-pipe mast;
And everyone said, who saw them go,
"O won't they be soon upset, you know!
For the sky is dark, and the voyage is long,
And happen what may, it's extremely wrong
In a Sieve to sail so fast!"
Far and few, far and few,
Are the lands where the Jumblies live;
Their heads are green, and their hands are blue,
And they went to sea in a Sieve.

The water it soon came in, it did,
The water it soon came in;
So to keep them dry, they wrapped their feet
In a pinky paper all folded neat,

And they fastened it down with a pin.
And they passed the night in a crockery-jar,
And each of them said, "How wise we are!
Though the sky be dark, and the voyage be long,
Yet we never can think we were rash or wrong,
While round in our Sieve we spin!"
Far and few, far and few,
Are the lands where the Jumblies live;
Their heads are green, their hands are blue,
And they went to sea in a Sieve.

&

And all night long they sailed away;
And when the sun went down,
They whistled and warbled a moony song
To the echoing sound of a coppery gong,
In the shade of the mountains brown.
"O Timballo! How happy we are,
When we live in a Sieve and a crockery-jar.
And all night long in the moonlight pale,
We sail away with a pea-green sail,

In the shade of the mountains brown!"
Far and few, far and few,
Are the lands where the Jumblies live;
Their heads are green, and their hands are blue
And they went to sea in a Sieve.

෮

They sailed to the Western Sea, they did,
To a land all covered with trees,
And they bought an Owl, and a useful Cart,
And a pound of Rice, and a Cranberry Tart,
And a hive of silvery Bees.
And they bought a Pig, and some green Jackdaws,
And a lovely Monkey with lollipop paws,
And forty bottles of Ring-Bo-Ree,
And no end of Stilton Cheese.

Far and few, far and few,
Are the lands where the Jumblies live;
Their heads are green, and their hands are blue,
And they went to sea in a Sieve.

∾

And in twenty years they all came back,
In twenty years or more,
And everyone said, "How tall they've grown!
For they've been to the Lakes, and the Terrible Zone,
And the hills of the Chankly Bore."
And they drank their health, and gave them a feast
Of dumplings made of beautiful yeast;
And everyone said, "If we only live,
We too will go to sea in a Sieve –
To the hills of the Chankly Bore!"
Far and few, far and few,
Are the lands where the Jumblies live;
Their heads are green, and their hands are blue,
And they went to sea in a Sieve.

Edward Lear

The Ant &
the Grasshopper

In warm sunshine, the ant was working hard, gathering food. As she bustled to and fro, she passed a grasshopper, who was lying in the shade, singing a merry tune.

"Relax!" the grasshopper said. "Why the panic? There's plenty to eat."

"Sorry, no time to chat. I must get this back to my nest before winter," panted the ant. And off she went, heaving her huge load.

The grasshopper shrugged. "Winter is ages away. Some people just don't know how to have fun!" he remarked and went back to his singing.

Gradually, summer faded. The leaves drifted down

from the trees and cold winds began to blow. Soon, winter arrived, smothering the ground with snow.

The grasshopper no longer felt like singing. He huddled under a dried leaf, hugging himself and shivering. Just then, the ant strolled past.

"What's the matter?" she asked, seeing his miserable face.

"I'm so hungry," the grasshopper moaned. "I should have been like you, spending the summer getting ready for winter. I expect your nest is full of food," he added wistfully.

"It is," said the ant. She smiled. "Would you like to come home with me? I have enough for two."

∾ 4 ∾

Eat, Coat, Eat!

Nasreddin Hodja had been invited to a grand banquet. Not liking to show off, he wore his normal clothes. Nobody came to talk to him, the servants ignored him and the host didn't even seem to know he was there. So the Hodja walked out, went home, changed into his finest coat and returned to the banquet.

"Good evening, sir," said the servant at the door, bowing low.

"My dear fellow, what a pleasure to see you," said a well-dressed guest.

"So glad you could make it," called the host. "You must try the lobster soup. It's delicious."

The Hodja took his seat at the banquet table and a servant instantly served him some soup. Then the

Tales of Nasreddin Hodja are popular across the Middle East. Hodja is a title meaning teacher or wise man.

Hodja dipped his coat sleeve into the bowl and commanded: "Eat, Coat, eat!"

The other guests were baffled.

"What game is this?" asked the host, with a frown.

"No game at all," the Hodja replied. "It is simply that when I came to the banquet without my coat, nobody wanted to know me. Now I'm wearing my coat, I'm suddenly very popular. So it must be my coat, not me, who is welcome at this banquet. Eat, Coat, eat!"

∾ 5 ∾

There was an Old Man of Apulia,
Whose conduct was very peculiar;
He fed twenty sons
Upon nothing but buns,
That whimsical Man of Apulia.

Edward Lear

❦ 6 ❦

Nail Soup

Tom Patch was a poor man who spent his days searching the countryside for work. One evening, he came to a cottage.

"Do you have a bed for the night?" he asked the old woman who answered the door.

"As long as you pay for it," snapped the woman.

"I don't have any money," said Tom. "But I could make you some soup. All I need is this magic nail."

"Magic nail?" said the woman in disbelief.

"Yes," said Tom. "Just pop it in a pot of boiling water and it will make the most scrumptious soup you ever tasted."

The woman didn't really believe Tom's story, but she decided to give it a try. She filled a pot with water and placed it on the stove.

Tom dropped in his nail.

"A little seasoning will help the taste," said Tom, as the water bubbled away.

The old woman wasn't convinced, but she sprinkled salt and pepper into the pot all the same.

"Mmm, that's better," said Tom. "Pity you don't have an onion. It goes really well with the nail."

"But I do have one," said the old woman. She peeled it, sliced it and dropped it into the pot.

"Fantastic," said Tom. "This is going to be the best soup yet. The only thing that could make it better would be potatoes."

"Wait a moment," said the old woman. She rummaged in a sack and pulled out a handful of fresh new potatoes. Moments later, they were scrubbed and in the pot too.

"Perfect," said Tom. "Although I don't suppose you have any meat...?"

By now, the soup was smelling mouthwatering. The old woman's stomach gurgled with hunger. She ran to her pantry, grabbed a plate of meat, chopped it into pieces and flung them into the pot.

Soon the soup was ready. The old woman ladled it into two big bowls and the pair slurped happily.

"That was wonderful," sighed the old woman as she swallowed her last mouthful. "For such a treat, you must take my bed tonight. I'll sleep in the living room."

So Tom had a full tummy and a night in a comfy bed – all thanks to his magic nail.

∾ 7 ∾
For Want of a Nail

For want of a nail the shoe was lost,
For want of a shoe the horse was lost,
For want of a horse the rider was lost,
For want of a rider the battle was lost,
For want of a battle the kingdom was lost,
And all for the want of a horseshoe nail.

∾ 8 ∾

Brer Rabbit Hears a Noise in the Woods

Brer Rabbit was hoppity-hopping through the woods one morning when he heard a sawing noise, followed by a loud CRASH. He leaped into the air in surprise, and raced away at top speed.

On his way out of the woods, he passed Brer Raccoon who asked, "What's the hurry, Brer Rabbit?"

"I heard a big noise in the woods," Brer Rabbit called over his shoulder.

"A big noise in the woods?" Brer Raccoon thought to himself. "I'm not sticking around to find out what it is." And he scampered away after Brer Rabbit.

As he sped over the meadow, he passed Brer Fox, who asked, "What's the hurry, Brer Raccoon?"

"There was a huge noise in the woods!" Brer

Raccoon shouted, as he ran.

"I hope whatever made it isn't coming this way," thought Brer Fox, and he chased after Brer Raccoon.

Up the hill he passed Brer Wolf, who asked, "What's the hurry, Brer Fox?"

"Something's making a huge noise in the woods, and it's coming after us!" panted Brer Fox, not slowing for a second.

"I don't want to be the first to meet it," thought Brer Wolf, and he ran after Brer Fox.

On the way down the hill he passed Brer Bear, who asked, "What's the hurry, Brer Wolf?"

"A massive monster has broken out of the woods and is coming to get us!" Brer Wolf called back.

Brer Bear took off as fast as he could behind the wolf, the fox and the raccoon.

They were all crossing the stream, when they passed Brer Turtle, who asked, "What's the hurry?"

"A monster's coming to get us!" said Brer Bear.

"Yes, something is coming out of the woods," said Brer Wolf.

"Well, there was a huge noise in the woods, anyway," said Brer Fox.

"Yes there was a noise," said Brer Raccoon.

"A noise?" asked Brer Turtle. "What kind of a noise?"

"I don't know," said Brer Bear. "Brer Wolf told me." They all looked at Brer Wolf.

"I don't know," said Brer Wolf. "Brer Fox told me." They all looked at Brer Fox.

"I don't know," said Brer Fox, "Brer Raccoon told me." They all looked at Brer Raccoon.

"Well, I don't know," said Brer Raccoon. "Brer Rabbit told me." They all looked, but Brer Rabbit wasn't there.

"I suggest you go and see Brer Rabbit," chuckled

Brer Turtle. "Maybe he can tell you what it was."

So they trooped off to see Brer Rabbit. To their surprise, he was lying outside his house in the grass, as relaxed as can be.

"What's the big idea?" said Brer Bear. "Have you been playing tricks again?"

"It's the first time I've seen you today, Brer Bear," said Brer Rabbit.

"You've had us all running away from monsters," said Brer Wolf.

"I've done nothing of the kind," said Brer Rabbit.

"But you told me there was a big noise in the woods!" said Brer Raccoon.

Brer Rabbit nodded. "There was indeed and if you'd asked me then what it was, I'd have told you. It was a woodcutter cutting down a tree. I never said it was anything to worry about, did I?"

There was nothing the animals could say to that. One by one they slunk off home, feeling rather foolish, and Brer Rabbit watched them go with an amused twinkle in his eye.

Old King Cole

Old King Cole was a merry old soul,
And a merry old soul was he.
He called for his pipe,
And he called for his bowl,
And he called for his fiddlers three.

Every fiddler had a fine fiddle,
And a very fine fiddle had he.
Oh, there's none so rare,
As can compare,
With King Cole and his fiddlers three.

A tutor who tooted a flute
Tried to tutor two tooters to toot.
Said the two to their tutor,
"Is it harder to toot
Or to tutor two tooters to toot?"

∾ 11 ∾
Rags & Riches

Chaim Yankl never had any money. He lived with his hungry family in a house full of holes that let in the wind and the rain. "Enough!" announced Chaim Yankl, at last. "I am going out into the world and I'm going to make my fortune."

So he strode away one spring day, with his fiddle tucked under his arm. He journeyed from town to town, playing his fiddle wherever he went, performing teasing, haunting, jaunty, dancing, unforgettable tunes. Crowds gathered. They showered him with coins, until Chaim Yankl had so many he exchanged them for paper money and sewed it into the lining of his old patchwork coat.

The years passed... Chaim Yankl didn't notice how fast, he was so busy building his fortune, until, with a jolt, he realized twenty years had gone by and it was high time he went home.

Meanwhile, his wife had been scrubbing floors,

painting walls and washing clothes to make money, and as soon as the children were old enough, they worked too. No one recognized the well-dressed man in the fur-trimmed coat who came striding down their street one afternoon.

Chaim Yankl knocked on the door of his house. His daughter answered – long-legged and full-grown. "Where is your father?" asked Chaim Yankl.

"I have no father," his daughter replied. "He left twenty years ago, with only his fiddle and his old patchwork coat."

Chaim Yankl opened his arms wide. "I am your father come home!" he said, embracing his daughter. He embraced all his children. Then he went off to the synagogue to give thanks for his blessings.

Soon after that, his wife came home. "Have you heard the news?" cried his children. "Father is back and he is rich!"

As they rejoiced, there came a knock at the door. An old beggarman stood outside. "Have you anything for the poor?" he asked.

Chaim Yankl's wife looked around their spare, empty house. All she could see was her husband's patchwork coat, hanging on a peg on the wall. "Take this," she said. "I hope it will help."

When Chaim Yankl returned, his family was overjoyed. "Now," he said. "Where is my old patchwork coat? Let me show you my wealth!"

"Oh, I gave that to a beggarman," said his wife.

Chaim Yankl fainted clean away. When he came to, he picked up his fiddle, walked out into the street and sang: *Fiddle-dee-dee, life is a riddle! I am a fool, a fool with a fiddle!*

But then, across the street, he caught sight of his patchwork coat. He ran after the beggarman. "Would you like to change coats with me?" he suggested.

The beggarman looked at the rich fur trim as if he couldn't believe his luck. Chaim Yankl went home, unpicked the lining of his old coat and showed his family their fortune. And so they lived for the rest of their days in happiness and wealth.

Spring

Sound the flute
Now 'tis mute;
Birds delight,
Day and night –
Nightingale,
In the dale,
Lark in sky –
Merrily,
Merrily, merrily to welcome in the year.

Little boy,
Full of joy;
Little girl,
Sweet and small;
Cock does crow,
So do you;
Merry voice,
Infant noise;
Merrily, merrily to welcome in the year.

Little lamb,

Here I am;

Come and lick

My white neck;

Let me pull

Your soft wool;

Let me kiss

Your soft face;

Merrily, merrily we welcome in the year.

William Blake

~ 13 ~
Robin Hood &
Little John

All was quiet in Robin Hood's hideout – too quiet for Robin's liking.

"I'm bored," he told his gang of outlaws. "I'm going in search of adventure."

"Don't forget your horn," called his friend Will. "Three blasts and we'll come running."

Robin set off through the thick undergrowth of Sherwood Forest. He knew every twist and turn, every tree stump and thicket. He knew where the river ran and the best place to cross it. Only today when he reached the river there stood a large man blocking his way.

"Let me pass," Robin called.

"I shall do no such thing," came the reply.

"Then I'll make you move," said Robin, raising his bow and arrow.

Robin Hood was a legendary English outlaw – a wanted criminal who lived in Sherwood Forest and stole from the rich to give to the poor.

"Coward!" cried the man. "Threatening me with a bow and arrow when I have only a wooden staff to protect myself!"

Now Robin Hood was many things, but he most definitely wasn't a coward. He lay down his bow, darted into the bushes and came out with a hefty wooden stick.

"Now we are evenly matched," he cried, leaping onto the narrow bridge. "Take that!"

A long, hard fight ensued, but for every blow that Robin landed on the stranger, he received a harder one back.

Finally, the stranger struck Robin low and hard and toppled him into the river below.

"Where have you gone?" teased the stranger. "I was just warming up..."

Robin heaved himself dripping wet onto the bank. "You won a fair fight," he spluttered. "I accept defeat." Then he put his horn to his lips and gave three sharp blasts.

Robin's men rushed to the scene.

"What's the matter?"

"You're all wet!"

"Did he hurt you? We'll duck him in the river."

Robin laughed. "This man is far too strong to be our enemy. Tell us your name, stranger."

"John Little," replied the large man.

"Well this is your forest as well as ours," said Robin. "Why don't you join our merry band and we can protect it together? We'll call you... Little John."

Little John chuckled and gave Robin a bone-crunching handshake. "I'd be delighted," he said.

The Emperor's Moustache

Emperor Akbar strode into the courtroom, where his nine advisors were waiting. "I have a question for you all," he announced. "Suppose someone pulled the emperor's moustache... What should be their punishment?"

Eager to impress him, his advisors began to call out suggestions.

"A hundred lashes of the whip!"

"He should be trampled by elephants!"

"Burn off his toes!"

But the emperor shook his head. He turned to his most trusted advisor, who had not yet said a word. "Birbal, what do you think?" he asked.

"Give him sweets, sir," came Birbal's reply.

The other advisors looked shocked.

Akbar was a real emperor who lived in 16th century India, and Birbal was one of his nine advisors, prized for his wisdom and wit. Akbar and Birbal stories are still very popular throughout India.

"Why do you say that?" demanded the emperor.

"Because the only person who would dare pull your moustache, sir, is your little grandson," Birbal replied. "So it would seem cruel to do otherwise."

The emperor smiled broadly. "Exactly, Birbal! Well done."

∽ 15 ∾

How Many Miles to Babylon?

How many miles to Babylon?
Three score miles and ten.
Can I get there by candlelight?
Yes, and back again.
If your heels are nimble and light,
You may get there by candlelight.

∽ 16 ∾
Hans the Hedgehog

Once, there lived a wealthy merchant, who was desperate to have a child. "Even a hedgehog would be better than nothing," he sighed one day.

When he returned home, he found his wife had given birth to baby who was a hedgehog from the waist up. They called him Hans and gave him some straw for a bed but they couldn't help feeling disappointed.

Hans grew older and wiser, but he was still half-hedgehog and his parents were embarrassed to have him around the house. "Give me some bagpipes and a rooster and I will leave you in peace," he promised.

Hans' parents eagerly agreed and the next day he rode his rooster deep into the forest. He made himself a shelter, foraged for food and was happy enough.

Then, one afternoon, a king got

lost in the forest. He followed the sound of bagpipes and found Hans and his rooster perched in a tree. "Will you show me the way to my palace?" he pleaded.

"Certainly," replied Hans, "if you reward me with the first thing we see when we get there."

"Of course," promised the king, though he didn't really mean it.

When they arrived at the palace gates, the king's daughter rushed out to greet them. The king quickly ushered her inside, saying nothing about his promise, and Hans went back into the forest.

Time went by and another king got lost in the forest. He too followed the sound of bagpipes and promised Hans the first thing he saw if he would show the king back to his castle. When they arrived, the second king's daughter rushed out to greet him.

The king looked downcast and immediately told his daughter of the promise he'd made. But when he turned around, the hedgehog-man was nowhere to be seen. Hans had scampered back to the forest.

Eventually, Hans felt ready to marry. He went to

the first king to claim his daughter. The king refused, so Hans pricked him with his spikes, before heading off to see the second king.

The second king's daughter saw him striding to the castle from her window.

"We must keep your promise," she told her father, and she went to the gates to meet the strange hedgehog-man.

They were married the very next day. That evening, Hans asked the servants to make a big fire. When it was time for bed, he took off his hedgehog skin, as easily as if it were a jacket. Then he gave it to a servant to burn in the fire. His new wife gasped as he transformed into a handsome young man.

"Now I'm Hans the Husband!" he announced and the couple were happy as can be.

∾ 17 ∾

The Bird Who Could Only Smile

Bushbird was feeling lonely. He called out to the leaping monkeys, the chattering toucans and the slithering snakes, but they all passed him by with a smile and a wave. "Don't you look happy today!" they said. For Bushbird had a problem... His beak curved up in an upturned line, so no matter how hard he tried to frown, he could only ever smile.

"I'm not happy. I'm lonely," he cried. But no one took any notice. So instead Bushbird sat on his branch and covered his head with his wing.

At last, a little howler monkey stopped to look at the sooty bundle of feathers, bunched down at the end of a branch. "Is that you, Bushbird?" he asked.

Under his wing, Bushbird nodded.

"Are you alright?" asked the howler monkey.

"No," croaked Bushbird. "I'm sad."

"Come quick!" howled the monkey, as loud as he

could. "Bushbird is feeling sad."

There was a flurry of wings, a pounding of feet, as all the animals came rushing.

"Poor Bushbird. Come out from under your wing. We'll comfort you," they said.

So Bushbird peeked out from his feathers to show his beaming, curving smile.

"You tricked us!" cried the animals.

"No..." called Bushbird. "Come back..."

But everyone had gone. As night fell, and the moon sank down behind the clouds, Bushbird began to sing. He sang of lonely days and long dark nights and the sadness behind his smile.

The animals woke and heard his haunting song. Babies crept closer to their mothers, and mothers hugged them closer still. "Who could be singing this sad, sad song?" they wondered.

And they followed the sound to the bamboo bush where the bushbird sang in the dark. But as they gazed up at him, the clouds began to part.

A glimmer of moonlight lit up the bushbird's smile.

"He's tricked us again!" cried the animals. "You're not sad at all. Get away! Get away! Get away!"

So Bushbird flew all through that night. When morning broke, he had reached the most secret part of the forest. The only sounds came from a strange creature, rooting around on the ground. It had funny pointed feet and a stubby little tail. But strangest of all was its droopy snout, that dangled down past its chin. It had the saddest face Bushbird had ever seen.

"Who are you?" asked Bushbird.

"I'm a tapir," the creature replied.

"You look just how I feel," remarked Bushbird.

"This is how tapirs always look, no matter how happy we feel. I think you need to look in a creature's eyes, to see how he feels inside."

From that day on, the bushbird and the tapir were the best of friends. Each knew exactly how the other felt... even though one always wore a frown, and the other a glorious, curling smile.

∞ 18 ∞

Caterpillar

Brown and furry
Caterpillar in a hurry,
Take your walk
To the shady leaf, or stalk,
Or what not,
Which may be the chosen spot.
No toad spy you,
Hovering bird of prey pass by you;
Spin and die,
To live again a butterfly.

Christina Rossetti

∞ 19 ∞

March winds and April showers
Bring forth May flowers.

∾ 20 ∾

The Runaway Pancake

There was once an old woman who made a hot buttery pancake and left it by the window to cool. But there must have been some magic in the mix because, when she turned her back, the pancake leaped up and rolled away.

"Come back, little pancake," called the woman. "I want to eat you!" But the pancake kept on rolling, and as it rolled, it sang:

"I'm the runaway pancake, fast and free,

I'm so fast, you can't catch me!"

It rolled and rolled, right into the forest – where a bright-eyed rabbit saw it. "Come here, little pancake," squeaked the rabbit. "I want to eat you."

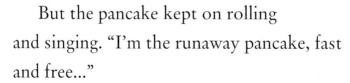

But the pancake kept on rolling and singing. "I'm the runaway pancake, fast and free..."

A grizzled old wolf saw the pancake. "Come here, little pancake," it growled. "I want to eat you."

The pancake rolled swiftly past. "I'm so fast, you can't catch me!"

It was rolling so fast, it almost didn't see the hungry fox sitting by the path.

"Hello, little pancake," said the fox, with a crafty smile. "What a lovely song that was. Would you sing it again for me?"

The pancake stopped, puffed up with pride and began. "I'm the runaway..."

"No, no," interrupted the fox. "I can't hear you. Come closer."

So the pancake rolled closer. "I'm the..."

"No, I still can't hear," said the fox. "A little closer, please."

The pancake rolled right up to the fox's sharp, shiny nose...

SNAP! GOBBLE! GULP! went the fox. And that was the end of the runaway pancake.

∽ 21 ∾
Rapunzel

Mrs. Wibley was expecting a baby. Every day, she had a craving for something new to eat.

"Look at that lovely rapunzel growing in the witch's garden next door," she exclaimed to her husband one evening. "It looks so green and tasty. Please get me some."

So, in the dead of night, Mr. Wibley crept into the garden. He had just picked a handful of rapunzel when the witch leaped out from the shadows.

"Ha! Caught you, Wibley," she shrieked. "I'm going to turn you and your wife to stone."

"Please don't," begged Mr. Wibley. "We'll give you anything you want."

"All right..." said the witch thoughtfully. "Give me your child when it's born."

He had no choice. A few months later, a tearful Mr. Wibley and his sobbing wife handed their baby daughter to the witch.

The witch named the girl Rapunzel and took her

to live with her in the forest.

On Rapunzel's sixteenth birthday, the witch locked her at the top of a tall tower with a single window, no staircase and walls as slippery as glass.

By now, Rapunzel had long, long, golden hair. Whenever the witch wanted to visit her, she would shout, "Rapunzel, Rapunzel, let down your hair!"

Rapunzel would lower her hair out of the window, and the witch would climb up it.

One morning, a prince rode through the forest. He heard the witch calling to Rapunzel and hid behind a bush to watch. As soon as he saw Rapunzel leaning out of the tower window, he fell in love.

The prince waited until the witch had gone. Then he croaked, just as the witch had done, "Rapunzel, Rapunzel, let down your hair!"

Rapunzel obeyed, and was amazed to see a

handsome prince clamber into her tower room.

She fell in love with him as quickly as he had with her. "But I'm trapped here," she explained, sadly.

"Don't worry," said the prince. "I'll come back with a rope ladder and help you escape."

Later that day, Rapunzel heard the familiar cry and let down her hair, calling, "You're back soon, Prince!" But it wasn't the prince. It was the witch – and she was furious. With an angry snarl, she hacked off Rapunzel's hair and cast a spell sending her to a far-off land. Then, clutching the hair, she waited...

When the prince returned and climbed up the golden tresses, he was confronted with an angry witch.

"Try to trick me would you?" she yelled, shoving him hard. The prince plummeted to the ground, landing in a spiky thorn bush that blinded him.

The prince staggered to his feet and stumbled away. He was left wandering the world in despair until, one day, he heard a familiar voice.

"Prince?"

"Rapunzel!" he cried and the pair fell into each other's arms. Rapunzel wept tears of joy that dropped on the prince's face. As they trickled into his eyes, the prince could see once more. Deliriously happy, they headed to his palace, where they married and were never parted again.

∾ 22 ∾

Curly Locks, Curly Locks,
Wilt thou be mine?
Thou shalt not wash dishes
Nor yet feed the swine,
But sit on a cushion
And sew a fine seam,
And feed upon strawberries,
Sugar and cream.

~ 23 ~
Daffodils

I wandered lonely as a cloud
That floats on high o'er vales and hills,
When all at once I saw a crowd,
A host, of golden daffodils;
Beside the lake, beneath the trees,
Fluttering and dancing in the breeze.

Continuous as the stars that shine
And twinkle on the Milky Way,
They stretched in never-ending line
Along the margin of a bay:
Ten thousand saw I at a glance,
Tossing their heads in sprightly dance.

The waves beside them danced, but they
Out-did the sparkling waves in glee.
A poet could not but be gay,
In such a jocund company:
I gazed – and gazed – but little thought
What wealth the show to me had brought.

For oft, when on my couch I lie
In vacant or in pensive mood,
They flash upon that inward eye
Which is the bliss of solitude;
And then my heart with pleasure fills,
And dances with the daffodils.

William Wordsworth

∽ 24 ∾
Fairy Gifts

The Flower Fairy Queen lived in a palace as lovely as herself. It was hidden among the flowers, and had a roof made of scented petals, with garlands of dewdrops strung between the windows. Princess Sylvia couldn't think of anywhere she would rather live. But she was almost grown up. Soon, she would have to go out into the wide world.

"Before you go," the Flower Fairy Queen said to her, "I will give you any fairy gift you choose, just like the princesses before you. You must think carefully and pick something that will help you."

"I'm not sure what to choose," said Sylvia. "I'd like nothing better than to stay here with you."

The queen hugged her. "Before you make your decision," she said, "why not visit four other princesses to see how they are getting along with the gifts they chose?"

"Very well," agreed Sylvia.

The queen summoned a butterfly-drawn carriage,

and Sylvia stepped inside. The butterflies whisked her over the flowers and far away, the Flower Fairy Queen waving her tiny cobweb handkerchief until they were out of sight.

A few weeks passed and Sylvia returned. "I'm so glad to be back," she said. Over a cup of flower nectar, she told the Flower Fairy Queen all about her trip. The first princess she had visited was Princess Iris. "She was breathtakingly beautiful!" Sylvia exclaimed.

"Beauty is the gift she chose," said the Flower Fairy Queen.

"Oh, but she's not very happy," said Sylvia. "She cares so much about how she looks that she has forgotten all her natural cleverness and kindness. While I was there, she was ill and her beauty was lost. She said life isn't enjoyable without being beautiful, and can you please give her beauty back?"

"I'm afraid the gifts I give can only be given once," said the Flower Fairy Queen sadly. "How was your next visit with Primrose?"

"She certainly has a way with words!" laughed Sylvia.

The Flower Fairy Queen nodded. "That's what she asked for."

"But Primrose doesn't know when to stop," said Sylvia. "After an hour in her company you are quite worn out and have to stop listening to her."

"Oh dear," said the Flower Fairy Queen. "What about Jasmine? She was always so amiable. And she asked for the gift of pleasing."

"She went out of her way to make me feel at home," said Sylvia. "And at first I thought she was lovely. I still do, only I pity her too."

"Why?" asked the Flower Fairy Queen.

"Because she has dark circles around her eyes,

and she seems rather sad. She is so busy running around pleasing everyone that she is worn out," said Sylvia.

"What a shame," said the Flower Fairy Queen. "Was Pansy any happier with her gift of cleverness?"

"She was happy," said Sylvia, sounding doubtful. "But I'm not sure people around her were quite so satisfied."

"Why not?" asked the Flower Fairy Queen.

"Because she had a habit of turning every occasion into a chance to show off her cleverness. Even fairly serious situations seem to be just an excuse for some clever argument," Sylvia replied.

After a day or two, the Flower Fairy Queen asked Sylvia to come and see her. "It's nearly time for you to find your place in the world," she said. "Have you thought about what you'd like me to give you as a parting gift?"

Sylvia paused a moment and then nodded. "I think a peaceful heart would be best for me," she said. And the Flower Fairy Queen granted her wish.

When she went out into the world, Sylvia was loved by everyone she met. Her gentle contentment shone beautifully in her face. If she was ever sad, the worst people would say was, "It hurts me to see her like that." But most of the time, her companions basked in the sunshine of her happiness.

∾ 25 ∾
Under the Greenwood Tree

Under the greenwood tree,
Who loves to lie with me,
And turn his merry note
Unto the sweet bird's throat?
Come hither, come hither, come hither;
Here shall he see,
No enemy,
But winter and rough weather.

William Shakespeare

Answer to a Child's Question

Do you ask what the birds say? The sparrow, the dove,
The linnet and thrush, say, "I love and I love!"
In the winter they're silent – the wind is so strong.
What it says I don't know, but it sings a loud song.
But green leaves and blossoms, and sunny warm weather,
And singing and loving – all come back together.
But the lark is so brimful of gladness and love,
The green fields below him, the blue sky above,
That he sings, and he sings; and for ever sings he,
"I love my Love, and my Love loves me!"

Samuel Taylor Coleridge

∽ 27 ∾
The Shepherdess Princess

Once upon a time there lived a king with two
daughters. He loved them with all his heart,
but when they grew up, he longed to know if they
truly loved him. So he asked his elder daughter,
"How much do you love me?"

"You are like the apple of my eye," she said.

"Ah!" said the king, kissing her tenderly. "You are
a good daughter."

Then he sent for his younger daughter. "How
much do you love me?" he asked.

"Oh Father, I look on you as I do salt in my
food," she replied.

The king was not at all pleased with this answer.
"Go away from my Court and never return!"
he bellowed.

The poor princess wept all the way to her room.
There, she made a bundle of her jewels and her best
dresses and left her castle home. "I must work for
my living now," she realized. "But no one will take

me dressed as a princess."

So she found some rags, dirtied her face, tangled her hair, then wandered from farm to farm, until at last she found work as a shepherdess.

The princess worked as hard as any village maiden, but every now and then she would long for all her fine things. Then she would walk to a stream, shake off her rags, clean her face and dress once again as a princess.

One day, as she skipped among the sheep, dressed in her finery, a prince rode past and saw her. He came closer... but the princess fled into the woods as swiftly as a bird. The prince searched for her everywhere, but could not find her.

"There are no fine ladies here," a farmworker told him, laughing. "Only a shabby shepherdess."

The prince returned home, where he pined for the lovely maiden. "How can we make you happy again?" asked his parents. The prince thought hard, then asked for some bread, baked by the shepherdess on the far-off farm.

When the princess received the order, she set to work right away. But while she kneaded the dough, one of her rings slipped into the mixture.

The loaf was taken to the king's son as soon as it was done. As he bit into it, he found the ring. A smile lit up his face. "I'll marry the girl who fits this ring!" he declared.

Maidens came from far and wide to try the ring, but it was too small for all of them. "I haven't yet seen the girl from the distant farm," said the prince.

She was soon fetched, and came to the palace dressed in rags. The ring fit perfectly. "Marry me?" asked the prince.

"But she's only a shepherdess!" cried his parents.

"A moment, if you please," said the girl. She left the room and returned in all her finery.

"It *is* you!" said the prince. And the princess told him her story.

They were married that spring, and among the guests were the princess's father and sister. But on the bride's orders, the king's food was served without salt. "Is it to your liking?" she asked.

"I cannot eat it," the king replied. "It's tasteless."

"Did I not try to tell you, Father, that salt was one of the most important things in life?"

The king embraced his daughter. "I'm sorry," he said. "Can you forgive me for sending you away?"

"I do, Father," said the princess. "After all, it was only by becoming a shepherdess that I found my prince."

∽ 28 ∽
Piping Down
the Valleys Wild

Piping down the valleys wild,
Piping songs of pleasant glee,
On a cloud I saw a child,
And he laughing said to me:

"Pipe a song about a Lamb!"
So I piped with merry cheer.
"Piper, pipe that song again;"
So I piped: he wept to hear.

"Drop thy pipe, thy happy pipe;
Sing thy songs of happy cheer!"
So I sang the same again,
While he wept with joy to hear.

"Piper, sit thee down and write
In a book, that all may read;"
So he vanished from my sight;
And I plucked a hollow reed,

And I made a rural pen,
And I stained the water clear,
And I wrote my happy songs
Every child may joy to hear.

William Blake

∞ *29* ∞
A Parrot

Clothed in yellow, red and green,
I prate before the king and queen.
Of neither house nor land possessed,
By lords and knights I am caressed.

∞ 30 ∞

There was an Old Man with a beard,
Who said, "It is just as I feared!
Two Owls and a Hen,
Four Larks and a Wren,
Have all built their nests in my beard!"

∞ 31 ∞

There was a Young Lady of Turkey,
Who wept when the weather was murky;
When the day turned out fine,
She ceased to repine,
That capricious Young Lady of Turkey.

∞ 32 ∞

There was a Young Lady whose chin
Resembled the point of a pin;
So she had it made sharp,
And purchased a harp,
And played several tunes with her chin.

∾ 33 ∾

There was an Old Man with a nose,
Who said, "If you choose to suppose
That my nose is too long,
You are certainly wrong!"
That remarkable Man with a nose.

∾ 34 ∾

There was an Old Man of the coast,
Who placidly sat on a post;
But when it was cold
He relinquished his hold
And called for some hot buttered toast.

∾ 35 ∾

There was an Old Person of Slough,
Who danced at the end of a bough;
But they said, "If you sneeze,
You might damage the trees,
You imprudent Old Person of Slough."

all by Edward Lear

～ 36 ～

The Good-luck Horse

In the shadow of the Great Wall of China lived a poor farmer and his son, Lee. It was hard scraping a living from the stony soil, but one thing made it easier – their strong farm horse, who tilled the hard ground and carried heavy loads as easily as stepping through a summer meadow.

One morning, Lee went to fetch the horse only to find his field empty. "He's gone," wailed Lee. "What shall we do? It's such bad luck!"

"Maybe, maybe not," said his father calmly. "Who knows? Perhaps some good will come of this."

Sure enough, a few days later the horse returned, followed by another – a beautiful cream mare. He had found a mate in the wilds beyond the Wall.

"Two horses," crowed Lee. "What good luck!" His father frowned.

"Maybe, maybe not," he said. "Who knows how this will turn out?"

Lee wasn't listening. "I wonder what she's like to ride?" Impatient to find out, he vaulted up...

"Careful!" warned his father – too late. The mare had never had anyone on her back before and bucked wildly. Lee clutched her tossing mane but it slipped through his fingers. He fell heavily, his leg twisting under him.

"Aaargh! I think it's broken," sobbed Lee. "That mare is nothing but bad luck."

"Maybe, maybe not," replied his father. "Who can tell what the future holds?" And he helped his son to hobble home and bind his leg.

A few weeks later, a general came to order all the young men to join the army. Lee had no love of fighting, but the general would have taken him anyway – except for his twisted leg.

"You're right," Lee told his father with relief, as the general left their farm empty-handed. "You never can tell!"

~ 37 ~

Fidgety Philip

"Let me see if Philip can
Be a little gentleman;
Let me see if he is able
To sit still for once at table."
Thus Papa bade Phil behave;
And Mamma looked very grave.
But fidgety Phil,
He won't sit still;
He wriggles,
And giggles,
And then, I declare,
Swings backwards and forwards,
And tilts up his chair,
Just like any rocking horse –
"Philip! I am getting cross!"

See the naughty, restless child
Growing still more rude and wild,
Till his chair falls over quite.
Philip screams with all his might,

Catches at the cloth, but then
That makes matters worse again.
Down upon the ground they fall,
Glasses, plates, knives, forks, and all.
How Mamma did fret and frown,
When she saw them tumbling down!
And Papa made such a face!
Philip is in sad disgrace.

Where is Philip, where is he?
Fairly covered up you see!
Cloth and all are lying on him;
He has pulled down all upon him.
What a terrible to-do!
Dishes, glasses, snapt in two!
Here a knife, and there a fork!
Philip, this is cruel work.
Table all so bare, and ah!
Poor Papa, and poor Mamma
Look quite cross, and wonder how
They shall have their dinner now.

Heinrich Hoffmann

~ 38 ~
Sinbad: Voyage One

Welcome dear reader! My story begins many moons ago in the fair city of Baghdad. I wasn't always the wealthy man you see in this picture.

My father died when I was young, and left me a small fortune. But rather than invest it wisely I spent it quickly and soon I had almost nothing.

"Time for an adventure," I thought, exchanging my belongings for a selection of silks and spices, and heading for the port of Basra. It was easy to befriend a group of merchants and we were soon onboard a trade ship, sailing into the Arabian Sea.

"Land ahoy!" shouted the captain the next day.

I followed the sailors onto the sandy island and helped collect firewood to cook our dinner. No sooner had we lit the fire than the whole island

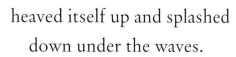

heaved itself up and splashed down under the waves.

It wasn't an island at all but a mighty whale! We were

scattered into the sea and many men drowned. Others made it to the ship and sailed away.

I was left floundering in the waves, a pitiful swimmer at the best of times, until a piece of flotsam saved my life. It carried me to a distant shore where I spied a handsome horse tangled up in seaweed. With the last of my strength, I freed the horse, which took me to a fabulous royal palace.

"My horse!" cried the king. "I must reward you. Become my advisor and I will make you rich."

I eagerly agreed and spent many months working for the king. I was happy enough, until one day a familiar ship weighed anchor in the port...

"The ship that fled whale island!" I gasped.

Sure enough, it was the same ship and the same captain. "Sinbad!" he called when he saw me. "I still have your silks and spices. Let me take you home."

"I suppose you must go," said the king, when he heard the news, "but take these jewels with you."

So I returned to Baghdad a rich man – and that is the end of the first chapter of my story...

A Boy's Song

Where the pools are bright and deep,
Where the grey trout lies asleep,
Up the river and over the lea,
That's the way for Billy and me.

Where the blackbird sings the latest,
Where the hawthorn blooms the sweetest,
Where the nestlings chirp and flee,
That's the way for Billy and me.

Where the mowers mow the cleanest,
Where the hay lies thick and greenest,
There to track the homeward bee,
That's the way for Billy and me.

Where the hazel bank is steepest,
Where the shadow falls the deepest,
Where the clustering nuts fall free,
That's the way for Billy and me.

Why the boys should drive away
Little sweet maidens from the play,
Or love to banter and fight so well,
That's the thing I never could tell.

But this I know, I love to play
Through the meadow, among the hay;
Up the water and over the lea.
That's the way for Billy and me.

James Hogg

∽ 40 ∽

Kite

A kite on the ground is just paper and string
But up in the air it will dance and sing.
A kite in the air will dance and will caper
But back on the ground is just string and paper.

Douglas & the Dragon

Douglas Dingle had a problem. In fact, he had one hundred. A wizard had granted his wife a wish, and she'd wished for a hundred children.

"How can I afford to feed them all?" Douglas asked his friend, Osric the shepherd.

"A dragon has been scaring my sheep," said Osric. "If you can get hold of the dragon's treasure, you could sell it to buy food."

It took all day, but Douglas eventually tracked down the dragon to its cave.

"I bet you all your treasure that I'm stronger than you," he boasted.

"You?" laughed the dragon, "Stronger than me?"

"I'll prove it," said Douglas, taking a lump of cheese from his pocket. "Can you squeeze a stone until it drips? I can."

And he did. Or so the dim dragon thought.

The dragon picked up a club. "I bet you're not strong enough to throw a club further than me."

"Oh yes I am," said Douglas. "But you throw first. The moon is blocking my throw right now."

The dragon gulped. Could Douglas really throw a club further than the moon? "I suppose you win," he grumbled, tossing down his club. "But if you want my treasure, you must spend a night in my cave."

Douglas agreed, but he didn't trust the dragon. So, before he went to sleep, he put a log under the sheets, and hid under the bed.

That night, the dragon crept up to the bed and whacked it hard with his heavy club.

When Douglas appeared, safe and well the next morning, the dragon couldn't believe his eyes.

"You really are stronger than me," he gasped. "Here, take my treasure and go!"

With the sacks of gold and jewels, Douglas could buy enough food to feed his family – for the next month or so, anyway.

∽ 42 ∾

Aunt Eliza

In the drinking-well
(Which the plumber built her)
Aunt Eliza fell –
We must buy a filter.

Harry Graham

∽ 43 ∾

Appreciation

Auntie, did you feel no pain
Falling from the apple tree?
Will you do it, please, again?
'Cos my friend here didn't see.

Harry Graham

∞ 44 ∞

At the Zoo

"First I saw the white bear, then I saw the black,
Then I saw the camel with a hump upon his back.
Then I saw the grey wolf, with mutton in his maw;
Then I saw the wombat waddle in the straw;
Then I saw the elephant a-waving of his trunk,
Then I saw the monkeys – mercy,
how unpleasantly they – smelt!"

William Thackeray

∞ 45 ∞

There was an Old Man on the Border,
Who lived in the utmost disorder;
He danced with the cat, and made tea in his hat,
Which vexed all the folks on the Border.

Edward Lear

46
The Monkey
& the Crocodile

Down by the banks of the Ganges, among the branches of a rose-apple tree, lived a sleek and golden monkey. Every day, his friend, the crocodile, came to talk and feast on the juicy apples.

"Have you a wife?" asked the monkey one day.

"I do," said the crocodile.

"Then you must take her my very best rose-apples," declared the monkey.

The monkey filled his friend's jaws with fruit and off he swam. The crocodile's wife was overjoyed.

"How delicious!" she cried, crunching on the apples. "Where did you get them?"

"My friend the monkey throws them down for me to eat."

"Ooh," said Mrs. Crocodile, clicking her jaws. "A monkey that lives off rose-apples must have such sweet flesh. I bet his heart tastes like heaven. Bring it to me!"

"But I can't," cried the crocodile. "The monkey is my friend."

"BRING IT TO ME!" snapped his wife. "Or I'll starve myself to death."

"Dear Monkey," said the crocodile the next day, his voice rather sad and gloomy. "My wife invites you to lunch. Come! Ride on my back."

The monkey smiled and clambered down the tree, his arms full of fruit for the crocodile's wife. Then off they went across the wide, wide river. But the nearer they came to the crocodile's wife, the worse the crocodile felt.

"I have to tell you, my friend," said the crocodile at last, "my wife has only invited you to lunch because she wants to eat your heart."

"But don't you know," said the monkey quickly, "I don't keep my heart with me. It's safe at the top of my tree."

"Then let us go back and get it," said the crocodile. And the monkey happily agreed.

Back on dry land, the monkey dashed up the tree… and didn't come down.

"What are you doing?" asked the crocodile.

"My foolish friend," said the monkey. "My heart is in my body, of course. Go away, and tell your wife I'm never giving either of you a rose-apple again."

❦ 47 ❦

A Daffodil

Daffy-down-dilly is new come to town,
With a yellow petticoat, and a green gown.

$\backsim$ 48 $\backsim$
The Twelve Huntsmen

There was once a prince who was to be married to Elsie, whom he loved very much. But before their wedding day, he received news that his father, the king, was very ill, and that he needed to go to him. He reached his father as he lay dying.

"My dearest son," said the king. "Promise me one thing – marry the princess of my choosing."

The son was so grieved that he promised without thinking. Then the king closed his eyes and died.

The prince was proclaimed king in his father's place, and he kept his word. He proposed marriage to the princess his father had chosen, and she was promised to him. When Elsie heard the news, she sobbed as if her heart would break.

Then her father said to her, "Dearest child, why are you so sad? What can I do to make it right?"

Elsie thought for a moment. "Dear father, I want to take eleven of my friends and go to the court of the king. But first we must be dressed as huntsmen."

Her father thought it a strange request, but agreed. So the twelve girls were dressed as huntsmen and rode away to the court of the new king. "Will you take us into your service?" asked Elsie.

"Yes," replied the king, without recognizing her. But the king had a lion who knew all secret and hidden things. "You think you have twelve huntsmen," he said to the king one evening, "but you are mistaken. They are twelve girls."

"I don't believe it," scoffed the king. "How can you prove it to me?"

"Scatter some peas on your floor," replied the lion, "and then you shall see. Men have a firm step, but girls tread lightly. They trip and skip and will spread the peas all over the place."

So the king took the lion's advice and ordered his servants to scatter peas on the floor. But one of the king's servants, who liked the huntsmen, had overheard the conversation. He told Elsie all.

"We must be strong," Elsie said to her eleven friends, "and step firmly on the peas."

When the king called the huntsmen before him, they stepped so firmly, none of the peas rolled at all.

"Lion! You lied to me," said the king, once the huntsmen had gone. "They walk just like men."

"They must have found out about the test," declared the lion. "Have twelve spinning plates brought to your chamber, then call for your huntsmen. They are sure to admire them. No man would do that."

So the king had spinning plates set up in his chamber, but again the servant had overheard.

"Remember," Elsie said to her eleven friends, "do not look at the spinning plates."

The next morning, when the king had the huntsmen summoned, they walked through his chamber without once glancing at the plates.

"You lied to me," the king told the lion again.

"They knew about that test too," replied the lion, but the king refused to listen to him any more.

The king went out riding with the huntsmen every day, and the more he knew them, the more he liked them. But one day, as they hunted, news came that the king's bride was approaching. Hearing the news, Elsie fell to the ground, clutching her broken heart.

The king ran over, only thinking to help his huntsman. But as he leaned down, he pulled off Elsie's glove, and saw the ring he'd given her long ago. Then he looked in her face, and recognized her at last. His heart was so touched that he kissed her, and when he drew back, he said, "You are mine, and I am yours, and no one in the world can change that."

His other bride was sent away, and the king and Elsie were married the next day.

∾ 49 ∾

The Lost Doll

I once had a sweet little doll, dears,
The prettiest doll in the world;
Her cheeks were so red and so white, dears,
And her hair was so charmingly curled.
But I lost my poor little doll, dears,
As I played in the heath one day:
And I cried for her more than a week, dears,
But I never could find where she lay.

I found my poor little doll, dears,
As I played in the heath one day:
Folks say she is terribly changed, dears,
For her paint is all washed away,
And her arm trodden off by the cows, dears,
And her hair not the least bit curled:
Yet for old sakes' sake she is still, dears,
The prettiest doll in the world.

Charles Kingsley

The Way Through the Woods

They shut the road through the woods
Seventy years ago.
Weather and rain have undone it again,
And now you would never know
There was once a road through the woods
Before they planted the trees.
It is underneath the coppice and heath
And the thin anemones.
Only the keeper sees
That, where the ring-dove broods,
And the badgers roll at ease,
There was once a road through the woods.

Yet, if you enter the woods
Of a summer evening late,
When the night-air cools on the trout-ringed pools
Where the otter whistles his mate,

(They fear not men in the woods,
Because they see so few.)
You will hear the beat of a horse's feet,
And the swish of a skirt in the dew,
Steadily cantering through
The misty solitudes,
As though they perfectly knew
The old lost road through the woods...
But there is no road through the woods.

Rudyard Kipling

∽ 51 ∾

Everyone is Right

In a village long ago, two men were having a heated argument. Neither would give in and accept that the other man was right. It so happened that Nasreddin Hodja was the local judge at the time. Surely he could come up with a solution?

First, one of the men went to the Hodja's house to explain his side of the argument. The Hodja listened, nodding wisely. When the man finished, the Hodja concluded:

"Yes, of course, you are absolutely right."

The man left the Hodja's house feeling very pleased with himself.

Next, the other man came to seek the Hodja's wisdom and judgement. He explained his side of the argument and the Hodja listened again. When the man had finished, the Hodja concluded:

"Yes, of course, you are absolutely right."

The man left the Hodja's house feeling very pleased with himself.

Then the Hodja's wife, who had been serving them all tea, turned to her wise husband. "They can't both be right," she pointed out.

"My dear," replied the Hodja, with a smile, "of course, you are absolutely right! But this way," he added, "at least they are both happy."

∾ 52 ∾
What Do You Suppose?

What do you suppose?
A bee sat on my nose.
Then what do you think?
He gave me a wink
And said, "I beg your pardon,
I thought you were the garden."

A Tree Toad Loved a She-Toad

A tree toad loved a she-toad
Who lived up in a tree.
He was a two-toed tree toad,
But a three-toed toad was she.

The two-toed tree toad tried to win
The she-toad's friendly nod;
For the two-toed tree toad loved the ground
That the three-toed tree toad trod.

But the two-toed tree toad tried in vain –
He couldn't please her whim;
From her tree toad bower
With her three-toed power,
The she-toad vetoed him.

∾ 54 ∾

Lavender's Blue

Lavender's blue, dilly dilly, lavender's green,
When I am king, dilly dilly, you shall be queen;
Who told you so, dilly dilly, who told you so?
'Twas mine own heart, dilly dilly, that told me so.

Call up your men, dilly dilly, set them to work,
Some with a rake, dilly dilly, some with a fork;
Some to make hay, dilly dilly, some to thresh corn,
Whilst you and I, dilly dilly, keep ourselves warm.

If you should die, dilly dilly, as it may hap,
You shall be buried, dilly dilly, under the tap;
Who told you so, dilly dilly, pray tell me why?
That you might drink, dilly dilly, when you are dry.

∾ 55 ∾

Roses are red, violets are blue,
Sugar is sweet and so are you.

∽ 56 ∾
Twigmuntus

There was once a king who was so clever and wise, that very few people could understand him. He spent his days with seven almost-as-wise professors. He would tell them his complicated plans for the country and they translated them into words that ordinary people could understand.

"The king is looking for a suitable husband for his daughter," they announced one day. "He must be so clever and wise that he can silence us with his words. Anyone is welcome to try, but if he wastes our time, we will chop off his head."

Now you might think that no one would be fool enough to risk their necks, but then you've never set eyes on the beautiful princess. Men from around the country lined up to try their luck. They spoke the wisest words they could muster, but the king was not impressed.

One by one, the poor men lost their heads. Eventually, the king's announcement reached the ears of a bright young man named Sven.

"I can easily bamboozle those professors with poppycock and twaddle," Sven thought, and he set out immediately for the royal palace.

On the way, he took a shortcut through a thick forest. He snapped off a twig and imagined he was presenting it to the king. "Twigmuntus, Your Majesty," he said with a smile.

Next he came to a meadow where a cow was bellowing. "Cowbelliantus, Your Majesty," Sven announced, chuckling.

On he ran to a river, with no obvious crossing, so he balanced his boots and clothes on his head and swam across. Mid-stream, a perch nibbled him on the nose.

"Perchnosius!" cried Sven in delight.
He was getting the hang of this
scholarly nonsense.

Even the heads on stakes at the entrance to the palace couldn't dampen Sven's spirits. He joined the line of suitors and waited his turn.

"Next," called a guard.

Sven was led into a grand room where the seven professors and the king sat looking important. One of them stood up and began spouting gibberish. Minutes went by and Sven couldn't understand a word. Eventually the professor turned to Sven. "What do you say to that then?"

"Very interesting," said Sven confidently, "if a little obvious. But the question I want to put to you is this: Twigmuntus, Cowbelliantus, Perchnosius?"

There was silence. The professors stretched their necks, adjusted their spectacles, looked uncomfortably at each other and then at the king.

Finally the king spoke. "Professors," he said, "behold the man my daughter will marry!"

∽ 57 ∽
Robin Hood Meets Friar Tuck

Robin Hood and his merry gang were seeing who could hit the trickiest target with their bows and arrows. First Will hit a leaping deer, then Little John hit a goose flying high above the trees.

"Bravo, Little John!" cheered Robin Hood. "You're almost as good an archer as me!"

"I've heard Friar Tuck at Fountains Abbey is better than both of you," said Will.

"Is he indeed?" replied Robin. "Then I must meet him."

And without delay Robin hurried through the forest to Fountains Abbey. There he found a short, plump friar strolling by a river. In one leap, he was on the friar's back.

"Take me across this river," he ordered, "and I shall let you go."

The friar did as he was told, wading through the water without saying a word. When Robin jumped down at the far bank, the friar promptly leaped onto *his* back.

"Take me back across the river," the friar ordered, "and I shall let *you* go."

Robin admired the friar's spirit and decided to test him further. No sooner were they on dry land than Robin leaped once more onto the friar's back. This time, the friar waded into the middle of the river and flung Robin into the water.

"Well if that game's over," said Robin, "I shall challenge you to another one. Archery."

"With pleasure," replied the friar.

They chose targets and fired arrows. To Robin's amazement, the friar hit them all – even a falling leaf from a distant tree. Soon Robin was out of arrrows.

"Now for a sword fight," he announced.

"With pleasure," said the friar again.

Although he was smaller and heavier than Robin Hood, he was surprisingly nimble and quick-footed.

The clang of metal filled the forest and the fight lasted well into the evening.

Eventually, Robin sank to his knees and asked for a moment's rest. He put his horn to his lips and gave three shrill blasts. Fifty of his merry men appeared, armed with bows and arrows.

"Wait," said the friar. He whistled loud and high, and fifty dogs appeared, snarling fiercely.

"You are a hard man to beat," Robin conceded. "And we'd rather have you as a friend than a foe. Will you join us?"

"With pleasure!" he replied.

And from that day on, Friar Tuck was one of Robin's band of merry men.

∞ 58 ∞

There was an Old Man with a flute.
A serpent ran into his boot;
But he played day and night,
Till the serpent took flight,
And avoided that Man with a flute.

∞ 59 ∞

There was an Old Man of Kilkenny,
Who never had more than a penny;
He spent all that money
In onions and honey,
That wayward Old Man of Kilkenny.

∞ 60 ∞

There was an Old Person of Ischia,
Whose conduct grew friskier and friskier;
He danced hornpipes and jigs,
And ate thousands of figs,
That lively Old Person of Ischia.

all by Edward Lear

∾ 61 ∽

If all the world were paper,
And all the seas were ink,
If all the trees
Were bread and cheese
What should we have to drink?

∾ 62 ∽

from The Walrus &
the Carpenter

"The time has come," the Walrus said,
"To talk of many things:
Of shoes – and ships – and sealing-wax –
Of cabbages – and kings –
And why the sea is boiling hot –
And whether pigs have wings."

Lewis Carroll

∾ 63 ∾

The Magic Kettle

Jimmu was trundling his junk cart up a steep mountain path. He hadn't sold anything that day, but he whistled a tune as went. Then over the whistling came a wailing sound, from within the thorny bushes beside the path. Jimmu rushed to investigate and found a tanuki, caught in a trap.

"Your poor thing," he said, freeing the creature and setting it on its way.

That night, as Jimmu unpacked his cart, he found an old, black kettle. "I don't remember seeing that before," said Jimmu, scratching his head.

He put it down and saw, to his amazement, that it was changing shape. The handle turned into a head, the spout grew into a tail and out of the sides sprang four little paws. Suddenly, the kettle wasn't a kettle at all. It was a tanuki.

"You helped me, now I want to help you," said the tanuki. "I'll

A tanuki is a Japanese raccoon dog, a small wild dog that looks a little like a raccoon.

change back into a kettle and you can sell me."

The next day, Jimmu sold the kettle to a monk for a fine amount of money. When the monk got home he set the kettle over the fire to boil... but the tanuki couldn't stand the heat. Out came his legs and he scuttled away, with the monk chasing after him.

"Give me back my money," the monk said to Jimmu. "I don't want a kettle with legs!"

"I'm sorry," said the tanuki, once the monk had gone. "I was trying to help and I failed. But I have an even better idea..."

And so the next day, Jimmu and his kettle went to market, and Jimmu called in the crowds. "Come and see the most wonderful transformation on earth," he cried.

A small group of people gathered. Jimmu pointed to the kettle. "Change!" he said. Before everyone's eyes, out sprang four little legs, the handle turned into a head and the spout grew into a tail.

"A tanuki!" clapped the crowd.

"Now dance," said Jimmu, and the tanuki began

to dance, this way and that, until the crowds couldn't resist dancing too.

"What a wonderful show!" everyone cheered, leaving Jimmu with a pile of gold coins.

After that, Jimmu went here, there and everywhere with his wonder-kettle, performing tricks for the crowd. Sometimes the tanuki would somersault. Sometimes he'd stay half-kettle, half-tanuki and walk a tightrope. Sometimes he would play the drums. Always, the crowds applauded in amazement.

Jimmu and the tanuki fast became famous throughout Japan, and both were as rich and as happy as could be.

∽ 64 ∾
The Fox & the Crow

"It's my lucky day!" thought Crow. She had found a piece of cheese, and was settling on a branch, high in a tree, to enjoy her tasty snack.

Just then, Fox came past. "Hello, Crow!" he called. The crow couldn't reply – she was holding the cheese tightly in her beak – but Fox carried on.

"How fine you look," he said. "What sleek, glossy feathers! What a smooth, shiny beak! Do you have a good, strong voice as well?"

Crow was delighted. "I do!" she cawed. "I do!" But the moment she opened her beak to speak, out fell the cheese.

Fox pounced on it instantly. "You may have a strong voice," he said, as he gobbled it up, "but the way you fell for my flattery, I can see you don't have brains to match!"

∽ 65 ∾
Toads & Diamonds

Kate was struggling to heave a pail of water from the old well in the woods. "If only my sister, Claire, would help with the chores once in a while," she thought, sighing as she pictured Claire lazing around at home.

"Excuse me, dear…" came a quavery voice. Kate jumped, almost spilling the water. Out from among the trees tottered an old woman with silver eyes and three long hairs on her chin. "Would you help an old lady to a drink?"

Kate offered her the pail, and the old woman took a long swig – so long that, by the time she was finished, not a drop of water remained.

"Your kindness is worth an ocean of jewels," said the old woman, wiping her mouth with the corner of her sleeve. "Now, forever speak your kindness to the world."

Kate gave a doubtful smile, and turned back to the well to refill her pail.

"And where do you think you've been?" snapped her mother, when Kate finally arrived home, lugging the heavy pail.

Kate opened her mouth to explain and out gushed a sparkling river of diamonds, rubies and gemstones.

"What…? How…?" babbled her mother, snatching up several diamonds in delight. Through a mouthful of jewels, Kate told her all about the strange old woman.

"What luck!" her mother exclaimed, and turned to her second daughter. "Claire, go and find that old woman too. See what she gives you."

By now, the sky was dark, and the trees echoed with ghostly hoots and howls.

"Where is that old woman?" moaned Claire, thinking of her snug home and warm bed.

When at last the old woman appeared, and again asked for water, Claire had lost patience. "Get it yourself," she said sulkily, kicking the empty pail.

The old woman plucked one of the hairs from her chin, raised her hands and proclaimed: "Lazy as a toad, now speak your laziness to the world!"

Claire just laughed – a dry, croaky laugh.

"Well?" demanded her mother, when Claire returned without the pail. The girl's face turned white. She opened her mouth and her mother shrieked as frogs and toads sprang out.

"It could have gone better," Claire said.

∾ 66 ∾
The Miller with the Golden Thumb

A rich merchant was unimpressed to find himself seated next to a poor miller at the mayor's annual feast. He decided to mock the miller, to make himself feel better.

"Master Miller," he began, "I've heard that every miller who is honest and good has a golden thumb to match. Is that true?"

"Indeed it is," replied the miller.

"In that case," the merchant went on, "I'm sure you won't mind showing me your thumb."

The miller did as he was asked.

"I knew it," piped the merchant with glee. "Your thumb is just the same as mine."

"That's where you're wrong, sir," replied the miller. "My thumb is made of solid gold, but only merchants who are honest and good can see it."

They spent the rest of the feast in stony silence.

∽ 67 ∽
The Old Horse

The war was over and an old soldier had come home, riding his tired old warhorse. But now he didn't know what to do with the animal. "I don't need a horse any more," he sighed. "And I've nowhere to keep one. It's time for you to fend for yourself, my friend." He slapped the horse on the flank and watched it clip-clop away.

The horse wandered slowly through the streets, looking for something to eat. Eventually, it found itself beside a bell tower. Now, in this town, if someone needed help, they could ring the bell and the rest of the townsfolk would gather to hear their troubles. But today, the rope that usually hung from the bell had been taken for mending – so a long, curling vine dangled in its place.

The horse saw the juicy green stem and gave a pleased whinny. It trotted over and took a bite.

Ding-dong! Ding-dong! With each tug of its teeth, the bell rang out. *Ding-dong! Ding-dong!*

The townsfolk came running – and stopped in astonishment when they saw who had fetched them.

"It's a horse!" they cried. "Calling for help. He needs looking after. Who does he belong to?"

The soldier stepped forward. "He's mine," he admitted. "I turned him loose because I had nowhere to keep him."

"I can help you build a stall," offered a carpenter.

"He can graze in my field," added a farmer.

"Thank you," said the soldier, patting the horse's nose. "Truth be told, I was missing my old friend."

And the horse whinnied softly, as if to say, "I missed you too."

∾ 68 ∾

Cinderella

Cinderella spent every day cooking and cleaning for her spiteful stepmother and two stepsisters.

One morning, an invitation arrived at the house.

"The prince is giving a grand ball at the palace," announced Cinderella's stepmother, in delight.

"How super!" shrieked her stepsisters. "We'll need gorgeous new ballgowns – and shoes to match."

"May I go?" asked Cinderella.

"You?" boomed her stepmother. "Certainly not. You're just a sooty, silly serving girl."

A week later, Cinderella sobbed as she watched her stepmother and stepsisters ride off to the ball. Curling up by the fireplace, she tried to sleep.

She was woken by a rumble and a flash of light. There in the kitchen, in a cloud of silver smoke, stood a sweet-looking old lady with bright pink wings.

"Who are you?" asked Cinderella nervously.

"I'm your fairy godmother, dearie," the old lady

replied. "And I see you've been crying."

Cinderella told her about the ball.

"Hmm," said the fairy. "Well, you must go too."

"But I can't let the prince see me in this ragged dress," sighed Cinderella.

"Of course not," smiled the fairy, waving her wand over Cinderella's head. There was a shower of stars and Cinderella found herself wearing a silken ballgown, embroidered with tiny flowers.

"Mustn't forget shoes," added the fairy, waving her wand again. Cinderella looked down to see a pair of glass slippers sparkling on her feet.

"Now, transport," the fairy declared. "That pumpkin in the garden will do." She aimed her wand and, with a *pop*, the pumpkin became a golden coach.

Then the fairy transformed three lizards into footmen, and a rat from a trap into a carriage driver. "I think you're ready to go," she said.

"But you must leave the ball at the first stroke of midnight. After that, my magic stops."

Bubbling with thanks, Cinderella stepped into the golden carriage and set off for the ball.

When she arrived, everyone whispered about this beautiful, mysterious girl. No one could remember meeting her before – and even her stepmother and stepsisters didn't recognize her.

As soon as the prince saw Cinderella, he fell in love. They danced all night. But as the clock struck midnight, Cinderella fled.

"Wait," the prince called. "I don't even know your name." He ran after her, but all he found was a single glass slipper, on the grand staircase leading from the palace. It gave him an idea.

"I shall marry whoever fits this glass slipper," he declared.

So the prince visited every home in his kingdom until, eventually, he came to Cinderella's house.

Cinderella's stepsisters grabbed the slipper, but their fat feet were far too big for it.

"May I try?" asked Cinderella, popping her head around the sitting room door.

Her stepmother was about to scream at her to get back to work, when the prince interrupted.

"Of course," he said kindly.

Cinderella slid her dainty foot into the slipper. It was a perfect fit.

"So she was the girl at the ball?" cried Cinderella's shocked stepsisters. "But she's just a servant."

"Marry me?" said the prince, ignoring them.

"Oh yes," said Cinderella, and they lived happily at the palace for the rest of their lives.

∾ 69 ∾

Tinker, tailor, soldier, sailor,
Rich man, poor man, beggarman, thief.

∞ 70 ∞
The Bedtime Fairy

The Bedtime Fairy was looking through her book of bedtime stories, wondering what to read to the littlest fairies. Magic crackled as she turned the pages. Elves waved, mice danced and a genie popped up in a billow of smoke. Here, a dragon snorted sparks. There, a bear padded through sparkling snow.

"Brrr," shivered the fairy, as snowflakes blew out of the book. Then she yawned. "All these bedtime stories are making me sleepy. I'll just shut my eyes..." A moment later, she was sound asleep.

A breeze stirred the curtains, fluttering pages. Curious faces peeked out of the book. Then, a naughty elf jumped off the page and into the room. "Come on," he whispered. "Let's explore!"

One by one, the other story creatures followed. On the table, a heap of baking ingredients had been left out. "Let's make a cake," giggled the elf. "Flour, eggs, sugar... what else can we add?"

"Raisins," said the genie, holding out a cupful.

"What about this?" called another elf, waving a little pot. "Atishoo! Oh no, that's pepper."

"Cheese," squeaked the mice, who had sniffed out a block of hard yellow cheese. "It'll be cheese cake!" So the cheese went in too.

"Now it needs cooking," said the dragon. "Allow me." He opened his mouth and hot flames licked the bowl. The smell of burnt cheese filled the air.

The naughty elf backed away and bumped into the fairy's wand – which clattered to the floor, shooting out spells. Suddenly, chairs came to life and chased each other around the table. Pots and pans banged and clanged, and the cake exploded in a shower of crumbs.

The Bedtime Fairy woke with a start. "What's happening?" She grabbed her wand. "Abracadabra, cadabra, cazoom!" There was a flash of light, a puff of smoke... and when the smoke cleared, everything was back to normal.

"You saved us!" sighed the story creatures.

"But not our cake," added the mice sadly.

"Look again," said the fairy, smiling.

The mice looked – and cheered. There, on the table, was a perfect cake with cherries on top.

After they had all had a slice, the Bedtime Fairy opened the book again. One by one, the creatures dived inside and curled up comfortably between the covers. Then a clock chimed.

"Five minutes to bedtime," cried the Bedtime Fairy. "The littlest fairies will want their story. Time to go!" And with a wave of her wand, she went.

∽ 71 ∽

A Book

The land was white,
The seed was black.
It would take a good scholar
To riddle me that.

∽ 72 ∽

Star Light, Star Bright

Star light, star bright,
The first star I see tonight;
I wish I may, I wish I might,
Have the wish I wish tonight.

∽ 73 ∽

Monday's Child

Monday's child is fair of face,
Tuesday's child is full of grace,
Wednesday's child is full of woe,
Thursday's child has far to go,
Friday's child is loving and giving,
Saturday's child works hard for its living;
But the child that is born on the Sabbath day
Is fair, and wise, and good, and gay.

The Dawn Wind

At two o'clock in the morning, if you open your
   window and listen,
You will hear the feet of the Wind that is going to call
   the Sun.
And the trees in the shadow rustle and the trees in the
   moonlight glisten,
And though it is deep, dark night, you feel that the
   night is done.

So do the cows in the field. They graze for an hour
   and lie down.
Dozing and chewing the cud; or a bird in the ivy wakes,
Chirrups one note and is still, and the restless Wind
   strays on,
Fidgeting far down the road, till, softly, the darkness
   breaks.

Back comes the Wind full strength with a blow like
    an angel's wing,
Gentle but waking the world, as he shouts:
    "The Sun! The Sun!"
And the light floods over the fields and the birds
    begin to sing,
And the Wind dies down in the grass. It is day and
    his work is done.

So when the world is asleep, and there seems no
    hope of her waking
Out of some long, bad dream that makes her
    mutter and moan,
Suddenly, all men arise to the noise of fetters
    breaking,
And every one smiles at his neighbour and tells
    him his soul is his own!

Rudyard Kipling

~ 75 ~
The Sunchild

There was once a woman who longed for children, but had none. So one day she spoke to the Sun. "Please," she begged him, "send me a little girl of my own."

"I will," replied the Sun. "But when she is twelve years old, you must give her back to me."

The woman promised and soon the Sun sent her a daughter. The woman was filled with joy and named her Letiko. She watched over Letiko, loved her and cared for her, until she was twelve years old. "Perhaps the Sun has forgotten my promise," she thought to herself. "Perhaps I can keep Letiko forever."

But one morning, while Letiko was out collecting herbs, the Sun came to her and said, "Go home and tell your mother she must remember her promise."

When the woman heard this, her heart fluttered with fear. She ran to the doors and bolted them, closed the shutters and stopped up every chink and hole in her home. But in her haste she forgot to close up the keyhole, and through it the Sun sent a ray into the house. The ray encircled Letiko and stole her back to the Sun.

There she lived in his splendid palace among the clouds where everything glinted with gold. But Letiko longed for her mother.

"Sing for me, Letiko," said the Sun. "You are the Sunchild." But Letiko never sang.

"Dance for me, Letiko," said the Sun. "You are the Sunchild." But Letiko never danced. Instead, she lay on her back and gazed at the sky and spun wisps of curling clouds. Everywhere she went, she wore her sadness like a heavy cloak, until at last the Sun knew – he must send Letiko back to her mother. And so he called two ravens to him.

"Will you take Letiko home?" he asked them.

"We will," replied the ravens.

The Sun cast Letiko and the ravens onto the topmost mountain and from there they came down into the valley where Letiko's mother lived.

But almost as soon as the Sun had let Letiko go, he became angry and longed for her to come back again. "Why should the old woman have her?" he thought crossly, "when she was promised to me all along? I'm sure I can make her happy in my splendid palace in the clouds."

And when Letiko next looked up, she saw the clouds skip past the Sun and his golden rays began to flood the valley. They danced here, there and everywhere. "He is trying to catch me," said Letiko, hiding in the shadows of a tree. "How will I ever get back to my mother?"

"We will shield you," said the ravens. And they held out their wings and flew over Letiko, so she was safe in their shadow. At last they came to Letiko's mother's house. When she saw them coming, she cried out for joy. She opened the door to her daughter and hugged her close. And when the Sun saw

Letiko's smile, he knew all the palaces in the world could never make her as happy as she was at home. And so Letiko stayed with her mother and never again had to fear being stolen away by the Sun.

∽ 76 ∽
Tweedledum & Tweedledee

Tweedledum and Tweedledee
Agreed to have a battle,
For Tweedledum said Tweedledee
Had spoiled his nice new rattle.

Just then flew down a monstrous crow,
As black as a tar-barrel,
Which frightened both the heroes so,
They quite forgot their quarrel.

Lewis Carroll

∽ 77 ∾
Hansel & Gretel

Hansel and Gretel lived with their father, a poor woodcutter, and their cruel stepmother, in a cottage on the edge of a forest.

"We can't afford to feed those two," snapped the stepmother to her husband, one evening. "They'll only starve if they stay with us. You'd better take them out with you tomorrow and leave them in the forest. I'm sure someone will rescue them."

Hansel overheard his stepmother and quickly hatched a plan. Sneaking into the kitchen later that night, he grabbed a small lump of bread.

The next morning, the woodcutter led his children deep into the forest, his heart breaking. "Wait there while I chop some wood," he said. "I'll be back later."

At dusk, he still hadn't returned. "How will we find our way home?" asked Gretel, in tears.

"Don't worry," Hansel said. "I left a trail of breadcrumbs behind us as we walked here. All we have to do is follow it."

But when they tried to retrace their steps, they discovered that birds had eaten every crumb.

Soon, they were hopelessly lost. The more they walked, the deeper into the forest they went.

At last, they came to a clearing – and there stood a house. The two children couldn't believe their eyes.

The walls were made of gingerbread. The roof tiles were sticky toffee, topped with marshmallow. The window frames were strips of liquorice and the door was carved from rich, dark chocolate.

An old woman opened the door and beckoned to

them. "Welcome!" she croaked with a grin. "There are plenty more sweet treats inside."

By now, Hansel and Gretel were starving, so they ran in. With a clang, a cage came clattering down, trapping Hansel.

"Ha, ha!" cackled the old woman, who was unmistakably a witch. "Now you're my prisoner. I'll fatten you up to eat." She grabbed Gretel's wrist. "And you can be my slave."

For the next week, the witch stuffed Hansel full of candies and cakes, while poor Gretel slaved away in the kitchen.

"You must be fat enough to eat now," the witch told Hansel one morning. She turned to Gretel. "See if the oven is hot enough to cook him, girl."

"Um, how do I do that?" said Gretel, pretending to be baffled.

"It's easy, foolish girl," sighed the witch, opening the vast oven door. "You just look inside and..."

Quick as a flash, Gretel shoved the witch into the

oven and slammed the door. The cage around Hansel dissolved and the pair raced out of the house.

As they ran through the forest, they bumped into their father.

"Thank heaven!" he cried. "I've been searching for you all week. Please forgive me for abandoning you. I should never have listened to your stepmother. I've told her to leave and never come back."

With that, he swept them up in a huge hug and all three agreed that no one would ever part them again.

∾ 78 ∾

Mix a Pancake

Mix a pancake,
Stir a pancake,
Pop it in the pan;
Fry the pancake,
Toss the pancake –
Catch it if you can.

Christina Rossetti

Betty Botter

Betty Botter bought some butter,
"But," she said, "this butter's bitter;
If I put it in my batter,
It will make my batter bitter,
But a bit of better butter –
That will make my batter better."

So she bought a bit of butter
Better than her bitter butter,
And she put it in her batter,
And the batter wasn't bitter.
So, 'twas better Betty Botter
Bought a bit of better butter.

The Brave Little Tailor

There was once a tailor who was eating bread and jam when a cloud of flies appeared. *Buzz, buzz, buzz...* around the jam pot they swarmed, until the tailor could stand it no longer. He swatted at them with a cloth – and seven fell to the ground.

"Seven with one blow," cried the tailor with pride. "The whole world shall hear of this!" He embroidered a sash with the words and put it on. Then he packed up a chunk of old cheese and his pet canary, and set out in search of adventure.

He had not walked far when he met a giant, who roared with laughter at his sash.

"Seven with one blow?" sneered the giant. "A little fellow like you... ha, ha, ha. Can you do this?" And he scooped up a rock and squeezed it, until it dripped water.

"That's nothing," said the tailor. And he took out his chunk of cheese and squeezed so it dripped too.

"Hmph," snorted the giant. "Well, can you do this?" And he picked up a boulder and threw it so high, you could hardly see it.

"Easy-peasy," scoffed the tailor. And he took out his canary and threw it into the air. "Look, mine doesn't come down at all. Not until I call for it, anyway."

He whistled loudly and a small yellow shape darted quickly back to him.

The giant scratched his head. He hated being beaten. "I must get rid of this upstart," he decided. So he invited the tailor to spend the night in his cave.

"You can sleep there," he said, pointing to an enormous, giant-sized bed.

The tailor lay down but couldn't get comfortable. "This bed is too big," he thought. So he crept out and curled up on the floor behind it. As soon as he began to snore – *whaaam!* The giant's club smashed the bed to pieces.

"What was that little bump?" yawned the tailor, sitting up and rubbing his head.

This was too much for the giant. He fled and never dared to return. But the brave little tailor lived long and happily, known by everyone he met as the mighty warrior who killed seven with one blow, and defeated a giant too.

∽ 81 ∾

Hot Cross Buns

Hot cross buns!
Hot cross buns!
One a penny, two a penny,
Hot cross buns!
If your daughters do not like them
Give them to your sons;
But if you haven't any of these pretty little elves
You cannot do better than eat them yourselves.

∞ 82 ∞

There was a Young Person of Crete,
Whose toilette was far from complete;
She dressed in a sack
Spickle-speckled with black,
That ombliferous Person of Crete.

∞ 83 ∞

There was an Old Person of Philae,
Whose conduct was scroobious and wily;
He rushed up a palm
When the weather was calm,
And observed all the ruins of Philae.

∞ 84 ∞

There was an Old Man of the West,
Who never could get any rest;
So they set him to spin
On his nose and his chin,
Which cured that Old Man of the West.

~ 85 ~

There was an Old Person of Hurst,
Who drank when he was not athirst;
When they said, "You'll grow fatter!"
He answered, "What matter?"
That globular Person of Hurst.

~ 86 ~

There was a Young Lady of Poole,
Whose soup was excessively cool;
So she put it to boil
By the aid of some oil,
That ingenious Young Lady of Poole.

~ 87 ~

There was an Old Person of Rheims,
Who was troubled with horrible dreams;
So, to keep him awake,
They fed him on cake,
Which amused that Old Person of Rheims.

all by Edward Lear

∾ 88 ∾
The Trapped Tiger

A man was walking through the woods one day, when he came across a tiger trapped in a cage.

"Excuse me," said the tiger. "Please would you let me out?"

"No chance," said the man. "You'd eat me alive."

The tiger widened its amber eyes. "I'd do no such thing," it said. "I'd be in your debt forever."

The idea of having a tiger at his beck and call was an attractive one. "Promise?" said the man.

"Promise," said the tiger.

So the man unlocked the door. As soon as the tiger sprang out, he knew he'd made a mistake.

"I haven't had a good meal in days," the beast growled, staring straight at him.

"You promised not to eat me," squealed the man.

"What's a promise to a hungry tiger?" the beast snarled, prowling closer.

"It's not fair!" wailed the man.

Just then, a jackal came trotting past. "What's all this then?" it asked cheerily.

The man told the whole story while the tiger waited, its tail twitching with impatience.

"So, let me get this straight," said the jackal when the man had finished. "You were in the cage–"

"No, it was the tiger," said the man.

"You were in the tiger?" the jackal gasped.

"No, no," said the man. "I was just passing."

"Oh, I see," the jackal said. "The cage was in the tiger–"

"NO," interrupted the tiger, who wanted to get on with its lunch. "I was in the cage, and this man let me out."

"Sorry," said the jackal. "I'm a little confused... you say this man was in a cage–"

"It was ME in the cage," snapped the tiger.

The jackal paused, looking thoughtful. "You mean to say you were in this cage?" he said.

"YES," roared the tiger.

"But how?" the jackal asked, scratching its head. "How did you get into the cage?"

"How can you be so stupid?" the tiger roared, beside itself with frustration. "Like this of course!" And he leaped into the cage. "SEE?"

Quick as a dart, the jackal slammed the door and turned the key in the lock. "I see," he grinned. "Perhaps it had better stay that way, don't you agree?" With a wink to the man and a nod to the trapped tiger, the jackal continued on his way.

∞ 89 ∞

One-one was a Racehorse

One-one was a racehorse,
Two-two was one, too.
When One-one won one race,
Two-two won one, too.

❦ 90 ❦
The Flying Tortoise

The birds were having a feast. Tortoise watched them gathering together piles of delicious food.

"*I* want to go," said Tortoise.

Mrs. Tortoise tutted. "It's in the *sky*," she said. "You'll never get up there. And what if you fell? You might ruin your lovely smooth shell."

But Tortoise ignored her. "All that food..." he murmured, his eyes lighting up. "I want it all for me."

So he crept among the birds, surreptitiously plucking a feather from each one and tucking them under his shell. Then he flapped his legs... and flew off to the sky feast, way up high among the fluffy clouds.

"Who are you?" asked the birds.

"My name," said Tortoise, "is *All of us*. Who is the food for?"

"It's for all of us," the birds replied.

Tortoise smiled. "That's my name! That's me!"

Greedy Tortoise ate ALL the food – every last

crumb. The furious birds squawked and flapped and pecked at him. One by one, his feathers fell out.

"It's TORTOISE!" cried the birds. "He can't fly now. Let's leave him stuck up here in the sky."

"I'll jump!" said Tortoise. "But please," he begged, "at least give a message to my wife. Tell her to bring out all our pillows and mattresses." He looked down and gulped. "I'll need something soft to land on."

But the birds took a different message. "Quick!" they called to Mrs. Tortoise. "Tortoise wants you to spread all your hard things over the ground for him."

In a panic, Mrs. Tortoise didn't stop to ask why. She simply collected up pots and pans and wooden chairs and hurried outside.

Tortoise peered over the edge of the cloud. He could just make out a vague heap on the ground, far below. "Now or never," he muttered and jumped.

Wheeeeeeeeeeee.... SPLAT! His shell shattered.

Mrs. Tortoise stuck it back together, but it was never the same. And from that day to this, Tortoise has carried a cracked, bumpy shell on his back.

The Golden Windows

Hannah lived in a cottage on the side of a hill. She often spent the morning looking across the fields to the other side of the valley.

There stood a house just like hers, except this one had four, beautiful golden windows that glinted and sparkled. "I wish I lived there," she thought.

After lunch one day, she decided to take a closer look. So she hopped on her bike and cycled down the hill, across the bottom of the valley and up the other side. As she got nearer to the house, she felt her heart pounding. The golden windows looked amazing from a distance. How wonderful they must be close up.

But when she arrived at the house, her heart sank. The windows were plain old glass. As she turned to cycle home, she looked across at her own house in the distance. She gasped. The windows were golden. And then she realized what was happening. The windows reflected the rays of the sun. So she did live in a house with golden windows after all!

Eldorado

Gaily bedight,
A gallant knight,
In sunshine and in shadow,
Had journeyed long,
Singing a song,
In search of Eldorado.

But he grew old –
This knight so bold –
And o'er his heart a shadow
Fell as he found
No spot of ground
That looked like Eldorado.

And, as his strength
Failed him at length,
He met a pilgrim shadow:
"Shadow," said he,

The word bedight means dressed.

"Where can it be,
This land of Eldorado?"

"Over the mountains
Of the Moon,
Down the valley of the Shadow,
Ride, boldly ride,"
The shade replied,
"If you seek for Eldorado."

Edgar Allen Poe

∽ *93* ∽

There was a girl in our town,
Silk an' satin was her gown,
Silk an' satin, gold an' velvet,
Guess her name, three times I've telled it.

The girl's name is found in the phrases *silk an' satin* and *gold an' velvet*.
(Her name is Ann.)

∾ 94 ∾
The Lion & the Statue

Once, a circus lion and a ringmaster got into an argument. They had started talking about which of them was the stronger.

"Admit it," laughed the lion, "when it comes to strength, lions are far superior to men!"

"On the contrary," the ringmaster replied, "men are mightier – and I can prove it. Follow me." He led the lion to a statue of a muscled man overpowering a lion with his bare hands.

"There you are," said the ringmaster, "What did I tell you?"

"That proves nothing," the lion scoffed. "This statue was carved by a man. If a lion had made it, you can be sure it would show the man losing!"

"I hadn't thought of that," said the ringmaster. "It just shows there are two sides to every story."

Walnuts & Pumpkins

Nasreddin Hodja was lying in the shade of an ancient walnut tree. His body may have been resting, but his mind most certainly wasn't. He was an important man with important thoughts.

The Hodja looked at the sturdy branches of the tree and frowned. "Allah is great and Allah is good..." he thought, "but why hang little walnuts on a strong tree, and pumpkins on spindly vines that can't even take their weight. Why not swap them over?"

By and by, tired out by his thinking, the Hodja drifted off to sleep... only to be woken by a walnut dropping onto his head. He sat up with a smile.

"Allah is great and Allah is good!" he cried. "If the world had been created according to my ideas, a pumpkin would just have fallen on my head. Never again will I question the wisdom of Allah."

Allah is the word for God in Arabic.

∾ 96 ∾
The Robbers & the Donkey

A man was leading his donkey home one day, when two robbers crept up behind him. One loosened the rope around the donkey's neck and slipped it around his own, and the other quietly led the donkey away and hid.

The man walked on, none the wiser, until suddenly the rope went taut. "Come on," he urged, looking behind him. He was astonished to find a man standing there instead of his donkey. "Who are you?" he asked.

"I'm your donkey of course," said the man. "That is to say I was your donkey... I used to be a man, but I was terribly rude to my mother and she turned me into a donkey."

"How awful," said the man.

"Yes," agreed the robber. "And then she chased me out of the house, and I was found by a merchant who sold me to you."

"Oh dear," said the man.

"But you have been so kind to me, that finally you have broken the spell. I can't thank you enough," said the robber, slipping the rope from around his neck.

"Don't mention it," said the man, shaking his hand. "Goodbye."

He returned home without the donkey, much to his wife's displeasure. "You'll have to go to market and buy us another," she grumbled.

So the man hurried off to market. Imagine his surprise when he found his very own donkey for sale. He looked it over from head to foot, and shook his head. "You naughty rascal," he said to the donkey. "Have you been rude to your mother again? Well, I'm not saving you this time." And off he went to buy a different donkey.

Doctor Foster

Doctor Foster
Went to Gloucester,
In a shower of rain.

He stepped in a puddle,
Right up to his middle,
And never went there again.

Doctor Foster
Went to Oxford,
In a cloud of fog.

He just couldn't see,
Bumped into a tree
And splat! He fell into a bog.

Doctor Foster
Went to Gosport,
In a howling gale.

The wind was so strong,
It blew him along,
And he flew down the street with a wail.

Doctor Foster
Went to Stockton,
In the swirling snow.

The frost bit his nose,
His spectacles froze
And he couldn't see
Which way to go.

Doctor Foster
Went to Bognor,
In the sizzling heat.

He took off his socks,
Fell asleep on some rocks
And got sunburned
All over his feet.

Doctor Foster told his daughter,
"I'm not going to roam.
I'll see patients here,
With my family near.
From now on, there's
No place like home."

adapted by Russell Punter

The original version of Doctor Foster appeared in 1810. Some people think it is about King Edward 1 of England. There is a story that, on a visit to Gloucester, he fell off his horse into a puddle and swore he would never return.

∞ 98 ∞

Rain on the green grass,
And rain on the tree,
Rain on the house-top,
But not on me.

∞ 99 ∞

Rain, rain, go away,
Come again another day.

∞ 100 ∞

Goosey, goosey gander,
Whither shall I wander?
Upstairs and downstairs
And in my lady's chamber.
There I met an old man
Who would not say his prayers.
I took him by the left leg
And threw him down the stairs.

∞ 101 ∞

The Cat & the Rat

Believe it or not, once upon a
time, cats and rats were the
best of friends. But that all changed
one day, when a tabby cat and his ratty
companion wanted a change of scene.

The pair lived on an island. There was plenty to
eat and drink, but not much else to do.

"I'm bored," sighed the rat one day. "Let's
leave this island and go in search of adventure."

"Good idea," agreed the cat. "But how?"

"We could build a boat," suggested the rat.

So the rat gnawed down a tree trunk and
the cat scratched out a space for them to sit. Then
the rat used two branches to carve a pair of oars.

"Goodbye boring old island," cried the rat as she
pushed their little craft into the water. She leaped in
alongside the cat and paddled for all she was worth.

An hour later, the rat was exhausted. On top of
that, the lazy cat had fallen asleep and his snoring

was driving her crazy.

"I'm starving," she thought to herself. And then, "And we forgot to bring any food!"

She looked down at the juicy tree trunk. "Just one little nibble couldn't hurt," she told herself. She licked her lips and began gnawing through the wood.

After a while, the noise woke the cat. "What's going on?" he cried. Then he saw the huge hole in the side of their boat. "Oh no!" he yelled, as water began lapping in. "What have you done?"

"I couldn't help it," wailed the rat, paddling like fury to keep them afloat. "I was hungry."

As the boat slipped beneath the waves, the cat and the rat had to swim for their lives. Eventually, the bedraggled pair crawled back onto the island.

"That was all your fault, rat," spluttered the cat angrily. "I should never have listened to you!"

He chased the rat across the beach. She ran towards a sand hill and began digging frantically.

"Come back!" the cat

yelled, as the rat disappeared.

"No fear!" replied the rat, safely inside her tunnel.

And that's why, to this day, you will sometimes see a cat patiently waiting to pounce on a rat.

∾102∾
She Sailed Away

She sailed away,
One bright summer day
On the back of a crocodile.
"You see," said she,
"He's as tame as can be;
I'll ride him down the Nile."
The croc winked his eye
As she waved them all goodbye;
Wearing her happy smile.
At the end of the ride
The lady was inside;
And the smile was on the crocodile.

∾103∾

The Battle of the Crabs

Once upon a time, on an island in the Sulu Sea, the fiddler crabs came together for a meeting. One of them waved his great claw in the air and said, "What are we going to do about the waves? They sing so loudly, all through the day and all night, that we cannot get any sleep."

"There is only one answer!" said the oldest crab. "We must fight them."

So the crabs waved goodbye to their wives and scuttled out from their mudhole homes to line up on the shore in a great long row.

"What are you doing?" asked the sea turtles, watching them from the sandy banks. "It's high tide! Get back in your burrows or you'll be washed away by the waves."

"Nonsense," said the crabs. "This is war and we're going to win." So saying, they raised their claws at the ocean and as the waves rose up to meet them... they charged.

But their snapping pincers were powerless against the swell of the sea. The foam alone scattered the crabs across the sand, then the waves sucked them back and carried them away – far, far away – out into the open ocean.

As the sun slipped down the sky and lit the water with a fiery glow, the wives of the crabs began to worry. "Whatever has happened to our husbands?" they asked, peeking out of the burrows. "Why haven't they come back from battle?" They scuttled down to the shore in search of the missing men. But no sooner had they arrived than the waves came crashing down again, and took the wives the way of the husbands.

The sea turtles shook their heads sadly. "What fools those crabs were," they said, "to battle with the waves."

For a long time, no crabs could be seen on the shores of the Sulu Sea, and the mudholes were empty. Until... one day, at high tide, thousands of

little crabs came scuttling out of
the sea. They ran up the beach as
fast as their eight legs could take them.
The sea turtles watched with wonder.
For it seemed as if these little crabs knew what
had happened to their kind before. Every day
they would rush down to the water's edge, ready
to fight the waves. Then, their courage would fail
them and they'd flee back up the beach again.

They can still be seen today... running to and
fro... caught between the soft, safe sand and the
surging, singing sea.

∞ 104 ∞

Red sky at night, shepherd's delight,
Red sky in the morning, shepherd's warning.

∾ 105 ∾
Sinbad: Voyage Two

After my first voyage, I lived a life of luxury, until my jewels ran out, and I yearned for excitement again. So I joined a group of merchants sailing south, trading goods from place to place.

On one island, I was strolling along the beach to stretch my legs when I happened upon a massive white rock. It was smooth to touch and very round. Just as it dawned on me that it might be an egg, a gigantic bird swooped down and grabbed me.

It carried me across forests and plains, finally dropping down into a steep-sided valley. Luckily for me, the bird had spotted something more tasty for its dinner: a dead sheep. Unluckily for me, I was now trapped in a rocky valley with no food or water, just a few dead sheep for company... and what looked like thousands of sparkling diamonds.

I was stuffing handfuls of diamonds into my

tunic, when I heard a cry from above: "Watch out!"

A dead sheep came tumbling towards me. I jumped out of the way and looked up to see a group of men peering over the cliff edge. They cheered as a huge bird picked up the sheep and flew off with it.

"This could be my ticket out of here," I thought, as another sheep tumbled by. I quickly unwound my turban, tied one end to the sheep and waited. Sure enough, a huge bird soared into the valley and scooped up the sheep, dangling me below.

Once I was clear of the valley I let go and landed next to the men and their pile of dead sheep.

"What *are* you doing?" I asked, in confusion.

"Collecting diamonds!" the men replied. "They stick to the sheep we throw into the valley, then fall off when the birds carry the sheep away."

"I'll give you some diamonds," I said, reaching into my tunic, "if you'll take me back to Baghdad."

"It's a deal!" replied the men.

A month later, I was home again, with diamonds to spare, but that's not the end of my story...

∽ 106 ∽

There was an Old Man of Corfu,
Who never knew what he should do;
So he rushed up and down
Till the sun made him brown,
That bewildered Old Man of Corfu.

∽ 107 ∽

There was an Old Person of Gretna,
Who rushed down the crater of Etna;
When they said, "Is it hot?"
He replied, "No, it's not!"
That mendacious Old Person of Gretna.

∽ 108 ∽

There was an Old Man of Nepaul,
From his horse he had a terrible fall;
But, though split quite in two,
With some very strong glue
They mended that Man of Nepaul.

all by Edward Lear

∽ 109 ∽
Chillmore Castle

Barney Jones was on a school camping trip to crumbling Chillmore Castle. It should have been fun, but he had to share a tent with Pat and Pete Plank, the school bullies.

"This castle is too scary for a weed like you, Jones," sneered Pat, as they joined the guided tour.

"Yeah!" Pete jeered. "They say the place is haunted. You're too chicken to survive the tour."

The class was shown around the creepy old castle. Their final stop was the dank, dark dungeon.

"This is where the castle ghost, Sir Tom the Terrible, appears at midnight," said the guide.

"Really?" gulped Barney, with a shiver.

"So people say," the guide replied.

"Ha!" laughed Pat. "Jones could never stay here at midnight."

"He'd faint if he saw a ghost," Pete chuckled.

"I'll show you!" snapped Barney. "I'll come back

tonight and face Sir Tom."

"You won't last five minutes," Pat snorted.

That night, Barney crept back to the dungeon. It was even spookier at night, he thought – but still better than spending the evening with Pat and Pete.

The tower clock struck midnight. As the last chime died away, an eerie moan filled the room, and a ghostly figure appeared.

"Er, woo," said the ghost. "I am Sir Tom the Terrible. So be afraid, if you don't mind... and um, beware, and that sort of thing."

Barney couldn't help laughing at him.

"Everyone laughs at me," sniffed Sir Tom. "I'm supposed to be scary, but people think I'm feeble."

Barney felt so sorry for Sir Tom, he spent the night teaching him how to roar and shout and scare.

"How do you know all this stuff?" asked Sir Tom.

"I'm used to being bullied by the Plank brothers," sighed Barney.

The next morning, Barney went back to his tent, but Pat and Pete didn't believe he'd met the ghost.

"You're too wimpy to face a spook," said Pete, shoving Barney off his feet.

"Who dares to shove brave Sir Barney?" came a thundering voice.

Pete and Pat shrank back in terror, as Sir Tom materialized and began poking and prodding them with his sword.

"Help!" shrieked Pete, turning pale with fear.

"I'm scared!" wailed Pat, turning even paler.

The horrified brothers fled, promising never to bully anyone again.

With a wink to his new friend, Sir Tom faded away. No one ever laughed at him again, thanks to brave Barney Jones.

～ 110 ～
The Lucky Cat

One night, a young man, whose parents had recently died, had the strangest dream. An unknown man appeared to him and said: "Listen to me – now that your parents are gone, all your father's riches belong to you. Half of his wealth he stole, and you must give it back to the poor. The other half you must throw into the sea. But watch as the money sinks into the water. If anything stays afloat, catch it and keep it, even if it is nothing more than a piece of paper."

Then the man vanished and the youth awoke. "I don't want to give away my riches," he thought, "and be cold and hungry." But he was an honest man, and didn't want to live off money gained by wicked means. So he spent half the money helping the poor in his village. The other half he took down to the sea and flung it in. In a moment it was out of sight, except for a tiny scrap of paper floating on the water. He stretched down and plucked it out. Wrapped inside were six shillings. This was now all the money he had in the world.

"Better than nothing," he decided, slipping it into his coat pocket. That night, tired, hungry and with only six shillings, he knocked on the door of a small hut he passed and asked for a night's lodging.

A family invited him in and made room for him as they ate their supper. By the fire, he spied a creature – small and black, with large, bright eyes, different from any animal he had ever seen. "What is that?" he asked.

"We call it a cat," they replied.

"I should like to buy it," he said, "if it's not too much money. It would be company for me."

So for six shillings the young man bought the cat. The next morning he waved goodbye, the cat tucked snugly in his coat.

"Where are you going now?" one of the girls called after him.

"To seek my fortune," the young man said.

"Go to see the king," advised her mother. "He is kind and will try to help you."

The young man walked many miles to the king's palace, until at last he reached the great hall, where His Majesty was sitting down to dinner. The young man bowed low, then gazed in surprise at the crowd of little brown creatures running around on the floor, even on the table itself. They were so bold, they snatched food from the king's own plate, and if he drove them away, they tried to bite his hands, so he could not eat his food.

"What sort of animals are these?" asked the young man.

"Mice," said the king, with a sigh. "For years we have tried to get rid of them, but it's impossible. They even come into our beds."

As he spoke, something flew through the air. It was the cat, pouncing here, there and everywhere.

It darted around
the hall, swatting with
its paws, catching with its claws,
biting with its jaws. Mice lay dead all
around. In no time, the cat had killed every last one.

For some minutes, the king could only look on in astonishment. "What animal is that," he asked at last, "that can work such magic?"

"My cat, Your Majesty," said the young man.

"You have freed my palace from a plague of tiny beasts," returned the king, "so I will give you the choice of two things. Either you shall be my Prime Minister, or else you shall marry my daughter and reign after me. Which shall it be?"

"The princess and the kingdom if you please – if your daughter is happy to marry me," the young man answered.

And so it was.

∽ 111 ∽

Elsie Marley is grown so fine,
She won't get up to feed the swine,
But lies in bed till eight or nine.
Lazy Elsie Marley.

∽ 112 ∽
What Are Little Boys Made Of?

What are little boys made of?
What are little boys made of?
Frogs and snails and puppy-dogs' tails,
That's what little boys are made of.

What are little girls made of?
What are little girls made of?
Sugar and spice and all that's nice,
That's what little girls are made of.

∞ 113 ∞
The Fox & the Goat

Trip, slither, splash! One minute, Fox was bounding along, the next he had fallen down an old, crumbling well. It was far too high to climb out. He sat in the puddle at the bottom and sighed. As he despaired of ever escaping, he heard a polite cough.

"Excuse me," said a passing goat. "What are you doing down there?"

"Um... a drought is coming," replied Fox. "I came down here to be near this lovely, fresh water. But you can share it with me if you like," he added slyly.

"Thanks!" said the goat, and jumped down into the well. Quick as a flash, Fox climbed up onto the goat's back and out into the sunshine.

"Hey, where are you going?" bleated the goat.

"I'm off!" said Fox, with a grin. "You shouldn't have believed me. Next time, we should both remember: look before you leap."

Catching the Sun

Every morning the Sun rose, raced across the sky... and went back to bed again.

"Lazy Sun!" railed the god, Maui. "All you want to do is stay in bed. You're making us spend our days in darkness!"

He turned to his brothers. "We need to slow down the Sun," he said.

As the Sun set, Maui and his brothers followed him to the eastern mountains. Between them, they carried a vast net and threw it over the deep pit where the Sun slept. Then they waited.

Late the next morning, the Sun rose from its pit and tried to race across the sky. But it was caught, held back by the giant net.

"Let me go!" cried the Sun.

"Only if you promise to slow down when you're crossing the sky," demanded Maui.

"No!" roared the Sun. But the Sun was trapped, and Maui refused to let him go.

"Fine," grumbled the Sun. "I promise."

Maui and his brothers pulled back the net, and the Sun crept slowly across the sky, that day and the next and the next... so now there is time to fish and find food, and sit in the sunshine.

How Doth the Little Crocodile

How doth the little crocodile
Improve his shining tail,
And pour the waters of the Nile
On every golden scale!

How cheerfully he seems to grin,
How neatly spreads his claws,
And welcomes little fishes in,
With gently smiling jaws!

Lewis Carroll

The Dragon Princess

The Dragon Princess lived far beneath the sea, in a palace of glittering coral and glimmering shells. Her father, the Dragon King, thought it was time she got married – but the princess was not easy to please. "I won't marry," she insisted. "Not until I find a man with a heart of gold!"

The king snapped his fingers. "I know just the man – a poor woodcutter named Yan."

"How can I be sure?" asked the princess.

"We'll set him a test," promised her father. "Listen..."

That night, in his little wooden hut, Yan heard a soft whisper. "Come outside," it said. So Yan went – and his nosy half-brother Yu followed. "Wow!" It was the princess. Yan thought she was the most beautiful sight he had ever seen. "I'm looking for the woodcutter with a heart of gold," she said shyly, glancing at the brothers.

"That must be me!" Yu shouted.

"May we help you?" added Yan politely.

"Can you bring me the Dragon King's white pearl from his palace under the sea?" asked the princess. "I will marry the man who finds it." She pulled a pin from her hair. "Here, you'll need this."

Yu snatched the pin, and the brothers set off. Along the way, they passed a flooded village.

"Please help us," begged the villagers.

"I'm busy," snapped Yu, hurrying past.

Yan stopped. "I'll try," he said. "What can I do?"

"The water keeps rising. Only the Dragon King's black pearl will stop it," the villagers told him.

"I'll find it for you," promised Yan.

At last, the brothers reached the sea. "What now?" grumbled Yu.

"The pin," Yan reminded him. They held up the pin and the waves parted. "Look, there's the palace!"

The Dragon King welcomed them. Then he showed them his treasure. "You may each take one thing," he declared.

The brothers gasped. Gold and gems sparkled all around. In pride of place shone a huge white pearl...

Yu snatched it. "I'm going to get married!"

Yan kept looking until he found a tiny black pearl. "Please may I have this?" he asked.

The Dragon King nodded. Then he clapped his hands and the brothers found themselves back on the shore. They set off for home.

When they reached the village, Yan threw the black pearl into the water. Right away, the floods began to sink. "Thank you," cried the villagers.

The princess was there too. She smiled at Yan. "You really do have a heart of gold," she said.

"*I* found the white pearl," Yu interrupted. But when he looked, he found he was holding only a drop of muddy water. "What...?"

Now Yan's pearl began to glow under the water. The black had washed away, leaving the purest white.

"*That's* my pearl," the princess told Yan. "You shall be my husband." And they lived happily ever after. As for Yu – he was left all alone, just as he deserved.

∽ 117 ∽
from The Mermaid

Who would be
A mermaid fair,
Singing alone,
Combing her hair
Under the sea,
In a golden curl
With a comb of pearl,
On a throne?

Alfred Tennyson

The Frog Prince

Princess Posy was playing in the palace garden. Her father, the king, had given her a gleaming golden ball for her birthday.

"I wonder how high I can throw it?" thought Posy, and she hurled the ball way up into the sky. At first, it seemed as if it would touch the clouds, but then it plummeted like a stone, to land *splosh*, right in the middle of the palace pond.

"Oh no!" cried Posy. "Daddy will be furious if he finds out I've lost my golden ball."

At that moment, a little green frog hopped across the lily pads and onto the princess's hands.

"I'll get your ball," he croaked, "if you'll do something for me in return."

"Whatever you want," said Posy, in desperation.

"I want to be your friend," said the frog. "I want to eat from your plate and sleep on your pillow."

Posy couldn't think of anything worse than being friends with a horrible slimy frog, but she didn't say so. "Very well," she sighed. "Now hurry up and get my ball, before I'm called in for supper."

The frog was as good as his word. He dived down to the very bottom of the pond and tugged the ball from a tangle of weeds, before springing to the surface. "Here you are!" he said, handing it over.

"Thank goodness!" gasped Posy. She snatched the ball and ran home.

"Hey!" yelped the frog, as he hopped into the palace behind her. "What about your promise?"

"What's that frog doing here?" cried the king, as the frog leaped across the palace dining room.

"Your daughter promised to be my friend," croaked the frog. "She said I could eat from her plate and sleep on her pillow."

"Is this true, Posy?" asked the king.

"Of course not," lied Posy. "Who'd want to

be friends with a warty old frog?"

And with that, she picked up the frog and threw him out of the window.

"Don't be so cruel, Posy," cried the queen. "How would you like to be a frog?"

Posy suddenly felt ashamed. She rushed outside and picked up the frog from the flowerbed where he'd landed.

"I'm sorry I was so mean," she sniffed, cradling the limp, lifeless little frog in her hands. Posy lifted the frog to her lips and kissed him.

There was a whoosh, a bang and a cloud of swirling green smoke. As the smoke cleared, Posy saw that the frog had vanished. In his place stood a handsome young prince.

"A witch cast a spell on me and turned me into a frog," he explained. "Only a kiss from a princess could turn me back."

Posy smiled. "Do you still want to be friends?" she asked. "But you get your own plate!"

The prince grinned and followed her in for supper.

The Donkey Lie

"Nasreddin Hodja, may I borrow your donkey?" asked a friend one day. "It would only be for a few hours..."

"I would happily lend you my donkey," began the Hodja, trying to think of an excuse, "only he's not here right now."

Just then, the donkey gave out a loud BRRRAAAAYYYYYY!

"Shame on you," said his friend. "Now I know you're lying."

Nasreddin Hodja looked hurt by his friend's comment. "Are you going to believe the word of a Hodja?" he asked. "Or the word of a donkey?"

How the Rhinoceros Got His Skin

By the shores of the Red Sea, there lived a young man named Manee, who wore a wonderful hat that reflected the rays of the sun. He owned nothing more than his hat, his knife and his cooking stove.

One day, he took flour and water and currants and nutmeg and sugar and plums and made himself an enormous cake. He put it to cook on his piping hot stove, and cooked and cooked it, until it smelled most sensational.

But just as he was going to eat it, there came down to the beach a rhinoceros. He had a horn on his nose, two piggy eyes and very few manners.

In those days, Rhinoceros's skin was a snug, tight fit, with no wrinkles in it anywhere. All the same, he had no manners then and he has no manners now, and he never will have any manners.

"GRUNT!" went Rhinoceros, and Manee left the cake and shot up the nearest palm tree. Then Rhinoceros gobbled up the cake and went away, waving his tail behind him.

Manee came down from his palm tree and said:

Them that takes cakes
Which the great Manee bakes
Makes dreadful mistakes.

And he meant it.

Five weeks later, there was a heat wave in the Red Sea. Rhinoceros took off his skin and carried it over his shoulder as he came down to the beach to bathe. In those days it buttoned underneath with three buttons, just like a coat. He waddled straight into the water and blew bubbles through his nose, leaving his skin on the beach.

Manee waited until he was sure Rhinoceros wasn't watching. Then he rushed to his camp and filled his hat with cake crumbs. And he took that skin... and he scrubbed that skin... and he rubbed that skin full of old, dry, stale, tickly cake crumbs, as much as it could hold. When he was done, he climbed to the top of his palm tree and waited for Rhinoceros to come out of the water and put his skin back on.

And Rhinoceros did. He buttoned it up with the three buttons and right away it began to tickle him. He wanted to scratch, but that made it worse. Then he lay down in the sand and rolled and rolled, and every time he rolled, the cake crumbs tickled him worse and worse.

He ran to the palm tree and rubbed and rubbed himself against it. He rubbed so hard that he rubbed his skin into a great fold over his shoulders, and another fold underneath and he rubbed his three buttons right off.

Then he rubbed some more folds into his legs until he was quite out of temper. But it didn't make the least difference to the cake crumbs. They were right inside his skin and OH! how it tickled.

So Rhinoceros went home, very angry and horribly scratchy. And from that day to this, every rhinoceros has great folds in his skin and a very bad temper, on account of the tickly cake crumbs.

∽ 121 ∾

I do not like thee, Doctor Fell,
The reason why I cannot tell;
But this I know, and know full well,
I do not like thee, Doctor Fell.

Calico Pie

Calico pie, the Little Birds fly
Down to the calico tree,
Their wings were blue, and they sang "Tilly-loo!"
Till away they flew,
And they never came back to me!
They never came back! They never came back!
They never came back to me!

∽

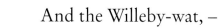

Calico Jam, the little Fish swam
Over the syllabub sea,
He took off his hat, to the Sole and the Sprat,
And the Willeby-wat, –
But he never came back to me!
He never came back! He never came back!
He never came back to me!

Calico Ban, the little Mice ran,
To be ready in time for tea,
Flippity flup, they drank it all up,
And danced in the cup, –
But they never came back to me!
They never came back! They never came back!
They never came back to me!

∾

Calico Drum, the Grasshoppers come,
The Butterfly, Beetle, and Bee,
Over the ground, around and around,
With a hop and a bound, –
But they never came back to me!
They never came back! They never came back!
They never came back to me!

Edward Lear

Robin Hood & Marian

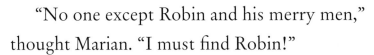

obin Hood had not always been an outlaw in Sherwood Forest. He had once lived a grand life next door to a beautiful girl named Marian.

Now that Marian was a young woman, she was more beautiful than ever, and the Sheriff of Nottingham had decided to marry her. Marian could think of nothing worse, but no one disobeyed the Sheriff and lived to tell the tale...

"No one except Robin and his merry men," thought Marian. "I must find Robin!"

That afternoon, while the Sheriff knocked on her front door, Marian crept out of the back. Disguised as a boy, with her hair tied up, she headed for Sherwood Forest.

As the trees grew thicker, Marian felt more lost and disorientated. At last, she found an old woodcutter in a clearing.

"Excuse me," she said, putting on a low voice. "I'm looking for Robin Hood."

"Fight me and I'll tell you where he is," said the woodcutter, sounding strangely familiar.

Marian wasn't afraid. Robin himself had taught her to fight. She could easily beat an old woodcutter. So she drew her sword and attacked with gusto.

An hour later, they were still fighting. Only when Marian slipped did she let out a cry – a cry which the woodcutter recognized.

"Marian?" he said in disbelief.

"Robin?" she replied, astounded.

The woodcutter took off his disguise and, sure enough, there stood Robin. The two were reunited and Marian instantly agreed to join Robin's band of merry men... and one merry woman.

❧ 124 ❧
The Tiger

Tiger! Tiger! burning bright
In the forests of the night,
What immortal hand or eye
Could frame thy fearful symmetry?

In what distant deeps or skies
Burned the fire of thine eyes?
On what wings dare he aspire?
What the hand dare seize the fire?

And what shoulder, and what art,
Could twist the sinews of thy heart?
And when thy heart began to beat,
What dread hand? And what dread feet?

What the hammer? What the chain?
In what furnace was thy brain?
What the anvil? What dread grasp
Dare its deadly terrors clasp?

When the stars threw down their spears,
And watered heaven with their tears,
Did he smile his work to see?
Did he who made the Lamb make thee?

Tiger! Tiger! burning bright
In the forests of the night,
What immortal hand or eye
Dare frame thy fearful symmetry?

William Blake

∽ 125 ∽

O Mistress Mine

O mistress mine, where are you roaming?
O, stay and hear; your true love's coming,
That can sing both high and low.
Trip no further, pretty sweeting;
Journeys end in lovers' meeting,
Every wise man's son doth know.

William Shakespeare

∽ 126 ∾
The Poor Man's Dream

Once, a poor man had a dream. In the dream, a genie told him, "Go to Cairo and seek your fortune. You will come home a rich and happy man."

In the morning, the man set off for Cairo on his donkey. It was a long way, and by the time he arrived, it was almost midnight. He didn't have money to pay for an inn, so he tied his donkey up outside a mosque and crept inside to sleep.

He was awoken by a loud noise. When he crept out to see what it was, he found a band of robbers breaking into the house next door. "Stop, thieves!" the man shouted, chasing after them.

The thieves fled, but people came running from houses down the street and found the man standing alone by the broken door. "You rotten thief!" shouted one. "You'll pay for this."

Before the man could say a word, he was dragged away and presented to the chief of police.

The chief of police took him aside to question

him. "Where are you from?" he asked.

"Baghdad," answered the poor man.

"Well, why come here?" asked the policeman.

"Because of my dream," the poor man answered miserably. "A genie told me I should come here and seek my fortune. But all I've found is trouble."

The chief of police burst out laughing. "You're a fool to take notice of a nonsense dream. I have a dream too. Every night in my dream a genie tells me to go to Baghdad and find a poor man's shabby blue house. Buried in the courtyard I will find riches beyond compare. Do you think I take any notice? Of course I don't. Now go home to Baghdad and don't let me catch you here again."

The poor man collected his donkey and rode home grinning from ear to ear. He went into his

shabby blue house, got a shovel, came outside and dug in the courtyard. There he found riches beyond compare, and he was happy to the end of his days.

Windy Nights

Whenever the moon and stars are set,
Whenever the wind is high,
All night long in the dark and wet,
A man goes riding by.
Late in the night when the fires are out,
Why does he gallop and gallop about?

Whenever the trees are crying aloud,
And ships are tossed at sea,
By, on the highway, low and loud,
By at the gallop goes he.
By at the gallop he goes, and then
By he comes back at the gallop again.

Robert Louis Stevenson

Is the Moon Tired?

Is the moon tired? She looks so pale
Within her misty veil:
She scales the sky from east to west,
And takes no rest.

Before the coming of the night
The moon shows papery white;
Before the dawning of the day
She fades away.

Christina Rossetti

The Flying Horse

A prince sat astride the brand new horse statue the royal sorcerer had given his father as a gift. "What happens if you push this button?" he asked. No sooner had he uttered the words than he was swept up into the sky. The wind rushed past his ears and he didn't hear the king shouting, "Stop!" beneath him.

"I wonder how you make it fly forwards," the prince said to himself, searching for more controls. "I wish I could see what lies beyond the sea." Before he had even finished his sentence, the horse was flying smoothly over the turquoise ocean.

"Aha," thought the prince, "it does whatever you wish..." Out loud he said, "I wish to fly lower!" In a heartbeat, he was skimming white-topped waves. "I wish to fly higher!" took him into the clouds.

After a few hours of amusing himself in this way, the prince sighed, "What I really wish for, is to find my one true love. I don't suppose you can do that, can you, flying horse?"

The horse sped on.

At nightfall, the prince found himself flying over a city with pretty domes and spires. Then, by itself, the horse landed gently on the flat roof of a palace.

The prince slipped off its back and looked around. Below him, the palace gardens lay dappled with silver moonlight. He caught his breath as a girl walked into view. "She is more beautiful than the moon itself," he thought.

Desperate to meet her, the prince climbed down the wall into the garden. "Excuse me," he called.

The girl gasped and spun around. "Who are you?" she asked. "Are you the suitor my father turned away? You are more handsome than he said."

The prince laughed, which made the girl laugh too. She looked even lovelier when she was smiling. They fell into talking – the prince told her all about the magic horse, and she told him about her father, the king, who didn't like visitors, certainly any who might ask to marry her. "In fact," she added, "he will be furious if he finds you here. You'd better go."

"I'd rather wait so I can ask him for your hand in marriage," said the prince. "If you'll marry me?"

"I will!" said the princess, turning pink.

The sun was already rising, and the couple sat and listened to the birds sing, until a gate burst open and in strode the king. "There you are, my blossom–" he began, but his face turned to thunder when he saw the prince. "Who are you?" he demanded.

"I'm a prince who wished for true love and have found it," said the prince. "May I have your daughter's hand in marriage?"

The king turned purple with rage. "I will have my army slay you for even thinking such a thing."

"That's no way to speak to an honest man," said the prince mildly. "But I'll fight your whole army, if that will help. I'll need my horse from the rooftop."

The king sent two soldiers to get it. They came back laughing, carrying the heavy statue between them. "This won't get you very far," giggled one.

The prince got on his horse on one side of the

battlefield, and the king's entire army gathered on the other. The princess was chalk-white and even the king was beginning to feel sorry for the prince. "You can't fight an army single-handedly," he said.

The prince smiled calmly. "It's no trouble."

Reluctantly, the king called, "Charge!"

The army charged. As they drew close, the prince rose up in the air on his horse. The soldiers fell over each other and landed in a heap.

The prince landed behind them. This time, the army surrounded him. But when the prince took off again, they all collided with one another and fell over. "This isn't fair!" shouted the general.

"No," the king laughed, "not fair at all for one man to defeat an entire army! I'd better save my army and accept this man as my son-in-law."

The very next day, the prince flew home with the princess. His father was delighted to see them. The sorcerer was given all the gold he could carry for helping the prince find his true love, and as for the happy couple, they were married on the spot.

Full House

One fine day, the local doctor came to visit Nasreddin Hodja. He was usually a calm man, but today he was tearing his hair out.

"Nasreddin Hodja," he cried. "You are very wise. Tell me what I should do. I have four children, a wife and a mother-in-law to house, but our home is tiny and I can't afford anything bigger."

The Hodja stroked his beard in thought. "Do you have any chickens?" he asked.

"Yes," replied the doctor. "I have five chickens and a rooster. Why?"

"Take them into your house as well, then come back to see me tomorrow."

The doctor was rather puzzled, but did as he was told. The next day he burst into the Hodja's house.

"It's worse than before!" he wailed. "Now there are chickens flapping everywhere!"

"Don't panic," said the Hodja. "Now, do you have any sheep or goats?"

"Yes," replied the doctor. "I have six goats..."

"Good, well take them into your house too and come back tomorrow."

As you can imagine, six goats, five chickens and a rooster don't leave much room for four children and three adults.

"I'm going crazy, Nasreddin!" the doctor exclaimed the next day. "Please do something to make it better, not worse."

"You have a donkey, don't you?"

"Don't tell me to take that in as well..."

"You'll thank me in the long run," advised the wise Hodja.

The man was so desperate, he would have tried anything. He squeezed his donkey into his house... and had the worst night of his life.

"Nasreddin!" he cried the next day. "I thought you were wise, but I've followed your advice and now my house is ruined, my wife wants to leave me and my mother-in-law wants to kill me!"

"Excellent," replied the Hodja. "Now take all the animals out of your house and come back tomorrow."

The doctor stared at the Hodja in disbelief before marching off, shaking his head and scowling. But by morning, he was grinning from ear to ear.

"Nasreddin!" he shouted, as he ran into the Hodja's yard. "You're a genius! My house has never seemed so big nor my family so happy. How can I ever thank you enough?"

"Oh, it was nothing," the Hodja said modestly.

∞ 131 ∞
The Magic Well

Beside a dusty track, in a distant part of China, stood a ramshackle tea house. The woman who ran it made very little money, for there were few passersby and fewer with money to spare for tea.

One scorching summer day, an old man with a long beard stopped outside. "I've come a long way," he said. "Please may I have some water?"

"Of course," said the woman. She went to the well and drew up a cupful of cold, clear water.

"I have no money," added the man.

"Don't worry," said the woman. "It's free."

"Tell me," said the man. "Why do you give drinks away when you have tea to sell?"

"People should help each other," said the woman.

The man smiled. "That is a good answer." He gulped down the water. "Now perhaps I can help you..." He waved his hand towards the well and a cool, sweet scent wafted up.

"That smells delicious!" cried the woman, running over. "What is it?" She drew up a cupful – and found the water had turned into iced tea. When she looked up, the old man had vanished.

Now people came from far and wide to taste the magical tea. The tea house thrived and the woman grew rich. But as she grew rich, she grew greedy.

A year later, the old man returned. When the woman saw him, she frowned. "Last time he filled my well with tea," she thought. "If only he'd filled it with something better..."

So she took him a cup of tea and, as he drank, she grumbled about how hard times were and how she wished she had a well full of wine. "I could make a lot more money from wine," she insisted.

The man listened in silence. Then he sighed, put down the cup and waved his hand at the well.

The woman ran to try it. "Pah! It's back to water."

There was a chuckle behind her. It was the old man. "Perhaps next time you will be grateful for what you have," he said.

∾ 132 ∾

What is Pink?

What is pink? a rose is pink
By the fountain's brink.
What is red? a poppy's red
In its barley bed.
What is blue? the sky is blue
Where the clouds float thro'.
What is white? a swan is white
Sailing in the light.
What is yellow? pears are yellow,
Rich and ripe and mellow.
What is green? the grass is green,
With small flowers between.
What is violet? clouds are violet
In the summer twilight.
What is orange? why, an orange
Just an orange!

Christina Rossetti

Shall I Compare Thee to a Summer's Day?

Shall I compare thee to a summer's day?
Thou art more lovely and more temperate:
Rough winds do shake the darling buds of May,
And summer's lease hath all too short a date:
Sometimes too hot the eye of heaven shines,
And often is his gold complexion dimmed;
And every fair from fair sometimes declines,
By chance or nature's changing course untrimmed;
But thy eternal summer shall not fade,
Nor lose possession of that fair thou owest,
Nor shall Death brag thou wanderest in his shade,
When in eternal lines to time thou growest:
So long as men can breathe, or eyes can see,
So long lives this, and this gives life to thee.

William Shakespeare

Upon Westminster Bridge

Earth has not anything to show more fair:
Dull would he be of soul who could pass by
A sight so touching in its majesty:
This City now doth, like a garment, wear
The beauty of the morning; silent, bare,
Ships, towers, domes, theatres, and temples lie
Open unto the fields, and to the sky;
All bright and glittering in the smokeless air.

Never did sun more beautifully steep
In his first splendour, valley, rock, or hill;
Ne'er saw I, never felt, a calm so deep!
The river glideth at his own sweet will:
Dear God! the very houses seem asleep;
And all the mighty heart is lying still!

William Wordsworth

∾ 135 ∾
The Wind & the Sun

The Wind was in the mood for an argument. "Hey, Sun!" he blustered, "I'm much stronger than you!"

"Whatever you say!" replied the Sun politely.

The Wind wasn't satisfied. "Let's have a contest," he demanded. "There's a man down there. We'll see which of us is strong enough to get his coat off." And the Sun agreed.

"Me first!" the Wind shouted, and he started to blow. He blew so hard that clouds scudded crazily across the sky and birds were blown off course. But the man just wrapped his coat more tightly around himself. "I can't see you doing any better, Sun," puffed the Wind grumpily.

The Sun simply smiled and started to shine. She shone so brightly that flowers opened their petals and lizards came out to bask in her warmth. The man wiped his forehead and took off his coat.

The Sun smiled another beaming smile. "You certainly are strong," she said to the Wind, "but you'll find you get what you want more easily if you use kindness rather than strength."

∞136∞
The Eagle

He clasps the crag with crooked hands;
Close to the sun in lonely lands,
Ring'd with the azure world, he stands.

The wrinkled sea beneath him crawls;
He watches from his mountain walls,
And like a thunderbolt he falls.

Alfred Tennyson

∞ 137 ∞
The Jade Leaf

A Chinese prince wanted a leaf carved out of precious jade. "And I want it perfect in every way," he insisted.

Now, what a Chinese prince wants, a Chinese prince gets, but jade is a very hard gemstone to carve. It took the country's best craftsman three whole years to make a thin, delicate leaf shape. It was so perfect, no one could tell the difference between the jade leaf and a real one.

The prince was overjoyed. He paid the craftsman handsomely and proudly displayed the leaf to his friends. They oohed and aahed at the intricate work – all except for a thoughtful man named Lieh Tzu.

"Thank goodness nature doesn't take three years to make a single leaf," he observed, "or our trees would all look rather bare..."

138

The Bear & the Wren

One summer, a bear was out walking with a wolf when he heard the most delightful song.

"Tell me, Wolf," he cried, "who is that singing?"

"It's the king of the birds," the wolf said for fun, when in fact it was only a little wren.

"Where does he live?" asked the gullible bear.

"Why, in a magnificent palace of course."

The bear's eyes grew wide with wonder. He followed the birdsong and saw two little birds flying in and out of a hole in a tree.

"There's a palace in *there*?" growled the bear.

"Take a look and see," teased the wolf, before slinking off into the shadows.

The bear waited until the birds had flown away, then peered inside the hole. All he could see was some messy moss and five very ugly chicks gaping up at him.

"This is a pigsty, not a palace," huffed the bear "and you're far too shabby to be royal children."

The bear stomped back to his den, leaving five very indignant chicks. They squawked and squawked until their parents returned, and then they squawked some more. "How *dare* that bear call us shabby!"

"How dare he indeed," the parents agreed.

They flew directly to the bear's cave and called out to him. "Old Growler, you have insulted our children and our home. We have no choice but to declare war on you."

The bear grew alarmed and summoned his four-legged friends. Meanwhile, the wrens called together all who flew in the sky.

"We need to know their tactics," said the father wren. "Little gnat, go and listen in on their meeting."

So the gnat flew off and hid under a leaf outside the bear's cave.

"Fox, you shall be my general," the bear was saying, "If the battle's going well, hold your tail up high. Only let it down if all is lost, then we shall surrender."

The gnat hurried back
to the flying animals' camp
and shared what she had heard.

"Excellent work," said the
wren. "Now here's *our* plan."

(But let's not listen too
closely – it might spoil the story.
Instead we'll race forward to the day of the battle...)

"CHARGE!" warbled the wren.

A buzzing-chirping swarm of insects and
birds descended on the army of four-legged
animals. Except, that is, for the hornet. She had
orders to attack a different target. With a sudden
*bzzzzzzzzzzzzzz s*he darted towards the fox and
stung him viciously on his bottom.

"Ouch!" yelped the fox, accidentally letting
his tail drop. The bear saw the fox's sign and
immediately surrendered. As for the wrens, they
returned victorious to their children.

"We still think he needs to say sorry," chirped the
chicks, but they never saw the bear again.

∾ 139 ∾
A Rainbow

Purple, yellow, red, and green,
The king cannot reach it, nor yet the queen.

∾ 140 ∾
Where the Bee Sucks

Where the bee sucks, there suck I:
In a cowslip's bell I lie;
There I couch when owls do cry.
On the bat's back I do fly
After summer merrily.
Merrily, merrily shall I live now
Under the blossom that hangs on the bough.

William Shakespeare

The Three Wishes

Bob Knot was a penniless woodcutter. One morning he was about to chop down a massive oak tree, when a fairy fluttered out from a hole in the trunk.

"Please don't chop down this tree!" she begged. "It's my home."

"But I need to sell wood, so I can buy food," Bob explained. "My wife and I haven't eaten properly in days."

The fairy thought for a moment. "Spare this tree," she said, "and I'll give you and your wife three wishes."

"It's a deal!" declared Bob excitedly. He rushed home to tell his wife the good news.

"I don't believe it," Mrs. Knot said, when she heard what the fairy had promised.

"I'll prove it," said Bob, licking his lips. "I wish for a big fat sausage!"

The next second, a sausage appeared, *ping*, on the kitchen table.

"Hooray!" cried Bob with delight. "It worked."

"You silly man," grumbled his wife. "Why wish for a *sausage*? I wish the stupid thing was stuck to your nose."

The next second, *ping*, the sausage was stuck fast to Bob's nose.

"You silly woman," Bob retorted. "You've wasted another wish. And I look completely ridiculous. I wish this had never happened."

With a *ping*, the sausage was back on the kitchen table.

"We had three wishes," sighed Mrs. Knot. "And all of them were completely wasted."

"Oh well," said Bob, grabbing a pan. "At least we have a sausage for lunch."

The Quangle Wangle's Hat

On the top of the Crumpetty Tree
The Quangle Wangle sat,
But his face you could not see,
On account of his Beaver Hat.
For his Hat was a hundred and two feet wide,
With ribbons and bibbons on every side
And bells, and buttons, and loops, and lace,
So that nobody ever could see the face
Of the Quangle Wangle Quee.

The Quangle Wangle said
To himself on the Crumpetty Tree –
"Jam; and jelly; and bread;
Are the best of food for me!
But the longer I live on this Crumpetty Tree,
The plainer than ever it seems to me
That very few people come this way,
And that life on the whole is far from gay!"
Said the Quangle Wangle Quee.

But there came to the Crumpetty Tree,
Mr. and Mrs. Canary;
And they said, "Did ever you see
Any spot so charmingly airy?
May we build a nest on your lovely Hat?
Mr. Quangle Wangle, grant us that!
O please let us come and build a nest
Of whatever material suits you best,
Mr. Quangle Wangle Quee!"

~

And besides, to the Crumpetty Tree
Came the Stork, the Duck, and the Owl;
The Snail and the Bumble-Bee,
The Frog, and the Fimble Fowl;
(The Fimble Fowl, with a Corkscrew leg);
And all of them said, "We humbly beg,
We may build our home on your lovely Hat,
Mr. Quangle Wangle, grant us that!
Mr. Quangle Wangle Quee!"

~

And the Golden Grouse came there,
And the Pobble who has no toes,
And the small Olympian bear,
And the Dong with a luminous nose.
And the Blue Baboon, who played the flute,
And the Orient Calf from the Land of Tute,
And the Attery Squash, and the Bisky Bat,
All came and built on the lovely Hat
Of the Quangle Wangle Quee.

And the Quangle Wangle said
To himself on the Crumpetty Tree,
"When all these creatures move
What a wonderful noise there'll be!"
And at night by the light of the Mulberry moon
They danced to the Flute of the Blue Baboon,
On the broad green leaves of the Crumpetty Tree,
And all were as happy as happy could be,
With the Quangle Wangle Quee.

Edward Lear

∞ 143 ∞

There was an old man from Montrose,
Who dozed off wherever he chose;
The fellow was able,
To sleep on a table,
Where he gave a loud snore through his nose.

Russell Punter

∾ 144 ∾

Prince Hyacinth
& his Enormous Nose

There was once a king who loved a princess, but he couldn't marry her, for she was under an enchantment. Eventually, he went to a fairy for help.

"The princess has a cat," said the fairy. "Step on the cat's tail and you will break the spell."

The king rushed to the princess's palace, certain of success. But every time he reached out for the cat's tail, the cat flicked it away. Finally, the king came upon the cat lying fast asleep. "Aha!" he cried, and brought his foot crashing down. With a yell, the cat sprang up and instantly changed into a wizard with angry, flashing eyes.

"You've broken the enchantment," he fumed, "so you may marry the princess. But here's my revenge: you will have a son with an enormous nose! And he will never be happy until he realizes it."

With that, the enchanter vanished, and the king, laughing at the ludicrous threat, made haste to marry the princess.

But all too soon the king died, and his wife was left with nothing but their little son, who was called Hyacinth. The little prince had large eyes of the prettiest cornflower blue but alas! his nose was so enormous it covered half his face.

The queen was wracked with worry. "Oh dear!" she cried, every time she looked at it, sobbing loudly. "He is cursed!"

"It's really not as large as it looks," promised her maids. And from that moment, everything was done to make Prince Hyacinth's nose seem normal. No one was ever allowed to come near him who didn't have a nose which resembled his own. Great princes, he was told, *always* had huge noses. As a result, the prince grew up convinced that his nose was a thing of great beauty and never wished it any smaller.

Upon his twentieth birthday, the queen decided it was time her son married. She ordered portraits of the prettiest princesses to be sent to the palace, so her son could choose between them.

"This is the one for me!" cried Prince Hyacinth, pointing to the portrait of Princess Esme, and he rode off to meet her. But just as he reached her palace, the wizard appeared in a clap of thunder, and whirled her away.

Prince Hyacinth was devastated. "I'll keep looking until I find her!" he declared. He rode away for a week and a day, until at last, exhausted and starving, he came upon a cavern. Inside sat a little old woman, who looked at least a hundred years old.

It was, in fact, the fairy who had once helped his father, the king, and was now determined to help Hyacinth, too. As soon as she saw Prince Hyacinth, she started laughing at his nose.

"It is no funnier than your own," snapped the prince. They sat down for supper, and though the fairy did all she could to point out the extraordinary nature of his nose, Prince Hyacinth wouldn't believe a word. Instead, he grew so fed up of the fairy's remarks that he rode hastily away.

"If I can't *tell* him about his ridiculous nose," thought the fairy, "I'll have to *show* him."

After another week and a day, Prince Hyacinth found Princess Esme at last. But she was trapped in a golden cage. Prince Hyacinth tried all he could to free her, but nothing would work. In despair, she reached out her hand so that he might kiss it, but whichever way he turned, he could never raise it to his lips, as his nose always got in the way.

"Well," said Prince Hyacinth at last, "I must admit my nose *is* too long."

No sooner had he spoken the words, than the golden cage opened like a flower and out stepped the princess.

The fairy appeared and took Princess Esme by the hand.

"You see," she said to Prince Hyacinth, "how important it is to know the truth about yourself."

Prince Hyacinth always remembered this lesson, and he and Princess Esme lived happily ever after.

∞ 145 ∞

Moses supposes his toeses are roses,
But Moses supposes erroneously.
For nobody's toeses are posies of roses,
As Moses supposes his toeses to be.

∞ 146 ∞

Peter Piper picked a peck of pickled peppers;
A peck of pickled peppers Peter Piper picked;
If Peter Piper picked a peck of pickled peppers,
Where's the peck of pickled peppers Peter Piper picked?

Little Miss Muffet

Little Miss Muffet,
Sat on a tuffet,
Eating her curds and whey.

Along came a spider,
Who dropped down beside her
And frightened Miss Muffet away.

"Help!" cried Miss Muffet.
She ran from her tuffet
And into the woods down below.

"Come back!" called the spider.
He rushed off to find her.
"I'm sorry for scaring you so."

The little girl sighed.
"What a bad place to hide.
Now I'm lost! I'll be stuck here all night."

When milk turns sour, it separates into solids known as curds, and a watery liquid named whey.

Then she heard a deep growl
And an ear-splitting howl.
They gave poor Miss Muffet a fright.

A big wolf jumped out.
He said with a shout,
"It's time for my dinner, my dear.

I'll have little girl pie!"
"Put her down!" came a cry.
"Don't worry – Seb Spider is here."

The wolf gave a smile.
"I do like your style.
But what can you do against me?"

"I'll show you," said Seb.
He spun a strong web
And tied the bad wolf to a tree.

Miss Muffet said, "Seb,
What a wonderful web.
Now let's go!" So Seb showed her the way.

Now she's friends with Seb Spider.
He hangs down beside her,
And spins for Miss Muffet all day.

adapted by Russell Punter

∽ 148 ∾
The Mice That Ate Iron

One day, a young merchant brought his iron weighing scales into a shop. "I'm going away for a while," he told the shopkeeper, "and these are too heavy for me to carry. Please could you look after them until I return?"

"No problem," said the shopkeeper. "They might be rather useful," he thought.

When the merchant returned from his long trip, he went to collect the scales. "Sorry," the shopkeeper said, "the mice ate them."

"But they were made of iron!" exclaimed the merchant. "Mice can't chew through metal."

The shopkeeper shrugged. "We have big, strong mice around here..." he said.

The merchant frowned, and left the shop without his scales. The very next day, however, he came rushing back. "Something terrible has happened," he panted. "I just saw a bird swoop down in the street and steal your donkey and cart!"

"What?" cried the shopkeeper, running outside in a panic. Then he stopped. "Wait a minute. Birds aren't strong enough to carry off a whole donkey and cart."

"In a place where mice are strong enough to eat iron, I shudder to think what the birds could do," the merchant observed.

"I see," said the shopkeeper, turning red. "I'll just go and get your scales."

∞ 149 ∞

Six little mice sat down to spin,
Kitten passed by and she peeped in.
"What are you doing, my little men?"
"Weaving coats for gentlemen."
"Shall I come in and cut off your threads?"
"No, no, Mistress Kitty, you'd bite off our heads."
"Oh no I'll not. I'll help you to spin."
"That may be so, but you don't come in."

∽ 150 ∽
Brer Rabbit & the Moon in the Pond

Brer Rabbit was a tricksy sort of a fellow, who liked nothing better than a laugh at someone else's expense. One fine day in May, he was busy plotting some fun. "I haven't had a giggle for weeks," he realized. "I'd better do something about it."

After a little more thinking, a grin spread across his whiskered face, and he hopped off into the woods.

That evening, a crowd of animals gathered at the pond. "Did Brer Rabbit invite you too?" asked Brer Fox as he joined them. The others nodded.

Just then Brer Rabbit himself came sauntering down the lane. "Good evening, everyone," he called. He was carrying a bundle of fishing lines and a big net, which he set down on the bank. "It's the perfect evening for a little fishing," he announced. "I've brought plenty of nets so we can all fish together."

"What a nice idea," said Brer Fox.

Brer Rabbit peered into the pond, and his smile turned to a frown. "Heavens, what a disaster!" he shouted.

"What's wrong?" asked Brer Bear.

"Just look for yourself," said Brer Rabbit. "The Moon has fallen right out of the sky." He pointed to the middle of the still pond at the Moon's round, silvery reflection.

"Well I never," said Brer Fox, staring hard.

"Deary me," Brer Rabbit said sadly. "If the Moon sinks to the bottom of the pond, that will be the end of it. There'll be no more moonlit walks at night..."

"Can't we stop it?" said Brer Fox, who loved walking in the moonlight.

"Nothing left to sing to..." Brer Rabbit went on.

"We must save it!" said Brer Wolf, who loved nothing better than singing to the Moon.

Brer Rabbit rubbed his chin thoughtfully. "Unless..." he started. Then he shook his head, "No, it's no use. I'm just not tall enough."

"What is it?" urged Brer Bear. "I can help."

"Well..." said Brer Rabbit, "we could try catching the Moon in this net..."

Before long, Fox, Bear and Wolf were all inching into the chilly water, each holding part of the net.

"Brrr, this water is cold," Brer Fox shivered.

"F-freezing," Brer Wolf quivered.

"I can't feel my legs," Brer Bear shuddered.

"Just a little further," urged Brer Rabbit.

Quaking with cold, the three animals waded deeper. When they were up to their waists, Brer Rabbit said, "Now spread out the net. You'll have to bend all the way down to scoop up the Moon."

The animals winced as they bent down in the cold water to spread the net under the Moon.

"That's it," said Brer Rabbit. "Next, you need to pull the net up to lift the Moon back into the sky. I expect it's going to be very, very heavy. So each of you pull as hard as you can on my count of three. Are you ready?"

The animals braced themselves.

"One, two, three... LIFT!" called Brer Rabbit.

The three animals heaved the net up with all their might. The net flew up in the air, scattering the moon's reflection into a thousand silver droplets, and all three animals fell backwards – SPLASH! – into the water.

The animals on the bank fell around laughing.

"Well done, well done!" chuckled Brer Rabbit.

"Did it work?" spluttered Brer Fox, as he and his dripping companions struggled back to shore.

"Oh, it worked," grinned Brer Rabbit. "I haven't laughed as much in a long time."

"What did you say?" Brer Bear glowered.

"Look up, look up," said Brer Rabbit. "The Moon is safe and sound."

Sure enough, when everyone looked up, they saw the Moon safely shining in the sky.

The Animals Went In Two By Two

The animals went in two by two,
Hurrah! Hurrah!
The animals went in two by two,
The elephant and the kangaroo,
And they all went into the ark
For to get out of the rain.

The animals went in three by three,
Hurrah! Hurrah!
The animals went in three by three,
The wasp, the ant and the bumble bee,
And they all went into the ark
For to get out of the rain.

The animals went in four by four,

Hurrah! Hurrah!

The animals went in four by four,

The great hippopotamus stuck in the door,

And they all went into the ark

For to get out of the rain.

∾ 152 ∾
Whether the Weather

Whether the weather be fine

Or whether the weather be not,

Whether the weather be cold

Or whether the weather be hot,

We'll weather the weather

Whatever the weather,

Whether we like it or not.

∾ 153 ∾
Strange Story

I saw a pigeon making bread
I saw a girl composed of thread
I saw a towel one mile square
I saw a meadow in the air
I saw a rocket walk a mile
I saw a pony make a file
I saw a blacksmith in a box
I saw an orange kill an ox
I saw a butcher made of steel
I saw a small knife dance a reel
I saw a sailor twelve feet high
I saw a ladder in a pie
I saw an apple fly away
I saw a sparrow making hay
I saw a farmer like a dog
I saw a puppy mixing grog
I saw three men who saw these too
And will confirm what I tell you.

At first glance, this seems like a nonsense rhyme – but try reading it with
a pause after the word pigeon in the first line, and then reading the second
half of each line with the first half of the following line.

Duck's Ditty

All along the backwater,
Through the rushes tall,
Ducks are a-dabbling,
Up tails all!

Ducks' tails, drakes' tails,
Yellow feet a-quiver,
Yellow bills all out of sight
Busy in the river!

Slushy green undergrowth
Where the roach swim –
Here we keep our larder,
Cool and full and dim.

Everyone for what he likes!
We like to be
Heads down, tails up,
Dabbling free!

High in the blue above
Swifts whirl and call –
We are down a-dabbling
Up tails all!

Kenneth Grahame

∽ 155 ∽

AEIOU

We are little airy creatures,
All of different voice and features;
One of us in glass is set.
One of us you'll find in jet.
T'other you may see in tin,
And the fourth a box within.
If the fifth you should pursue,
It can never fly from you.

Jonathan Swift

Sinbad: Voyage Three

After my second trip, I lived in luxury – until my diamonds ran out and I sought adventure.

Off I went to the port of Basra. After several days at sea, a mighty storm blew our ship onto a strange shore. Immediately we were attacked by hundreds of monkeys so we fled to the hills and found ourselves in the courtyard of a castle.

Hungry and thirsty, we searched around for something to eat. Everything was gigantic, from the pots and pans lying around, to the monstrous shadow that appeared at the entrance. We looked up at the shadow's owner and screamed in fright.

As tall as a palm tree, and with one enormous eye, a ghastly giant stood towering over us.

He bolted the castle gate behind him, lit a roaring fire, eyed us hungrily, then roasted a whole sheep for his supper.

I shuddered in the shadows with the other men.

As darkness fell, the giant settled down to sleep and was soon letting out thunderous snores.

"We're doomed!" moaned the sailors.

"We need to escape," I murmured and quickly told them my plan. There was no time to spare...

First, we heaved a sharp metal roasting spit into the hot embers of the fire. Then we used our turbans to bind firewood together and make a raft. When the end of the spit was glowing red, we lifted it carefully, tiptoed up to the sleeping giant and, on the whispered count of three, poked his bottom.

"AIIEEEOOOOOOEEEEE!" yelled the giant, leaping to his feet. He ran to the gate, unbolted it and rushed down to the sea to plunge his bottom in the cool water.

We crept after him, carrying our raft. Silently, we pushed out to sea and mercifully were picked up by a passing ship. Back in Baghdad, the sailors were so grateful, they showered me with gold. I was a rich man yet again, but that's not the end of my story...

The Hares & the Frogs

The hares were feeling twitchy, as usual. Someone always seemed to be picking on them. Dogs chased them, people set traps for them and mischievous foxes crept up on them when they weren't looking. The hares sat huddled in a group, glancing around nervously for any sign of trouble.

"Look out," cried one, "Hawk overhead – take cover, quick!"

The hares scampered as fast as they could to a clump of thick bushes beside a pond. But, as they came near, they heard cries of panic and splashing.

"Dive, dive!" chorused a colony of frogs, plunging headlong into the pond. "Hare attack!"

From the bushes the hares began to laugh. "If they're afraid of us, they must get picked on even more than we do," said one of the hares.

"Yes, there's always someone worse off than yourself," another agreed.

The Magic Mulberry Tree

Once, in China, there were three sisters who lived in a cottage beside a large, leafy mulberry tree. The tree shaded them in summer and sheltered them in winter, and they loved to climb its branches and eat its sweet purple berries.

One day, as the sun was setting, there was rap on their door. "Hello dears," muttered a low voice. "It's your granny come to visit."

The girls glanced at each other in surprise. "We didn't know you were coming," exclaimed the youngest, opening the door.

A stooped figure shuffled in, wrapped in shawls. In the darkening room, it was hard to see.

The eldest sister, whose name was Shan, began to feel suspicious. "Let me light a candle," she said.

"No, I like the dark," growled a husky voice.

"Let me take your shawl," said Shan.

"No, I'm too cold."

"Let me get you a chair," said Shan. As she brushed past the visitor, she felt something hairy. "Fur?" she thought, peering closer. "Fangs? That's not Granny, that's a wolf!"

'Granny' wolf looked at the girls and licked his lips. "I'm hungry," he rasped. "What shall I eat?"

Shan thought quickly. "How about berries?"

"Berries?" snorted the wolf. "I want meat!"

"Ah, but these berries are magic," promised Shan, winking at her sisters. "They become any food you want. Come and see." She picked up a basket and a rope, and beckoned everyone outside.

Quickly, the sisters climbed the tree and began eating the berries.

"Mmm, ice cream," sighed the youngest.

"Candied plums," giggled the second.

"Juicy steak," added Shan.

"Pass some to me," demanded the wolf, drooling.

"Oh no, you have to eat the berries up here," called Shan. "The magic only works in the tree."

"But I can't climb," moaned the wolf.

"We'll pull you up," said Shan. She let down the basket, the wolf leaped in and the girls began to haul him up. He was hardly halfway when – *whoosh BUMP!* They let go and the wolf plummeted to the ground and flew from the basket.

"Ouch!" he growled. "Be careful."

"Sorry, Granny," they called down. "The rope slipped. Let's try again."

The wolf clambered back in. This time he was three-quarters of the way when – *whoosh BUMP!*

"Ooooow!" howled the wolf. "Useless girls."

"Sorry, Granny," they called. "We'll try harder."

The wolf stepped gingerly into the basket. He was almost at the top when – *whoosh **BUMP!***

"Aaaaargh!" yowled the wolf. Before the sisters could say anything, he turned tail and fled. So the sisters went on living happily in their cottage, and the wolf never bothered them again.

A Good Play

We built a ship upon the stairs
All made of the back-bedroom chairs,
And filled it full of sofa pillows
To go a-sailing on the billows.

We took a saw and several nails,
And water in the nursery pails;
And Tom said, "Let us also take
An apple and a slice of cake;"
Which was enough for Tom and me
To go a-sailing on, till tea.

We sailed along for days and days,
And had the very best of plays;
But Tom fell out and hurt his knee,
So there was no one left but me.

Robert Louis Stevenson

~ 160 ~
Robin Hood & the Golden Arrow

The Sheriff of Nottingham spent many sleepless nights plotting how to capture Robin Hood, until finally an idea came to him...

"There's an archery competition taking place in Nottingham," announced Little John to Robin and his men, a few days later, "with a golden arrow for the winner!"

"Then that arrow is mine," said Robin, his eyes lighting up.

"Don't go," warned Friar Tuck, "it's sure to be some sort of trap."

"I'll go in disguise," said Robin, "and take Little John for support."

The two outlaws made their way to Nottingham, dressed as merchants. No one spotted them in the excited crowd.

As Robin won his way through the early rounds of the competition, the Sheriff looked over the crowd in disappointment.

"I was sure that rascal Hood would turn up," he grumbled. "I thought he'd love an opportunity to show off..."

Only three archers made it through to the final: the Sheriff's man Gilbert, a local man named Adam, and Robin, still in disguise. In front of a large crowd, Gilbert fired first. His arrow struck the target just a whisker away from the bull's eye. Adam went next, but his arrow strayed wide.

"We may not have caught Robin Hood," thought the Sheriff, "but at least my man will win the competition..."

Last of all, the merchant stepped forward, raised his bow and fired so accurately that his arrow split Gilbert's in two and pierced the bull's eye. The crowd cheered, and the Sheriff groaned as he handed over the arrow. Then the two merchants disappeared down the street.

"Three cheers for Robin!" whooped his merry men, back in their forest hideout.

But Robin was frowning. "I'm the best archer and I want the Sheriff to know it…"

So, that evening, he crept to the Sheriff's castle, fired an arrow through an open window and delivered a note to the Sheriff.

Thanks for the golden arrow! Robin Hood

∽ 161 ∽
Be Like the Bird

Be like the bird who,
Resting in his flight
On a twig too slight,
Feels it bend beneath him
Yet sings,
Knowing he has wings.

Victor Hugo

∽ 162 ∽

Godfrey Gordon Gustavus Gore

Godfrey Gordon Gustavus Gore –
No doubt you have heard the name before –
Was a boy who never would shut a door!

The wind might whistle, the wind might roar,
And teeth be aching and throats be sore,
But still he never would shut the door.

His father would beg, his mother implore,
"Godfrey Gordon Gustavus Gore,
We really *do* wish you would shut the door!"

Their hands they wrung, their hair they tore;
But Godfrey Gordon Gustavus Gore
Was deaf as the buoy out at the Nore.

When he walked forth the folks would roar,
"Godfrey Gordon Gustavus Gore,
Why don't you think to shut the door?"

They rigged out a Shutter with sail and oar,
And threatened to pack off Gustavus Gore
On a voyage of penance to Singapore.

But he begged for mercy, and said, "No more!
Pray do not send me to Singapore
On a Shutter, and then I will shut the door!"

"You will?" said his parents; "then keep on shore!
But mind you do! For the plague is sore
Of a fellow that never will shut the door,
Godfrey Gordon Gustavus Gore!"

William Brighty Rands

∽ 163 ∽
The Crow & the Jug

It was a scorching hot day and Crow was thirsty. She flapped her way wearily over fields and gardens, trying to find something to drink. But there was no water to be seen anywhere...

And then, in the corner of a garden, Crow spotted an old, chipped jug. "Aha! That might have some water," she croaked, and flew down to find out.

Crow looked inside. Sure enough, right at the bottom was some cool, fresh water – but she just couldn't reach it with her beak. She thought for a moment, then flew around the garden collecting stones. One by one, she dropped them into the jug. As the stones filled the jug, the water rose up... and up... until, finally, Crow could reach it.

"I'll remember that," she thought, as she gulped down the water. "If you really need to do something, you can usually find a way."

∽ 164 ∽

The Hairy Toe

An old woman was in the woods searching for wild herbs to add to her stew.

"What's this," she muttered, holding up a hairy, bulbous object. "Is it a toe-shaped root or a root-shaped toe? No matter. It's big and fleshy and will be very tasty in my stew."

She took the hairy object home and cooked it for her supper.

That night she went to bed full and happy, but at midnight she stirred uneasily in her sleep. A howling wind was entering her dreams, carrying a booming voice with it.

"Where's my toe?" it called out. "I want my toe!"

The woman sat up in bed and pulled the covers around her. A dark shadow fell across the moon and a voice called out louder and nearer:

"Where's my toe? I want my toe."

Heavy footsteps stomped on the garden path. The old woman shuddered in her bed. "At least I locked the front door," she thought.

CRRASHHH! went the front door.

The old woman yanked the covers over her head.

Stomp, stomp, stomp, went the footsteps on the stairs. "Where's my toe?" a voice echoed around the landing. "I want my toe."

The old woman peeped out from under the covers. A massive figure was filling the doorway.

"I-I-I..." she stammered.

"You... *what*?" asked the deep voice.

"I ate it," said the woman hurriedly.

And softly, very softly, the giant figure replied, "I know."

No one ever saw the old woman again. The only clue to her disappearance was a large footprint in her garden – with its big toe missing...

∽ 165 ∽
The Body's Quarrel

The parts of the body were all grumbling. "That belly," they moaned, "it doesn't do a thing for us. It just sits there absorbing food!"

"It's so unfair!" piped up the mouth, "I have to do all the biting, chewing and swallowing for it."

"Good point," the hands and arms joined in, "but don't forget us! We get the food up to you, in the first place."

"Tell you what," the brain intervened, "let's teach that lazy belly a lesson. We'll go on strike – when it doesn't get any food, it will soon see that it needs to start doing something useful."

They all did as the brain suggested, and stopped eating. But things didn't go as they expected. The belly soon grew slack and empty, but the brain felt feeble and dizzy, the mouth became dry and parched, and the hands and arms were weak and trembly, too. In fact, the whole body felt terrible.

"What's going on?" the mouth mumbled faintly.

The brain thought as hard as it could manage, in its weakened condition. "We were wrong," it replied eventually. "All the time we thought the belly did nothing but take in food. But really, it was sending out nourishment, to keep us all going. It's true that the belly can't manage without us... but we can't manage without the belly either."

∞ 166 ∞

There was an Old Lady of Chertsey,
Who made a remarkable curtsey;
She twirled round and round
Till she sank underground,
Which distressed all the people of Chertsey.

Edward Lear

∾ 167 ∾

Ten Fools

"As Emperor, I only ever meet wise men. I'm tired of all their cleverness," Emperor Akbar complained to his best advisor, Birbal, one morning. "I want you to bring me ten of the biggest fools in my kingdom."

"That shouldn't be difficult," said Birbal, and he set out right away.

Just outside the palace, he met a man riding a horse, with a stack of firewood balanced precariously on his head.

"Why don't you put the firewood on the saddle behind you?" he asked the man.

"I don't want to tire out my horse," the man replied. "So I thought I'd simply carry the firewood myself."

Birbal smiled. "Come with me," he said. "The emperor wants to meet you."

Further along, he saw a man lying in a ditch with his arms in the air. "Help!" shouted the man.

"I fell in and can't get out. Don't touch my arms, though," he added quickly.

"Why not?" Birbal asked, hauling the man to his feet by his belt.

"My wife asked me to buy a pot this big. I can't move my arms or I'll forget the size," the man said.

"Come with me," said Birbal. "Emperor's orders."

No sooner had they set off, than another man came racing past.

"What's the hurry?" Birbal called.

The man stopped. "I was trying to see how far the sound of my voice carries," he panted. "So I was

chasing after it. But I think I've lost it now."

"Try another day," Birbal told him. "The emperor wants to meet you."

A little further on, they came to two men having a fierce argument. "What's wrong?" Birbal asked.

The first man explained. "We were both praying. I prayed for buffalo, but then my so-called friend here went and prayed for a tiger!"

"What's wrong with that?" Birbal asked.

"Isn't it obvious?" the man spluttered indignantly. "His tiger is going to eat my buffalo!"

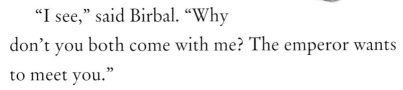

"Well it's hungry!" the second man shouted.

"I see," said Birbal. "Why don't you both come with me? The emperor wants to meet you."

Another man joined them, carrying a pot of oil on his head. "Those two have been fighting since the crack of dawn," he said. "No word of a lie. If

I'm lying, may my blood be spilled like this," and he poured his oil all over the ground.

"Oh dear," he said, as it sank into the dust. "Now I've lost all my oil."

"I think you'd better come with us too," said Birbal.

On the way back to the palace, they passed a man searching frantically on the ground. "Have you lost something?" Birbal asked.

"I lost a ring over there," said the man, pointing to the opposite side of the road.

"Why are you looking here, then?" Birbal said.

"The light's better here," replied the man.

"Join us," Birbal smiled. "Emperor's orders."

In front of the palace gates, they found a man digging hole after hole in the ground.

"Did you bury something?" Birbal asked him.

"My gold," said the man. "I can't find it."

"Didn't you mark the spot?" Birbal asked.

"I didn't need to," said the man. "There was a nice fluffy cloud right above it. But it's gone now!"

"Too bad," Birbal murmured. "Come with me. The emperor wants to meet you."

Birbal returned to the palace and presented the men, one by one, to Emperor Akbar and his court. By the time he had finished, the emperor was weeping with laughter.

"They shall each have a bag of gold for coming to see me," he said. "But Birbal, I asked for ten of the biggest fools in my kingdom. You have only brought eight. Where are the other two?"

Birbal bowed. "One is sitting on the throne, sir, and the other is bowing before it," he said.

"Explain yourself," demanded the emperor.

"If you'll forgive me, sir, you and I are the other two fools," said Birbal. "You for setting such a ridiculous task, and I for carrying it out."

There was a dangerous silence. Then, much to everyone's relief, the emperor roared with laughter.

"You have earned a bag of gold too, Birbal," he said. "But as far as I'm concerned, you're priceless."

∽ 168 ∾
A Man in the Wilderness

A man in the wilderness said to me,
"How many strawberries grow in the sea?"
I answered him, as I thought good,
"As many red herrings as swim in the wood."

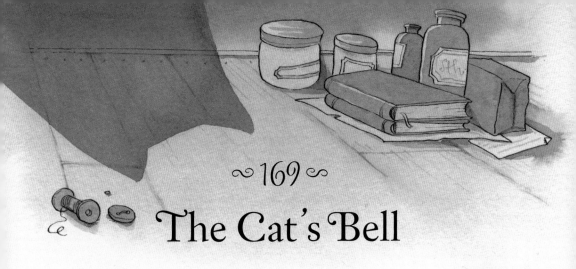

∽ 169 ∽
The Cat's Bell

All the mice lived in terror. Their enemy, the cat, stalked the house silently, pouncing on them one by one.

"It's an outrage!" the remaining mice squeaked. "Something should be done!"

So the oldest and wisest mouse called a meeting. "Any ideas?" she asked. A young mouse spoke up.

"The answer's obvious," he said. "We tie a bell around the cat's neck. That way, we'll always hear the cat coming and have time to run away."

The oldest mouse sighed. "Great idea," she said, "but will you volunteer to tie on the bell?" The young mouse turned pale and hurriedly backed away.

"You see," the oldest mouse explained, "some things are easy to say but not so easy to do."

∞170∞

Mr. Toad

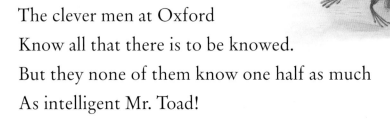

The world has held great Heroes,
As history-books have showed;
But never a name to go down to fame
Compared with that of Toad!

The clever men at Oxford
Know all that there is to be knowed.
But they none of them know one half as much
As intelligent Mr. Toad!

The animals sat in the Ark and cried,
Their tears in torrents flowed.
Who was it said, "There's land ahead."
Encouraging Mr. Toad!

The Army all saluted
As they marched along the road.
Was it the King? Or Kitchener?
No. It was Mr. Toad!

The Queen and her Ladies-in-waiting
Sat at the window and sewed.
She cried, "Look! who's that *handsome* man?"
They answered, "Mr. Toad."

Kenneth Grahame

∾ 171 ∾

There was an Old Man of the Isles,
Whose face was pervaded with smiles;
He sung "High dum diddle,"
And played on the fiddle,
That amiable Man of the Isles.

∾172∾

There was a Young Lady whose nose
Was so long that it reached to her toes;
So she hired an Old Lady,
Whose conduct was steady,
To carry that wonderful nose.

both by Edward Lear

The Donkey & his Shadow

One hot, bright day, a merchant hired a donkey and its owner to take him to a distant market. They set off early, but as they journeyed further, the sun began to beat down. There was no shade for miles around, and the sweltering heat was becoming unbearable. The merchant decided to shelter in the donkey's shadow... but there was only room for one.

"I hired this donkey," said the merchant, "so I am the one who gets to shelter in its shadow."

"Ah, but you only hired the donkey," said the owner. "You didn't say anything about its *shadow*!"

The two began to argue, shouting at each other right in the middle of the road. They were so busy fighting, they didn't notice the donkey seize its chance and gallop off, far over the horizon.

Clever Rabbit & the Lion

Long ago, a ferocious lion lived in a forest. Greedily, he began to eat the forest animals, one by one, until they feared that soon they would all be gone.

"Don't worry," said a wise old rabbit. "I have a plan that will save us all. Hide for now and put your trust in me."

The next morning, the lion stalked through the forest. "Where are you?" he called to the other animals. "Come out and be eaten! There is no escape. None of you can match me, for I am the king of the jungle."

In their hiding places, the forest animals quaked with fear. They trembled and shook. They quivered.

As for the wise old rabbit, he hopped out to face

the lion. He stood on his two hind legs, not a whisker out of place.

"You can eat me," he told the lion.

"Of course I can eat you," the lion snarled. He padded up to the rabbit, claws out, jaws open.

"I tried to come before," the rabbit went on, "but a huge lion stopped me."

"Nonsense," snapped the lion. "I am the only lion in this forest."

"I hate to disagree with you," said the rabbit, "but I saw the other lion only an hour ago. He was much bigger than you – about twice the size, I would say. And his claws, oh my! Sharp as knives. And his teeth! They are like shining daggers."

"Take me to him!" roared the lion. "I'll eat him up, and then I'll eat you."

"With pleasure," the rabbit replied, and he led the lion to a deep, wide river.

"He lives in there," said the rabbit, pointing to the flowing water.

"Not for much longer..." the lion declared,

walking up to the water, his mane full and proud. He stared into the river. Another lion looked back.

"How dare you live in *my* forest," stormed the lion, shaking his head with rage.

The lion in the water shook his head, too.

"Do you dare defy me?" the lion asked, his eyes ablaze.

The other lion stared back, defiantly.

"You won't get away with this!" cried the lion. He leaped at the other lion in the water... and was swept away by the wide, wide river.

"Ha!" laughed the rabbit. "You've been fooled by your own reflection."

As the lion disappeared around the bend in the river, the forest animals crept out from their hiding places. "Clever rabbit!" they cheered. "You did save us all!"

Where Stories Come From

A long, long time ago, in the vast grasslands of Africa, there lived a herd of elephants. Every night they would gather beneath the baobab tree and beg the oldest elephant to tell them a story. She would swish her trunk from side to side, searching her mind for a tale to tell. But she knew none.

"Sipho!" she said to her sister. "You must go into the world in search of stories."

And so Sipho set out, walking deep into the night. "Does anyone know any stories?" she called into the darkness.

"Whoo, hoo, hoo," hooted an owl. "Ask Fish Eagle. He flies higher and sees further than any other bird. He'll know where to find stories."

Sipho followed the river to the sea, and there she found Nkwazi, the fish eagle. "My herd is hungry for stories," she told him. "Do you know where I might find some?"

"I only know of things on the face of the Earth," Nkwazi replied. "And I've heard no stories there. But there is one who knows the secrets of the ocean. Perhaps he can help you."

Away Nkwazi flew, and after a while, Sipho watched as a great sea turtle heaved himself out of the ocean.

"Take hold of my tail with the tip of your trunk," said the sea turtle. "I will guide you to the land of the spirit people."

Down, down, down they went, right to the depths of the sea, where the king and queen of the spirit people sat on coral thrones, dressed in seaweed gowns.

"Do you have any stories to share?" begged Sipho.

"We have many," the king and queen replied. "But in return, you must tell us about your life."

So Sipho began to speak. She described the joy of wallowing in mud, the beating sun and the sound of animals, crying out in the stillness of the night.

"You have woven a spell with your words," said the king and queen, "and carried down to us an image of life in the sun. In return, we give you this shell. Whenever you want a story, just hold it to your ear and it will tell you a tale."

Sipho took the shell up to her own dry world. When she reached the shore, she followed the scent of her herd, and found them just as the sun was setting, gathered beneath the towering branches of the baobab tree.

"Tell us a story, Sipho," begged the elephants.

Sipho put the shell to her ear. "*Kwasuka sukela...* Once upon a time..." she began. And that is how stories came to be.

～176～

As I was Going Up the Stair

As I was going up the stair
I met a man who wasn't there.
He wasn't there again today –
Oh, how I wish he'd go away.

～177～

There was an Old Woman...

There was an old woman
Lived under a hill,
And if she's not gone
She lives there still.

Highwayman's Halt

Mr. Cook and his daughter Chloe were the owners of The Highwayman's Halt inn. But they had so few customers, they were losing money.

"What are we going to do?" sighed Mr. Cook, as they served lunch to Mr. Filch, their only guest.

"There's always Flintlock's gold," suggested Chloe, with a smile.

"Er, what's that?" Mr. Filch asked, trying to sound casual.

"Fred Flintlock was a highwayman who stayed here when he was on the run," explained Mr. Cook.

"They say he hid the loot from his robberies somewhere in the inn," Chloe added. "But no one's ever found it."

"I'm not surprised," said Mr. Cook with a shiver. "Flintlock's ghost will haunt anyone who dares to take his gold."

"Ghosts don't scare me," declared Chloe. "I'm going to find that treasure."

"Not if I find it first," thought Mr. Filch.

Chloe spent the next week searching the inn from roof to cellar, with no luck. Just as she'd given up hope, she noticed the wooden inn sign. It was a carving of a highwayman clutching a chest.

"I wonder..." thought Chloe.

She climbed up to the sign, and pried open the lid of the chest. Inside was a bag full of gold coins. Delighted, she grabbed it and scooted down to the ground.

"Hand that back!" wailed a spooky voice.

Chloe turned to see the ghost of Fred Flintlock. "Please Mr. Flintlock," she begged, "We really need the money," and she told him her story.

"Hmm," sniffed Flintlock. "I suppose I *might* let you have one or two coins..."

At that moment, the bag was whipped out of Chloe's hand by Mr. Filch.

"Thanks for leading me to the treasure," Filch laughed, as he ran to his car and drove off.

Flintlock gave a whistle, and Bess, his ghostly horse, appeared. He and Chloe climbed on her back and chased after Filch.

"Stop that scoundrel!" yelled Flintlock, as Bess caused chaos in the town in pursuit of Filch.

They chased Filch's car to the very edge of the local docks and blocked his path.

"Out of my way!" barked Filch, driving his car straight at Bess.

Flintlock tugged on the reins, and Bess floated into the air. Filch couldn't stop in time, and shot off the jetty. The police dragged him from the water, but Flintlock's gold was lost forever.

It didn't matter. The Cooks had to start a waiting list for all the people who wanted to stay at the Highwayman's Halt and meet its ghostly guests.

∾ 179 ∾

There was an Old Man who said, "Hush!
I perceive a young bird in this bush!"
When they said, "Is it small?"
He replied, "Not at all!
It is four times as big as the bush!"

∾ 180 ∾

There was an Old Person of Rhodes,
Who strongly objected to toads;
He paid several cousins
To catch them by dozens,
That futile Old Person of Rhodes.

∾ 181 ∾

There was an Old Man with a poker,
Who painted his face with red ochre;
When they said, "You're a Guy!"
He made no reply,
But knocked them all down with his poker.

all by Edward Lear

The Woman who Lived in a Vinegar Bottle

There was once an old woman named Mrs. Malt, who lived in a vinegar bottle. It was cramped and the wind whistled through it all day long.

"Oh, why do I have to live in an old vinegar bottle?" sighed Mrs. Malt. "I wish I had a cottage with a thatched roof and roses by the door."

At that moment, a good fairy fluttered by. She felt sorry for the old woman.

"Blink twice," she told Mrs. Malt, "and your wish will come true."

So Mrs. Malt did – and found herself standing

in front of a lovely cottage. She was delighted. But when the fairy visited her again, the old woman was less happy.

"This cottage is tiny," she moaned. "I wish I had a fancy town house on two floors, with four large bedrooms and a brass knocker on the door."

"Blink three times," the fairy told Mrs. Malt, "and your wish will come true."

Mrs. Malt blinked – and found herself inside a tall, red-brick town house.

Mrs. Malt was content for a while. But it didn't last. "What a shame I have to live on a street between other people," she grumbled to the fairy. "I wish I had a mansion in its own grounds."

"Blink four times," said the fairy, "and your wish will come true."

Mrs. Malt blinked. The next second, she stood before a huge mansion.

At last, she should have been happy.

But Mrs. Malt was *not* happy. "This house still isn't right," she wailed to the fairy. "I want my home to look down on the whole world!"

The fairy thought for a moment. "Blink once," she told Mrs. Malt, "and your wish will come true."

Mrs. Malt blinked. But when she opened her eyes, she found herself beside her old vinegar bottle. It was perched on top of a mountain.

"Now you *can* look down on the whole world," said the fairy, flying away.

And no matter how hard Mrs. Malt wished and blinked, she never saw the fairy again.

∾183∾

If wishes were horses
Beggars would ride.
If turnips were watches,
I would wear one by my side.

Jackal & the Well

When a beautiful valley was hit by a terrible drought, all the animals came together to dig a well. Only Jackal refused to help. After many hours spent snoring in the shade, he woke with a mouth drier than sand and headed for a drink.

"Not so fast," Rabbit squeaked, leaping between Jackal and the well. "No work means no water."

Jackal scowled. *I thought all the animals had gone home.* But Jackal was as cunning as he was lazy, and his scowl quickly changed into a big, toothy grin.

"Water?" Jackal scoffed. "Why would I need water when I have this lovely honeycomb?" He reached into a small bag at his side, pulled out a piece of golden honeycomb, and chomped on it greedily.

Rabbit's mouth watered. "May I have some?"

"I suppose so," Jackal decided. "Open your mouth, but close your eyes, so you can enjoy it more."

Rabbit did as Jackal asked and, quick as a flash, Jackal ran past him and drank from the well.

"Hey!" cried Rabbit, realizing his mistake. But it was too late – Jackal had gone. "He may have tricked me," thought Rabbit, "but he won't get past Hare."

The next day, Hare was on guard before dawn. But again, the honeycomb was just too tempting.

"You scoundrel!" shouted Hare as Jackal ran away, water trickling down his chin. "You may have tricked me, but you won't get past Tortoise!"

Jackal thought this was very funny, and laughed until the sun came up. He continued to chuckle to himself as he swaggered back to the well, where Tortoise sat waiting for him.

"Mmm, who needs water when you can have this delicious honeycomb?" Jackal said and smacked his lips together.

Tortoise ignored him.

"You're welcome to have some," Jackal went on.

Tortoise continued to ignore him.

"Oh, just get out of my way," Jackal barked, growing impatient. He kicked at Tortoise, but Tortoise was ready for him. In one swift move, Tortoise bit Jackal's leg – hard.

"Aah, let me go!" Jackal cried. He shook and he growled, but Tortoise only held on tighter. "I promise, I'll leave the well alone," Jackal pleaded. "But first, tell me why I couldn't fool you?"

Tortoise spat out Jackal's leg and smiled. "Why would I need honeycomb," he asked, "when I have this lovely well?"

The Elephant & the Ants

Two ants were scurrying along a jungle path, when a thumping sound made them look up.

Towering above was a wrinkly elephant. "This is *my* path," he barked. "Move or I'll squash you."

"This is our path too," spoke the bold little ants. "We may be small, but we're just as important as you."

"Nonsense," replied the elephant. "I'm bigger *and* better. Everyone knows that."

"Let's have a race then," said the ants, "and the winner will get to use the path."

The elephant let out a blast of laughter. "You're on," he said. "Ready, get set, go!"

Have you ever seen an elephant run? It's more of a lumbering, fast walk really. But an elephant is so big, it can easily outrun a tiny ant. Then again, these

ants weren't planning on running. They were much too clever for that.

Ants are everywhere, in their hundreds. Look closely at any patch of forest floor and you're sure to spot a couple. And that's just what the elephant saw whenever he stopped to look down at the ground. He lumbered as fast as his tree trunk legs could carry him, but the ants were always just ahead.

"I give up," he puffed. "You win."

And the message was passed down the trail of ants that they'd outwitted the elephant and the path was theirs.

THUD! CREAK! CRASH! (That's the elephant clearing himself a new path.)

∽ 186 ∽

Jack be nimble,
Jack be quick,
Jack jump over
The candlestick.

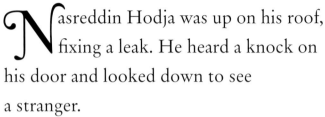

❧ 187 ❧
On the Roof

$\mathcal{N}$asreddin Hodja was up on his roof, fixing a leak. He heard a knock on his door and looked down to see a stranger.

"I'm up here!" he called out.

"Please come down," called the stranger. "I have something to say."

So the Hodja climbed all the way down his ladder to the ground below.

"What is it?" he asked.

"Could you spare me a few coins?"

The Hodja sighed. "Come with me," he replied, and headed back up the ladder.

The stranger followed and soon they were both standing, panting, on top of the roof. Only then did the Hodja turn to the stranger.

"I'm sorry," he said. "I don't have any coins on me. Why not try next door?"

Simple Simon met a pieman,
Going to the fair;
Said Simple Simon to the pieman,
"Let me taste your ware."

Said the pieman to Simple Simon,
"Show me first your penny."
Said Simple Simon to the pieman,
"Indeed I have not any."

There was a crooked man,
Who walked a crooked mile.
He found a crooked sixpence
Upon a crooked stile.
He bought a crooked cat,
Which caught a crooked mouse
And they all lived together
In a little crooked house.

The Miller, his Son & their Donkey

A miller and his son were taking their donkey to market to sell. As they led him along the dusty road, they met a group of young girls.

"Hee hee!" giggled one of the girls. "How silly to be trudging along when one of you could be riding the donkey."

"That's true," said the miller. "Hop up, son. I'll lead the donkey."

The boy did as he was told, and they went on their way.

A few minutes later, they met three old men.

"What a lazy boy," snorted one.

"Yes," agreed another. "Imagine making his poor old father walk, while he rides the donkey."

"They're right," said the son. "Climb up, Dad, and I'll lead the donkey."

So the miller and his son switched places, and they continued on their way.

A few minutes later, they met two women with their children.

"How unfair," cried one. "That man is making his poor little boy walk, while he gets to ride the donkey."

"She's got a point, son," said the miller. "Come up and ride with me."

Some time later, they met a farmer.

"Are you taking that donkey to market?" he asked.

"That's right," replied the miller.

"He'll be worn out, carrying you two," said the farmer. "Who will want to buy him then?"

"We hadn't thought of that," said the miller.

"Why not carry him?" suggested the farmer.

So the miller and his son tied the donkey to a pole and carried him along.

When they got to the market, everyone laughed.

"Look at that silly pair!" chuckled one man.

"Imagine trying to carry a donkey," roared another.

The donkey didn't like being laughed at. He struggled free of the pole and ran off down the road.

"We shouldn't have tried to please everyone," panted the miller, as they chased after him. "Now we're the ones who look like donkeys."

∞ 191 ∞

There wise men of Gotham
Went to sea in a bowl.
If the bowl had been stronger,
My story would have been longer.

❧ 192 ❧

The Pobble Who Has No Toes

The Pobble who has no toes
Had once as many as we;
When they said, "Some day you may lose them all;"
He replied, "Fish diddle de-dee!"
And his Aunt Jobiska made him drink,
Lavender water tinged with pink,
For she said, "The World in general knows
There's nothing so good for a Pobble's toes!"

❧

The Pobble who has no toes,
Swam across the Bristol Channel;
But before he set out he wrapped his nose
In a piece of scarlet flannel.
For his Aunt Jobiska said, "No harm
Can come to his toes if his nose is warm;
And it's perfectly known that a Pobble's toes
Are safe – provided he minds his nose."

The Pobble swam fast and well,
And when boats and ships came near him
He tinkedly-binkedly-winkled a bell,
So that all the world could hear him.
And all the Sailors and Admirals cried,
When they saw him nearing the further side,
"He has gone to fish, for his Aunt Jobiska's
Runcible Cat with crimson whiskers!"

But before he touched the shore,
The shore of the Bristol Channel,
A sea-green Porpoise carried away
His wrapper of scarlet flannel.
And when he came to observe his feet,
Formerly garnished with toes so neat,
His face at once became forlorn
On perceiving that all his toes were gone!

And nobody ever knew
From that dark day to the present,
Whoso had taken the Pobble's toes,
In a manner so far from pleasant.
Whether the shrimps or crawfish gray,
Or crafty Mermaids stole them away –
Nobody knew; and nobody knows
How the Pobble was robbed of his twice five toes!

The Pobble who has no toes
Was placed in a friendly Bark,
And they rowed him back, and carried him up,
To his Aunt Jobiska's Park.
And she made him a feast at his earnest wish
Of eggs and buttercups fried with fish;
And she said: "It's a fact the whole world knows,
That Pobbles are happier without their toes."

Edward Lear

∽ 193 ∾

Master of all Masters

Once, an intelligent girl became a servant for an eccentric old man.

"Should I call you Master?" she asked.

"No," he replied, "you shall call me Master of all Masters."

"Very well, Master of all Masters," she said respectfully. "Would you like me to make your bed?"

"It is not a *bed*," said the old man. "It is my barnacle."

"If you say so," replied the girl, slightly amused. "Now where should I put your clothes?"

"They are not *clothes*," insisted the old man, "they are my squibs and crackers."

"Of course they are," said the girl, "and is this your sweet little cat?"

"It most certainly isn't," said the man, indignantly. "She's a white-faced simminy. She likes to warm herself by the hot cockalorum," he explained, pointing to the fire.

"Oh I see," said the girl, trying not to giggle.

"You have a great deal to learn," said the old man with a sigh. "Tell me, what's this?" He indicated the water in his glass.

"Water?" suggested the girl.

"No, it's pondalorum," said the old man firmly. "You will kindly call things by their rightful names when you are in my high topper mountain."

"High topper mountain?" exclaimed the girl, almost bursting with laughter.

"Indeed that is where I live," the old man affirmed. "But I'm tired of all this teaching. I'm going to rest on my barnacle."

The servant girl was tidying the house when she had a fright. "Master of all Masters," she cried out. "Get out of your barnacle and put on your squibs and crackers. White-faced simminy has got a spark of hot cockalorum on her tail and unless you get some pondalorum quickly the whole high topper mountain will be on hot cockalorum!"

∽ 194 ∽

Gregory Griggs, Gregory Griggs,
Had twenty-seven different wigs.
He wore them up, he wore them down,
To please the people of the town.
He wore them east, he wore them west,
But he never could tell which he loved the best.

∽ 195 ∽

Bobby Shafto

Bobby Shafto's gone to sea,
Silver buckles at his knee;
He'll come back and marry me,
Bonny Bobby Shafto!

Bobby Shafto's fat and fair,
Combing down his yellow hair;
He's my love for evermore,
Bonny Bobby Shafto!

I Saw a Ship A-Sailing

I saw a ship a-sailing,
A-sailing on the sea;
And oh! it was all laden
With pretty things for thee.

There were comfits in the cabin,
And apples in the hold;
The sails were made of satin,
And the masts were made of gold.

The four-and-twenty sailors
That stood between the decks,
Were four-and-twenty white mice,
With chains about their necks.

The captain was a duck
With a jacket on his back;
And when the ship began to move,
The captain said, "Quack! Quack!"

∞ 197 ∾

The Wolf & the Crane

The wolf was the biggest, greediest animal in all the forest. He always gobbled down his food in two quick bites. And then he growled.

The wolf's growl was loud, it was deep and it was very, very scary. The other animals hid as soon as they heard it. They knew that the wolf was looking for his next meal – and it might be them.

But, one day, the wolf's growl sounded different. Just as loud, just as deep, but really rather sad. The other animals still hid, but they pricked up their ears to listen.

"Ow, ow!" howled the wolf. "I ate my dinner too greedily. There's a bone stuck in my throat and I can't get it out. If you help me, I'll give you anything you like!"

None of the animals moved. But the crane thought about the wolf's promised reward.

"Anything I like!" she said to herself. "That's tempting." And she stepped out of her hiding place.

"Open wide!" said the crane. "I can reach down your throat with my long beak. I'll have that bone out in no time." And she did.

"Right," said the crane, "time for my reward!"

The wolf grinned. His grin was big, it was wide, and it was very, very toothy.

"You put your head inside a wolf's mouth and lived to tell the tale! That's reward enough," he growled. And now his growl was back to normal. It was loud, it was deep and it was very, very scary.

The crane flapped quickly up into a tree. "I should have known," she thought, crossly. "Those who are greedy are never grateful."

∽ 198 ∽

Rain before seven,
Fine before eleven.

∾ 199 ∾

There was a Young Lady whose eyes
Were unique as to colour and size;
When she opened them wide,
People all turned aside,
And started away in surprise.

∾ 200 ∾

There was an Old Man in a boat,
Who said, "I'm afloat! I'm afloat!"
When they said, "No, you ain't!"
He was ready to faint,
That unhappy Old Man in a boat.

∾ 201 ∾

There was an Old Person of Leeds,
Whose head was infested with beads;
She sat on a stool
And ate gooseberry-fool,
Which agreed with that Person of Leeds.

∾ 202 ∾

There was an Old Man of the Hague,
Whose ideas were excessively vague;
He built a balloon
To examine the moon,
That deluded Old Man of the Hague.

∾ 203 ∾

There was an Old Person of Ware,
Who rode on the back of a bear;
When they'd ask'd, "Does it trot?"
He said, "Certainly not.
He's a Moppsikon Floppsikon Bear!"

∾ 204 ∾

There was a Young Lady of Bute,
Who played on a silver-gilt flute;
She played several jigs
To her uncle's white pigs,
That amusing Young Lady of Bute.

all by Edward Lear

~ 205 ~

Dino Diner

It was the opening night of Rick and Rob Raptor's Dinosaur Diner. The tables were laid, the glasses were polished. All they needed now were customers.

But when Rob went to the refrigerator to take out the meat, he got a nasty shock.

"It's all gone!" he wailed. "Every last steak."

At that moment, a little green blur carrying a string of sausages whizzed through Rick's legs and out of the kitchen door.

"A Compsognathus!" cried Rick.

"And he's eaten all our food," yelled Rob. "What are we going to do? Look, our first customer is here!"

Rick peered into the restaurant. "That's Egon Raptor from the Dino Dining Club," he exclaimed. "If he doesn't like our food, we're sunk."

Rob went outside to think. Moments later,

he rushed back with armfuls of plants.

"What's that for?" asked his brother, with a puzzled frown.

"I'm going to cook them," replied Rob.

Rick was amazed. "Are you crazy?" he gasped. "No dinosaur I know eats yucky green leaves or vegetables."

Rob had no time to argue. He chopped everything up, drizzled it with nettle juice and arranged it neatly on a plate.

"Dinner is served," announced Rick, as he presented Egon Raptor with the finished dish.

Egon took one bite, made a face, and ran out of the restaurant. "Yeucch!" he moaned. "That's the worst meal I've ever tasted."

"We're finished," sobbed Rick, waving the plate of greens in the air.

At that moment, a strange-looking dinosaur poked his head around the door. "Any chance of a bite to eat?" he asked.

"Not unless you want this," said Rick, plonking the plate down on a table.

"Mmm, that looks good," said the dinosaur. Seconds later, he'd eaten it all.

Rick couldn't believe his eyes. "You like leaves?" he goggled.

"Of course," replied the dinosaur. "I'm a Stegoceras. We never eat anything else."

The Stegoceras told all his friends about Rob's wonderful food. And from then on, every sitting was fully booked at the Green Dino Diner.

∾ 206 ∾

There was a young pirate named Stark,
Who dived off his ship for a lark.
He swam up and down,
But soon wore a frown,
When he got gobbled up by a shark.

Russell Punter

∾ 207 ∾

Jack Sprat could eat no fat,
His wife could eat no lean,
And so between them both, you see,
They licked the platter clean.

∾ 208 ∾

Pease porridge hot, pease porridge cold,
Pease porridge in the pot nine days old.
Some like it hot, some like it cold,
Some like it in the pot nine days old.

∾ 209 ∾
The Smell of Soup & the Sound of Money

Once, a beggar found a chunk of dry bread. He wanted something to go with it, so he went into an inn and asked for some soup.

"Go away," said the innkeeper. "I only serve paying customers."

The beggar pretended to leave but secretly he crept into the kitchen. A large pot of soup was simmering over the fire. It smelled delicious. The beggar carefully held his bread over the soup, hoping it would soak up the smell.

"Stop stealing my soup!" the innkeeper yelled from the doorway.

"I'm not," said the beggar. "I'm smelling it."

"Then you must pay for the smell," replied the innkeeper.

But the beggar had no money, so the angry innkeeper took him to see the local judge, who happened to be Nasreddin Hodja.

The wise Hodja listened to the innkeeper's story with one ear. Then he listened to the beggar's story with the other ear.

"Well, well," said the Hodja. "If the beggar owes the innkeeper money for the smell of his soup, then I shall pay it myself."

Both the innkeeper and the beggar looked at him in surprise.

The Hodja went on, "I shall pay for the smell of soup with the sound of money."

And with those words, the Hodja reached into his pocket, took out some coins and jangled them together. "There you are," he announced, "all paid for. Now be off with you."

∾ 210 ∾
Robin Hood & Alan a Dale

Out in the forest one day, Robin Hood came upon a young man dressed in fine clothes. He was strumming a small harp and looked so unhappy that Robin decided not to rob him.

"Who are you and what's the matter?" he asked.

"I'm Alan a Dale," said the young man, "and this should have been my wedding day, but an old knight has stolen my bride for himself."

"Where's the wedding taking place?" asked Robin. "We shall go there at once!"

Alan led the way to a pretty village church.

"Give me your harp and wait here," Robin ordered. Then he strode into the service.

"Just in time!" said the bishop. "We need some music for the bride's entrance."

At that moment, a beautiful young bride appeared on the arm of her father. They walked hesitantly down the aisle to where a stern old knight stood waiting at the altar. But instead of playing the harp, Robin blew three shrill blasts on his horn. In charged his merry men and dragged off the old knight, despite his protests.

"You had the wrong groom," Robin explained. "Step forward, Alan."

"I will not marry them!" said the bishop.

"Never mind," said Friar Tuck. "I will." And, pushing the bishop aside, he performed a short, sweet wedding ceremony.

So Alan was married to his bride, and all the merry men joined the celebrations.

He Wishes for the Cloths of Heaven

Had I the heavens' embroidered cloths,
Enwrought with golden and silver light,
The blue and the dim and the dark cloths
Of night and light and the half-light,
I would spread the cloths under your feet:
But I, being poor, have only my dreams;
I have spread my dreams under your feet:
Tread softly because you tread on my dreams.

W. B. Yeats

∽ 212 ∾
How the Moon
& Stars Came to Be

In the distant past, when the sky was very close to the ground, a young woman went into her yard to pound rice into flour.

It was an energetic job, so first she removed her necklace and her hair comb, and hung them on a cloud. Then she raised her pestle and brought it down heavily onto the rice. This action she repeated, again and again, breaking the rice into smaller pieces.

Carried away by the pounding rhythm, the woman didn't realize she was gradually reaching higher and higher... until her pestle struck the sky itself and knocked it far up into the heavens.

Unfortunately, the sky took her necklace and comb with it. The comb is now the Moon and the necklace beads have scattered to make the stars.

Sleeping Beauty

It was the day of Princess Aurora's christening and seven fairies had been invited to the celebration. The king and queen looked on proudly as the fairies fluttered up to the crib to shower the princess with gifts – beauty, grace, a kind heart...

BOOM! A sudden crack of thunder shook the castle and a furious fairy swept in. "Why wasn't I invited?" she shrieked. "You'll pay for this insult!"

Before anyone could move, the evil fairy hovered over Aurora and cast a spell. "One day, you'll prick your finger on a spindle and die!" she screeched. With that, she vanished.

The king and queen were horrified.

"Don't worry," said a fairy with silvery wings. "I can't completely break the spell, but I can change it." She looked down at the baby princess. "You won't die," she said softly. "Instead, you'll fall asleep for a hundred years, until a prince wakes you."

That very day, the king ordered all spindles in the kingdom to be destroyed. And so the princess grew up safely and happily until the eve of her fifteenth birthday.

She was exploring the palace's oldest tower, climbing up and up, until she reached a tiny room. Sat in the corner was an old woman, spinning away.

The old lady never left her tower, so she hadn't heard the king's order about spindles.

Aurora hadn't seen anyone spinning before. She reached out curiously to touch the spindle, and pricked her finger.

Instantly, she fell into a deep sleep. When the king and queen heard what had happened, they laid Aurora on her bed and sent for the silver-winged fairy.

There was nothing she could do. But she didn't want Aurora to be alone when she woke up, so she sent the king, the queen and the whole palace to sleep too. With a wave of her wand, the palace became entwined with thick brambles to protect the sleepers.

One hundred years passed...

Then a prince heard the story of the sleeping princess and set out to discover if it was true.

He slashed his way through the walls of brambles with his sword. Spiky thorns tore at his face, but he refused to give up.

At last, he reached the princess's room. With one glance, the prince fell helplessly in love. Kneeling down, he gave Aurora a gentle kiss.

In that instant, the spell was broken. The princess and the rest of the palace awoke.

Not long after, Princess Aurora married her prince and lived a long and happy life – though she was careful to stay well away from spindles.

Soldier Soldier

Soldier, soldier, won't you marry me,
With your musket, fife, and drum?
Oh! No, pretty maid, I cannot marry thee,
'Cause I've got no coat to put on.
So she went upstairs to her father's chest,
And she brought him a coat of the very, very best,
And the soldier put it on.

Soldier, soldier, won't you marry me,
With your musket, fife, and drum?
Oh! No, pretty maid, I cannot marry thee,
'Cause I've got no boots to put on.
She went upstairs to her father's chest,
And she brought him boots of the very, very best,
And the soldier put them on.

Soldier, soldier, won't you marry me,
With your musket, fife, and drum?
No, no, pretty maid, I cannot marry thee,
'Cause I've got a wife at home.

∽ 215 ∽

What Are Heavy?

What are heavy? Sea-sand and sorrow:
What are brief? Today and tomorrow:
What are frail? Spring blossoms and youth:
What are deep? The ocean and truth.

∽ 216 ∽

Flint

An emerald is as green as grass;
A ruby red as blood;
A sapphire shines as blue as heaven;
A flint lies in the mud.

A diamond is a brilliant stone,
To catch the world's desire;
An opal holds a fiery spark;
But a flint holds fire.

The Rainbow

Boats sail on the rivers,
And ships sail on the seas;
But clouds that sail across the sky
Are prettier far than these.

There are bridges on the rivers,
As pretty as you please;
But the bow that bridges heaven,
And overtops the trees,
And builds a road from earth to sky,
Is prettier far than these.

all by Christina Rossetti

∽ 218 ∾
Sinbad: Voyage Four

I had made three voyages and three fortunes – but when my gold ran out, I went to sea once more.

The sea was calm, the sky was blue. No one saw the jagged rocks ahead. All of a sudden we heard a wrenching sound as a deep gorge was cut into the ship's hull. We were letting in water and sinking fast.

Many men went down with the ship. I was luckier than most. I found an empty barrel and clung to it, hoping for the best. I passed out from exhaustion and when I awoke I thought I was still dreaming.

I was in an opulent hall, lined with lavish silks, a bowl of exotic fruit on one side and a beautiful woman fanning me on the other.

"At last you're awake!" called a voice. I looked up to see a kind-faced man wearing sumptuous robes. "I am King Fazar and you are my guest," he said.

In the days that followed I learned that the king's daughter had found me washed up on a beach and nursed me back to health. She'd taken a shine to me and the king asked if I would like to marry her.

"With pleasure," I said. "I owe her my life!"

Little did I know how true my words were. According to local custom, when a person died, their spouse was buried with them – alive. I prayed my wife would enjoy a long life.

Alas, one day, she caught a fever and died. Her burial chamber was dug, deep and wide. I was left beside her, clutching a chest of gems from the heart-broken king. But what use were gems to me now?

For days I sat in the dark, dying from hunger and thirst, until I heard an animal scrabbling in the dirt. I followed the sound, felt the entrance of a narrow tunnel and wriggled through. Imagine my delight when I saw a glimmer of light ahead.

I emerged by a river mouth as a ship went past and, with the last of my strength, I swam out to it. Gems from the treasure chest paid for my trip and finally I arrived home. But my story does not end there...

∽ 219 ∽

To a Fish

You strange, astonished-looking, angle-faced,
Dreary-mouthed, gaping wretches of the sea,
Gulping salt water everlastingly,
Cold-blooded, though with red your blood be graced,
And mute, though dwellers in the roaring waste;
And you, all shapes beside, that fish be, –
Some round, some flat, some long, all devilry,
Legless, unloving, infamously chaste: –

O scaly, slippery, wet, swift, staring wights,
What is it you do? What life lead? Eh, dull goggles?
How do you vary your vile days and nights?
How pass your Sundays? Are you still but joggles
In ceaseless wash? Still nought but gapes, and bites,
And drinks, and stares, diversified with boggles?

Leigh Hunt

220

A Fish Answers

Amazing monster! that, for all I know,
With the first sight of thee did make our race
Forever stare! O flat and shocking face,
Grimly divided from the breast below!
Thou that on dry land horribly dost go
With a split body and most ridiculous pace,
Prong after prong, disgracer of all grace,
Long-useless-finned, haired, upright, unwet, slow!

O breather of unbreathable, sword-sharp air,
How canst exist? How bear thyself, thou dry
And dreary sloth? What particle canst share
Of the only blessed life, the watery?
I sometimes see of you an actual *pair*
Go by! linked fin by fin, most odiously.

Leigh Hunt

∽ 221 ∽

from The Lighthouse

The rocky ledge runs far into the sea,
And on its outer point, some miles away,
The Lighthouse lifts its massive masonry,
A pillar of fire by night, of cloud by day.
Even at this distance I can see the tides,
Upheaving, break unheard along its base,
A speechless wrath, that rises and subsides
In the white lip and tremor of the face.
And as the evening darkens, lo! how bright,
Through the deep purple of the twilight air,
Beams forth the sudden radiance of its light
With strange, unearthly splendor in the glare!

Not one alone: from each projecting cape

And perilous reef along the ocean's verge,

Starts into life a dim, gigantic shape,

Holding its lantern o'er the restless surge.

And the great ships sail outward and return,

Bending and bowing o'er the billowy swells,

And ever joyful as they see it burn,

They wave their silent welcomes and farewells.

Henry Wadsworth Longfellow

∽ 222 ∾

Blow, Wind, Blow

Blow, wind, blow
And go, mill, go!
That the miller may grind his corn,
That the baker may take it,
And into bread make it,
And bring us a loaf in the morn.

∾ 223 ∾

The Dragon & his Grandmother

There was once a great war, and the king had many soldiers, but he paid them so little, they could not live on it. So three decided to run away.

"If we are caught, we'll be hanged," said one.

"We'll hide in that cornfield," said another. And there they hid, desperate with thirst and hunger.

As they sat waiting for the army to pass on, a fiery dragon came flying through the air. "I can take you to safety," he told them, "and then I'll let you live freely for seven years. But after that you'll be mine forever, unless you can solve my riddle."

The three men agreed – they had no other choice. So the dragon seized them in his claws, took them through the air, and set them down far away. He gave them each a whip, saying, "Whip and slash these and as much money as you want will jump up before you. You can then live as great lords, keep horses and drive around in carriages. But remember, after seven years, you will be mine, unless you solve the riddle."

For nearly seven years the men had as much money as they wanted, wore grand clothes, and lived in merrymaking and grandeur. But the time passed quickly and two of the men began to worry.

"Why are you so sad?" asked an old woman passing by.

"We are bound to a dragon," said the two. "And we will soon belong to him forever if we cannot guess his riddle."

"Well go into the woods beyond," said the old woman, "and you will see a little hut made of stones. Go in, and you will find help."

"That won't save us!" said the two sad men, despairingly. But the third jumped up and went into the woods to find the hut. There sat a very old

woman. She was the dragon's grandmother.

When the man had told her his tale, the old woman took pity on him. "Hide yourself here," she said, lifting up a large stone which lay over a cellar. "And listen to what the dragon says."

At midnight, the dragon flew in and asked for his supper. As they ate, the dragon told his grandmother about the three soldiers. "They are mine," he said. "I will give them a riddle they'll never guess."

"What sort of riddle?" asked the old woman.

"Well," said the dragon, "I will simply tell you this. In the North Sea lies a dead seacat – that shall be their roast meat; a rib of a whale shall be their spoon and the hollow foot of a horse their wineglass."

When the dragon fell asleep, the man climbed out of the cellar and went to meet his friends. Full of cheer, they waited for the dragon.

"I will take you underground with me," said the dragon when he arrived, "and you shall have a meal. If you can tell me what you will get for your roast meat, you shall be free."

"The dead seacat in the North Sea shall be our roast meat," said the first soldier.

The dragon hummed and hawed and then asked the second soldier, "But what shall be your spoon?"

"The rib of a whale," he replied.

The dragon made a face and growled three times. "Hmm, hmm, hmm," he said to the third soldier. "And what will your wineglass be?"

"An old horse's hoof."

Then the dragon flew away with a loud shriek, and that was the last they saw of him. The soldiers took out their whips, whipped as much money as they wanted and all three lived happily to the end of their lives.

∾ 224 ∾
A Star

Higher than a house,
Higher than a tree,
Oh, whatever can that be?

∾ 225 ∾
Spindle, Shuttle & Needle

An orphan girl lived all alone, with only a spindle, a shuttle and a needle, in the poorest house in the village. She worked hard all day, spinning and weaving and sewing... and dreaming of another life.

Now, at this time, the king's son was searching the country for a bride. "I want a girl who is neither rich nor poor, who is at the same time the richest and the poorest," he decided.

When he came to the village where the girl lived, he asked, as he did everywhere, who was the richest girl and who was the poorest. First, they named for him the richest girl. She sat in her doorway in all her finery. When the prince approached, she bowed before him. He looked at her, said not a word, and rode on to the poorest girl's house.

When the prince arrived, she was spinning in her kitchen, the sunlight streaming in, a blush on her cheeks. She continued to spin until the prince had ridden away. Then she sang to her spindle,

> *Spindle, spindle, go and roam,*
> *Bring a suitor to my home.*

With a twirl, the spindle jumped out of her hand and was through the door, dancing across the field and chasing after the prince, pulling a glistening golden thread behind it.

"What's this behind me?" cried the prince. "Is it a spindle showing me the way?" So saying, he turned his horse and followed the thread.

Without her spindle, the girl had picked up her shuttle, seated herself at her loom and begun to weave. To her shuttle she sang,

Shuttle, shuttle, weave with care,
Make me a carpet, fine and fair.

The shuttle leaped from her hand and began to weave a carpet on the doorstep, a more beautiful one than the girl had ever seen before. Roses and lilies blossomed at its sides. In the middle, trees twined their branches against a golden background, with birds nestled among them. The only thing missing was the birds' singing.

Without her shuttle, the girl sat down to sew. She held her needle in her hand and sang,

Needle, needle, sharp and fine,
Clean up the house for this suitor of mine.

The needle jumped out of her fingers and flew about the kitchen. It was as though invisible spirits were at work. The table and benches were soon covered with green cloth, the chairs with velvet, and silk curtains hung at the windows.

Just as the needle made its last stitch, the girl looked through the window and saw the prince, following the spindle's golden thread. He swung himself down from his horse and walked across the carpet into her house. The girl stood waiting for him, fairer than a rose.

"You are the poorest but also the richest," said the prince. "Come with me and be my bride."

The girl said nothing but reached out her hand to him. The prince led her outside, lifted her onto his horse and off they rode to the royal palace, where they were married the very next day.

As for the spindle, the shuttle and the needle... they were placed in a treasure chamber for all to see.

❀ 226 ❀
Clever Jackal Tricks the Lion...

"**K**wasuka sukela..." this story begins (that means "Once upon a time" in Zulu), the most cunning animal in all of Africa was trotting along with his nose to the ground. It was, of course, the mischievous, rascally, trickster Jackal. At that moment, he was sniffing around for his next meal. Sniff, sniff, sniff, he went. "Mmm, I smell lizard," he muttered, "that would make me a tasty snack. And can I smell antelope too? No, something bigger... something much bigger..."

Clever Jackal lifted his nose and came face-to-face with... Lion, or Great Bhubesi as he was known in that land.

"Oops," thought Clever Jackal. He had played one too many tricks on Great Bhubesi, and the snarly old lion was probably wanting revenge.

In a flash, Clever Jackal thought of a plan. He cowered at the side of the path, sending terrified, darting glances at the craggy rocks above. "Help!" cried Clever Jackal. "Help! Help!"

Lion stopped in surprise.

"Oh Great Bhubesi," said Clever Jackal. "There is no time to lose. See that great rock above us? It's about to fall! We'll both be crushed to death. Do something, mighty lion. Do something, or we shall both be killed."

Great Bhubesi looked up in alarm, while Clever Jackal cowered even lower to the ground, putting up his paws to protect his head. "Hurry," said Clever Jackal. "Hurry!"

So Great Bhubesi bounded over and put his strong shoulder beneath the rock, straining under its weight.

"Thank you, great king," said Clever Jackal. "I will go and find a log to put under the rock, so we can hold it up." And, the next moment, Clever Jackal was out of sight.

Five hours later, Great Bhubesi was still standing under the rock. "Jackal isn't coming back," he realized at last. "And this rock isn't coming down, is it?" He moved away from the rock. It stayed exactly where it was.

"A trick," growled Great Bhubesi. "A dastardly, jackally trick – and I fell for it. GRRRR!"

∽ 227 ∽

...and Warthog Tries to Copy Him

A few days later, Warthog was busy making himself a new home. It was inside an old termite mound and wonderfully spacious. Warthog bumbled around, widening the entrance and burrowing away, until... "Perfect," he declared. "Positively perfect."

He was very pleased with himself: snout tipped skywards, tail twitching, tusks up. "Even Clever Jackal doesn't have such a good home," he declared. "Mine is the most magnificent in all of Africa."

Every day, he stood in the entrance and watched the world go by, certain he must be the envy of all – until, one morning, he was horrified to spy Great Bhubesi, the lion, stalking stealthily up to him.

"Oh dear," muttered Warthog, backing away. He realized, too late, that he had made the entrance of his home so grand, Great Bhubesi would have no trouble following him inside.

"What can I do?" wondered Warthog, for he knew Lion would eat him in a flash. Then, with great relief, Warthog remembered the trick Clever Jackal had told him. Why, Jackal had been bragging about it only the other day.

The next moment, Warthog arched his back until it touched his roof and cried out, "Help! I am going to be crushed."

"The roof is caving in. Flee, Great Bhubesi, before you are crushed along with me."

Great Bhubesi looked down at Warthog and ROARED! "Do you think I am a fool?" he said. "I remember this trick of Jackal's. I'm not going to be caught out again."

Trembling with fear, Warthog dropped to his knees. "Oh, Great Bhubesi," he cried. "Have mercy on me. Don't eat me – please!"

"Luckily for you, I'm not hungry," said Great Bhubesi. "I have just dined on fresh antelope. But from now on, you must stay on your knees, you foolish beast."

Lion laughed to himself and stalked away. "Ha!" he thought. "What a dimwit! As if I'd fall for the same trick twice."

As for Warthog... he never forgot the lion's command. And to this day, you will see him feeding on his knees, with his snout to the ground and his bottom in the air, looking very undignified indeed.

The Man with the Coconuts

A man had worked hard all morning, climbing palm trees and collecting coconuts. He had just loaded up his horse when a small boy walked by.

"Excuse me," called the man. "How long will it take to get to the nearest market?"

"If you go slowly you'll be there very soon," replied the boy, "but if you go fast it will take you all day."

"Silly boy," thought the man. He set off quickly, but the coconuts soon fell off the horse's back and the man had to stop to pick them up.

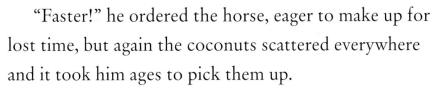

"Faster!" he ordered the horse, eager to make up for lost time, but again the coconuts scattered everywhere and it took him ages to pick them up.

When the man finally reached the market, it was nightfall and all the customers had gone home.

"If only I'd listened to that boy," he sighed.

The Duck & the Kangaroo

Said the Duck to the Kangaroo,
"Good gracious, how you hop!
Over the fields and the water too,
As if you never would stop.
My life is a bore in this nasty pond,
And I long to go out in the world beyond!
I wish I could hop like you!"
Said the Duck to the Kangaroo.

∾

"Please give me a ride on your back!"
Said the Duck to the Kangaroo.
"I would sit quite still, and say nothing but 'Quack,'
The whole of the long day through!
And we'd go to the Dee, and the Jelly Bo Lee,
Over the land and over the sea.
Please take me a ride! O do!"
Said the Duck to the Kangaroo.

Said the Kangaroo to the Duck,

"This requires some little reflection;

Perhaps on the whole it might bring me luck,

And there seems but one objection,

Which is, if you'll let me speak so bold,

Your feet are unpleasantly wet and cold,

And would probably give me the roo -

Matiz!" said the Kangaroo.

Said the Duck, "As I sat on the rocks,

I have thought over that completely,

And I bought four pairs of worsted socks

Which fit my web-feet neatly.

And to keep out the cold I've bought a cloak,

And every day a cigar I'll smoke,

All to follow my own dear true

Love of a Kangaroo!"

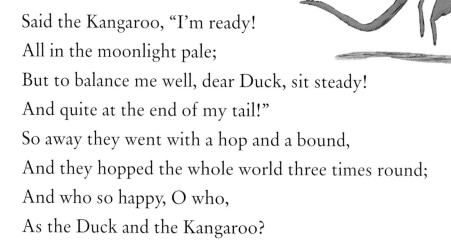

Said the Kangaroo, "I'm ready!
All in the moonlight pale;
But to balance me well, dear Duck, sit steady!
And quite at the end of my tail!"
So away they went with a hop and a bound,
And they hopped the whole world three times round;
And who so happy, O who,
As the Duck and the Kangaroo?

Edward Lear

∾ 230 ∾
Teeth

Thirty white horses
Upon a red hill,
Now they tramp,
Now they champ,
Now they stand still.

∽ 231 ∾

Angel

Angel was a fairy. But unlike most fairies, she wasn't kind and helpful. Angel was proud and spiteful.

One day, she was fluttering among some poppies when she noticed a human boy on his way home from school. Angel followed him to see where he lived.

She had thought of a sneaky trick to play on him, but first she needed to speak to her mother.

"Mother," she said innocently, when she got home, "if anyone hurt me, would you be angry?"

"Of course, darling," replied her mother.

"Would you punish them?" asked Angel.

"Yes of course I would!" said her mother.

Angel smirked to herself. It was just what she wanted to hear.

That evening, she visited the little boy's house, flapping down the chimney into his bedroom.

The little boy was amazed to see a real live fairy.

"Would you like to play a game?" asked Angel, beaming her sweetest smile.

"I suppose so," said the boy, warily.

"Good," said Angel. "What's your name?"

Something about this fairy made the boy feel cautious. "My name is Me Myself," he replied, even though his name was Oliver.

"'Me Myself'? What a stupid name," thought Angel, but she didn't say so. "Let's play tag," she cried, hovering over the boy's bed.

The boy stumbled around the room, trying to catch Angel. But she was too fast for him. Every time he went to touch her, she flew out of reach.

Angel had been teasing the boy this way for half an hour, when she suddenly fell to the floor, crying. "You hurt me!" she wailed.

"I never touched you," said the boy, shocked.

"Yes you did," pretended Angel. "I'm going to tell my mother. MOTHER!" she screamed.

Fairies have very good hearing. When she heard her daughter's cries, Angel's mother flew as fast as the wind to be by her side.

"Someone hurt my knee," sobbed Angel, when her mother appeared.

"Tell me his name," said Angel's mother, "and I'll punish him."

"It was Me Myself," said Angel.

"Really," said Angel's mother. "Well, in that case, I'll have to punish you yourself."

Before she had to time to argue, Angel found herself back at home and banished to her room.

"You can stay there until you've learned to behave," called her mother through the keyhole.

"Hmph!" said Angel, but there was nothing she could do – and she didn't play another trick for months.

The Sandman

Hal was snuggled sleepily in bed when he heard someone tiptoe into his room.

"Who's that?" he asked, sitting up.

"Oh!" cried a startled voice. A bag thumped to the floor, spilling glittering golden sand. Hal looked around and saw a little man with an umbrella.

"Hello Hal," said the man. "I'm the Sandman."

"I've heard of you," Hal cried. "You sprinkle your sand in people's eyes while they're asleep, to fill their dreams with stories."

"Yes," said the man. "I had some wonderful stories for you, but now they're all spilled. Oh dear, what shall I do?" He thought for a moment. "I know!"

He pointed his umbrella at a flowerpot on the windowsill. At once, the flower began to grow, until the room was filled with sweet-smelling blossom.

Next, the umbrella pointed at a picture on the wall. It showed a sailing ship on a sunlit sea – only now the sails were billowing and the deck bobbed up and down.

The Sandman lifted Hal up through the picture frame, into the sunlight. They sailed past green shores, where toy soldiers guarded fairytale castles. The soldiers saluted crisply while princesses waved from the windows. Here, a pirate dug for treasure on a desert island. There, dolphins splashed and played...

Then, somewhere, a clock chimed. "A quarter to midnight," exclaimed the Sandman. He snapped his fingers and they were back in Hal's room. Yawning, Hal got into bed. A moment later, he was fast asleep.

"Sweet dreams," said the Sandman softly. And with a twirl of his umbrella, he was gone.

∾ 233 ∾
Early to Bed

Early to bed and early to rise
Is the way to be healthy,
Wealthy and wise.

∾ 234 ∾

There was an Old Person of Dover,
Who rushed through a field of blue clover;
But some very large bees
Stung his nose and his knees,
So he very soon went back to Dover.

∾ 235 ∾

There was an Old Person of Woking,
Whose mind was perverse and provoking;
He sat on a rail,
With his head in a pail,
That illusive Old Person of Woking.

∾ 236 ∾

There was an Old Man who said, "How,
Shall I flee from that horrible cow?
I will sit on this stile,
And continue to smile,
Which may soften the heart of that cow."

∾ 237 ∾

There was a Young Lady of Dorking,
Who bought a large bonnet for walking;
But its colour and size
So bedazzled her eyes,
That she very soon went back to Dorking.

∾ 238 ∾

There was an Old Man in a tree,
Who was horribly bored by a bee;
When they said, "Does it buzz?"
He replied, "Yes, it does!
It's a regular brute of a bee!"

∾ 239 ∾

There was a Young Lady of Norway,
Who casually sat in a doorway;
When the door squeezed her flat,
She exclaimed, "What of that?"
This courageous Young Lady of Norway.

all by Edward Lear

❧ 240 ❧
The Midnight Circus

Ben Busby trudged home sadly. He'd come second in the school gym contest for the third year in a row. However hard he tried, he never won.

An impatient sigh made him look up. There was an old woman glaring at a tree.

"My cat's stuck up there and I can't reach her," grumbled the woman.

"I'll get her," Ben offered. "I'm good at climbing trees." He scampered up to the top branch and gently carried the cat back to earth.

"I suppose you want a reward now," the old woman snorted. "Come with me."

Ben followed her to a tall tower, with one little door and a single window right at the top. The woman went inside and emerged with a book.

"Spells?" thought Ben, reading the cover. The woman tugged a silver ticket from between the pages and handed it to him.

Starlight Circus: Midnight, Fen Field, he read.

"Enjoy it while you can," said the old woman, with a grin. She went inside and slammed the door.

That night, Ben crept out of his house and ran to Fen Field. It was empty.

"The old woman tricked me," he thought.

He had turned to go when, with a CRASH and a BANG, a swirl of stars surrounded the field. The next second, a circus big top shimmered into view.

"Come one, come all!" cried a ringmaster. "The Starlight Circus is about to begin."

Ben ran inside excitedly. He was the only one in the audience and chose a seat at the very front.

He gaped as the tightrope walker teetered high

above his head. He gulped as ten acrobats formed a wobbly human pyramid. And he gasped as trapeze artists flew through the air.

"I'll tell all my friends about your great circus," he told the ringmaster when the show ended.

"They'll never see us," sighed the ringmaster. "A witch saw our show and hated it. She put a spell on us, and now we only appear when someone brings a magic ticket to the field. When the sun rises, we'll disappear and so will your ticket."

"I think I met that witch today," said Ben, telling his tale. "If we get hold of her book of spells, we might be able to lift the spell on the circus."

An hour later, Ben and the circus troupe stood at the foot of the witch's tower. The door was locked but the window was open.

The acrobats sprang into action. In seconds, they'd formed a human ladder. Ben clambered up and peered through the window.

"I can see the spell book on a shelf above the witch's bed," he whispered. "But I can't reach it."

"Let me try," said Trixie the trapeze artist. She climbed to the window, leaped onto a chandelier and swung across the room. Reaching out, she grabbed the book and swung back again.

Ben and his new friends rushed back to Fen Field. It was nearly sunrise. Already the performers and the big top were starting to fade. Ben desperately looked through the book.

"I think I've found it," he cried at last. "Help me spirits, if you would, let the circus stay for good!"

There was a CRASH, a BANG and a swirl of stars. The sun rose, but the circus didn't disappear.

"You've done it!" cried the ringmaster in delight.

The Starlight Circus soon became the biggest attraction in town.

As a reward, Trixie and her friends gave Ben free acrobatic lessons. After that, he won the school gym contest every single year.

~ 241 ~
Robin Hood & the Butcher

One day, Robin Hood met a butcher going to market. This gave him an idea...

"Let me buy your meat from you here," he said. "It will save you a trip into town."

The butcher agreed and, for an extra fee, he sold Robin his apron as well.

So, dressed as a butcher, Robin made his way into Nottingham and set up a stall. His prices were so low that people started talking.

"If he can sell his meat this cheaply," they whispered, "he must already be rich."

"And own lots of land..."

"And many herds of cattle..."

When the Sheriff of Nottingham heard of this rich butcher, he decided to invite him to a feast.

Robin readily accepted and borrowed some fine clothes for the occasion. The Sheriff had no idea that the wealthy butcher at his table was really his arch enemy. He was far too preoccupied with becoming richer himself by buying up farmland and cattle.

"Have you any herds you can sell me?" asked the greedy Sheriff, between courses.

"Oh yes," said Robin. "There are hundreds of animals where I live, and lots of land too."

The Sheriff rubbed his hands in glee. "Then tomorrow we shall go on a little shopping trip."

The next morning, the Sheriff saddled up two horses and weighed them down with gold coins. Then he followed Robin out of Nottingham, eager to see his many fields and farm animals.

"This is the quickest route," said Robin, turning into Sherwood Forest.

"I hope we don't bump into Robin Hood and his outlaws..." the Sheriff muttered.

By and by, they came to a clearing in the forest, where a herd of wild deer stood grazing.

"Here are my animals, and here is my land," announced Robin.

The Sheriff's look turned from bafflement to outrage, as he realized he'd been duped. Robin lifted his horn and blew three times. Immediately a band of outlaws arrived, aiming their arrows at the Sheriff.

"Let us relieve you of your heavy burden," said Robin, taking the Sheriff's sacks of gold. "Now why don't you join us for a feast, after you treated me so kindly last night?"

The Sheriff scowled at Robin and his men. "I'll get you for this!" he yelled, kicking his heels into his horse and galloping away.

"He forgot his herd!" said Robin, with a smile.

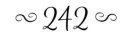

~ 242 ~
The Peacock & the Crane

A proud peacock lived on the banks of a lake. Every day, he preened his magnificent feathers, admiring his reflection in the still water.

One morning, a crane arrived. The peacock looked scornfully at her dull feathers. "What a sad life you must lead with such drab plumage!" the peacock sneered.

"Your feathers certainly look beautiful," replied the crane, "but they can't do this."

She spread her wings and, with a few skilled flaps, rose smoothly into the air. "You shouldn't judge things by their looks alone!" she called as she soared out of sight.

The Months

January brings the snow,
Makes our feet and fingers glow.

February brings the rain,
Thaws the frozen lake again.

March brings breezes, loud and shrill,
To stir the dancing daffodil.

April brings the primrose sweet,
Scatters daisies at our feet.

May brings flocks of pretty lambs,
Skipping by their fleecy dams.

June brings tulips, lilies, roses,
Fills the children's hands with posies.

Hot July brings cooling showers,
Apricots and gillyflowers.

August brings the sheaves of corn,
Then the harvest home is borne.

Warm September brings the fruit,
Sportsmen then begin to shoot.

Fresh October brings the pheasant,
Then to gather nuts is pleasant.

Dull November brings the blast,
Then the leaves are whirling fast.

Chill December brings the sleet,
Blazing fire, and Christmas treat.

Sara Coleridge

Hodja Borrows a Pot

One day, Nasreddin Hodja borrowed a friend's large cooking pot. The following week, he returned it.

"Wait a minute," said his friend, "there's another pot inside."

"Oh yes," said the Hodja. "While your pot was with me it gave birth to a baby pot. It would be wrong to separate a mother and child, so you should keep both."

His friend thought Nasreddin Hodja had gone crazy. On the other hand, he didn't own a small cooking pot, so he was happy to keep it.

A few months later, the Hodja asked to borrow his friend's pot again. This time he didn't return it.

Time went by and eventually the friend came to collect his pot.

"Oh, I'm so sorry," said the Hodja. "The pot died so I buried it."

"Don't be silly, pots can't die!"

"My dear friend," the Hodja said, "your pot gave birth to a shiny baby pot, a pot that you were happy to keep. If it can give birth, then it can also die. I'm very sorry for your loss."

The friend shook his head and walked away. He never let the Hodja borrow anything again.

∽ 245 ∽
As I was Going to St. Ives

As I was going to St. Ives,
I met a man with seven wives,
Each wife had seven sacks,
Each sack had seven cats,
Each cat had seven kits:
Kits, cats, sacks, and wives,
How many were going to St. Ives?

The answer is one – only I was going to St. Ives.

From a Railway Carriage

Faster than fairies, faster than witches,
Bridges and houses, hedges and ditches,
And charging along like troops in a battle,
All through the meadows, the horses and cattle:
All of the sights of the hill and the plain
Fly as thick as driving rain;
And ever again, in the wink of an eye,
Painted stations whistle by.

Here is a child who clambers and scrambles,
All by himself and gathering brambles;
Here is a tramp who stands and gazes;
And there is the green for stringing the daisies!
Here is a cart run away in the road,
Lumping along with man and load;
And here is a mill, and there is a river;
Each a glimpse and gone for ever!

Robert Louis Stevenson

∽ 247 ∾
The Two Frogs

Not so long ago in Japan there were two inquisitive frogs. One lived in the vibrant city of Osaka, the other lived among the beautiful temples of Kyoto. Although they'd never met, they shared a similar longing...

"How I'd love to see the bright lights of Osaka," thought the Kyoto frog.

"How I'd love to visit the temples of Kyoto," thought the Osaka frog.

Quite by chance, they both set off on the same day on the long journey to the other's city. They met halfway on a mountain and they soon got talking.

"If only I were a little taller," said the Kyoto frog, "I'd be able to see Osaka and decide whether it's worth the journey."

"That's easy," said the Osaka frog. "We just need to help each other balance on our hind legs."

And that's what they did. Only the foolish things forgot that their eyes were high up on their heads.

As they faced the way they were going, their eyes looked back at the cities they'd just left.

"Kyoto isn't so very different from Osaka after all," said the Osaka frog, sounding disappointed.

"And Osaka is exactly the same as Kyoto," frowned the Kyoto frog.

"At least that saves us a journey," they agreed. And off they hopped, back to their vastly different cities, believing them both to be exactly the same.

∽ 248 ∽

Handy dandy, riddledy ro,
Which hand will you have, high or low?

The 'Handy dandy' rhyme can be used when hiding a small object in one hand and asking someone to guess which hand they think it's in.

The Clever Tailor

There was once a very proud princess. If anyone wanted to marry her, she set them a riddle. If they failed, she laughed them out of town.

Three tailors heard this tale. The elder two were sure at least one of them would know the answer to the riddle. "Not you though," they said to the youngest. "You stay at home. Your brain is too small for this sort of thing."

But the little tailor was undaunted. He set off with the others, walking as if the whole world belonged to him.

"Here we are!" they announced as they arrived at Court. "We will guess your riddle, princess. Our wits are so fine you might almost thread a needle with them."

"We'll see," said the princess, who sat swathed in embroidered shawls. "Now, I have two different shades of hair on my head. What are they?"

"Most likely black and white," said the first tailor, "like the cloth we call pepper-and-salt."

"Wrong," said the princess.

"Then they are no doubt red and brown," said the second tailor, "like my father's Sunday coat."

"Wrong," said the princess.

The third little tailor stepped boldly to the front and said, "The princess has silver and golden hair upon her head."

"You are right!" cried the princess, turning pale. "But don't think you have won me yet. Below in the stable is a bear. If you can survive a night lying next to him, you shall marry me."

She was sure to be rid of him now, she thought. The bear had never left anyone alive who had come within reach of his claws.

"Bravely dared is half won," said the tailor cheerily, and went to find the bear.

The great beast tried to snatch up the tailor with his huge paws.

"Gently," said the tailor, and took some nuts

from his pocket, cracking the shells and eating the nuts as if he didn't have a care in the world.

"May I have some?" asked the bear, feeling rather hungry.

The tailor dived into his pocket and gave him a handful, only these weren't nuts, but pebbles.

The bear thrust them into his mouth, but couldn't crack them. He looked at the little tailor in wonder. What sharp teeth he must have, thought the bear. I won't try attacking him again.

When morning came, the princess came to the stables. She was shocked to see the tailor alive and untouched, as fresh and lively as a fish in water.

"Marry me!" said the tailor.

The princess smiled. At last, here was a man with courage and cleverness to match her own. "Gladly," she said.

And so, the princess and tailor lived together for many years, as happily and merrily as larks.

Alphabet

A was once an apple-pie,
  Pidy Widy Tidy Pidy
Nice insidy Apple-pie.

B was once a little bear,
  Beary! Weary! Hairy! Beary!
Taky cary! Little Bear!

C was once a little cake,
  Caky, Baky Maky Caky,
Taky Caky, Little Cake.

D was once a little doll,
  Dolly, Molly, Polly, Nolly,
Nursy Dolly, Little Doll!

E was once a little Eel,
  Eely Weely Peely Eely
Twirly, Tweely, Little Eel.

F was once a little fish,
    Fishy Wishy Squishy Fishy
In a Dishy, Little Fish!

G was once a little Goose,
    Goosy Moosy Boosey Goosey
Waddly-woosy, Little Goose!

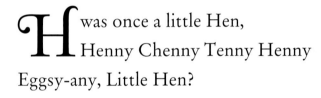

H was once a little Hen,
    Henny Chenny Tenny Henny
Eggsy-any, Little Hen?

I was once a bottle of ink,
    Inky Dinky Thinky Inky
Blacky Minky, Bottle of Ink!

J was once a jar of jam,
    Jammy Mammy Clammy Jammy
Sweety–swammy, Jar of Jam!

K was once a little kite,
　　Kity Whity Flighty Kity
Out of sighty – Little Kite!

L was once a little lark,
　　Larky! Marky! Harky! Larky!
In the Parky, Little Lark!

M was once a little mouse,
　　Mousy Bousey Sousy Mousy
In the Housy, Little Mouse!

N was once a little needle,
　　Needly Tweedly Threedly Needly
Wisky-wheedly, Little Needle!

O was once a little owl,
　　Owly Prowly Howly Owly
Browny fowly, Little Owl!

P was once a little pump,
　　Pumpy Slumpy Flumpy Pumpy
Dumpy, Thumpy, Little Pump!

Q was once a little quail,
　　Quaily Faily Daily Quaily
Stumpy-taily, Little Quail!

R was once a little rose,
　　Rosy Posy Nosy Rosy
Blows-y, Grows-y, Little Rose!

S was once a little shrimp,
　　Shrimpy Nimpy Flimpy Shrimpy
Jumpy, Jimpy, Little Shrimp!

T was once a little thrush,
　　Thrushy! Hushy! Bushy! Thrushy!
Flitty, Flushy, Little Thrush!

U was once a little urn,
   Urny Burny Turny Urny
Bubbly-burny, Little Urn!

V was once a little vine,
   Viny Winy Twiny Viny
Twisty-twiny, Little Vine!

W was once a whale,
   Whaly Scaly Shaly Whaly
Tumbly-taily, Mighty Whale!

X was once a great King Xerxes,
   Xerxy Perxy Turxy Xerxy
Linxy Lurxy, Great King Xerxes!

Y was once a little yew,
   Yewdy Fewdy Crudy Yewdy
Growdy, grewdy, Little Yew!

Z was once a piece of zinc,
Tinky Winky Blinky Tinky
Tinkly Minky, Piece of Zinc!

Edward Lear

❧ 251 ❧

The Lion &
the Unicorn

The lion and the unicorn,
Were fighting for the crown.
The lion beat the unicorn,
All around the town.
Some gave them white bread,
And some gave them brown.
Some gave them plum cake,
And drummed them out of town.

~ 252 ~
Molly & the Giant

Once upon a time, three sisters went out for a walk and got lost. They walked and walked, until the sun was setting. At last, they came to a massive house.

"We'll have to spend the night here," decided the eldest, whose name was Molly. She knocked boldly until a woman looked out.

"May we come in?" asked Molly.

The woman shook her head, frowning. "My husband is a giant," she said. "He'd eat you up!"

"Please," said Molly. "We're lost and tired."

The woman thought of her own three girls and her face softened. "All right – but you'd better go before he gets home." She let the girls sit by the fire and gave them each some bread and milk. They had hardly taken a bite when they heard a roar outside.

"Fee, fi, fo, fum, I smell the blood of some little ones!" The giant was home early.

"Now husband, don't shout," said the woman.

"These girls just came in to rest."

The giant gave a sly smile. "Of course," he said. "They can share our girls' bed tonight and go on their way in the morning."

Before the girls went to bed, the giant slipped a gold chain around each of his daughters' necks. For Molly and her sisters, he produced ropes of braided straw. Molly watched thoughtfully. She waited until the others were asleep, then took the chains for herself and her sisters, and put the ropes of straw around the giant's daughters instead.

In the middle of the night, a giant hand reached across the bed, feeling for the ropes... "Got you!" The giant tapped three girls on the head, scooped them up and dropped them into a cooking pot.

"You'll be a tasty breakfast," he chuckled. But when dawn broke, he saw to his fury that Molly and her sisters had fled, and it was his own daughters groaning and rubbing their heads inside the pot.

Molly and her sisters ran all the way to the king, who was very impressed to hear what Molly had done.

"The giant's house is full of stolen treasures," he told Molly. "If you can outwit him again and take back the silver sword that hangs above his bed, your youngest sister can marry my youngest son."

So Molly went back and hid beneath the giant's bed. Once he was snoring, she slipped out, lifted down the sword and was away through the door. But the sword rattled, and the giant leaped up with a roar and chased her. Molly ran and ran, until she reached a bridge so narrow that the giant couldn't follow her. And then she knew she was safe.

On her return, the king had another request. "If you can bring me the purse of gold the giant keeps under his pillow, your second sister can marry my second son."

So Molly went back and hid again. After the giant fell asleep, she slipped her hand beneath the pillow, pulled out the purse and was away. But it jingled as she ran, and the giant leaped up and chased her. Molly ran and ran, until she reached the narrow bridge and the giant had to stop.

The king had one last request. "If you can bring me the golden ring from the giant's finger, you can marry my eldest son and rule together after me."

So Molly went back and hid one last time. When she heard snores, she crept out and tugged off the ring...

"Got you!" shouted the giant, snatching the ring back and seizing her in a grip like iron. He had only been pretending to sleep. "Now, tell me what would *you* do with a thief like yourself?"

Molly thought fast. "I'd tie me in a sack and go into the woods to cut a stout stick to hit me."

The giant put down the ring, tied her in a sack and went to cut a stick.

While he was gone, Molly began to sigh loudly: "Oh, if you could see what I see in here!"

"What can you see?" the giant's wife wanted to know. But Molly wouldn't say. Eventually, the wife could stand it no longer. She opened the sack to have a look. Quick as a flash, Molly leaped out, grabbed the ring and ran. She didn't stop until she was safely over the bridge. And this time, when she reached the palace, Molly married the king's eldest son and left the giant in peace for good.

∾ 253 ∽

Hickety, pickety, my black hen,
She lays eggs for gentlemen;
Gentlemen come every day
To see what my black hen doth lay.
Sometimes nine and sometimes ten,
Hickety, pickety, my black hen.

∾ 254 ∾
The Turnip

O nce, there were two brothers: one rich, the other poor, and both of them soldiers.

The poor brother needed to earn more money, so he took off his red soldier's uniform and began tilling the soil. He planted some turnip seeds and watched them grow. One turnip just wouldn't *stop* growing. It grew bigger than a cat, bigger than a cow, big enough to fill a cart.

"It can't be worth much," thought the poor brother. "Smaller turnips are always tastier. But it's rather unusual, so I'll take it to the king."

The king was impressed. "You must be a very rich farmer," he exclaimed. When he heard that in fact the opposite was true, he took pity on the poor brother and gave him a vast area of land to farm.

The rich brother found out about the king's gift and was jealous. He decided to visit the king himself, bearing gifts of gold and fine horses, and hoping for even greater riches in return.

The king was extremely grateful. "I will reward your generosity with the most precious thing in my possession," he declared.

The rich brother rubbed his hands with glee. "Now my brother will be jealous of *me*," he smirked.

Imagine his dismay when the king's gift arrived on the back of a cart. The king had sent him the world's biggest turnip.

∞ 255 ∞

Peter, Peter, pumpkin eater,
Had a wife and couldn't keep her;
He put her in a pumpkin shell
And there he kept her very well.

∽ 256 ∽
The Magic Moneybag

A young couple lived in a very small hut on a mountainside. Every day, they ventured into the forest to collect two bundles of firewood. They brought one into their hut to use themselves. There was no room for the other one, so they left it outside to sell at the market the next day.

One morning, the husband opened the door and called out in dismay, "The firewood's missing!"

With no wood to sell at the market, they would have no food that evening, but there was nothing the couple could do except head into the forest as usual. They collected two bundles of firewood, left one outside and took the other one in to burn.

"The firewood's gone again," exclaimed the husband the next morning. For four days in a row, the bundle outside disappeared overnight.

"Enough's enough," decided the husband.

On the fifth day, he hid himself inside the bundle of firewood. In the dead of night, he felt himself being lifted higher and higher. Suddenly, the bundle came undone. The husband tumbled out and found himself on a soft cloud, face to face with an old man.

"Tell me," asked the old man, gently. "Why do you collect two bundles of wood but only use one?"

"So we can sell the second bundle at the market and buy enough food to live," replied the young man. "We are very poor you see..."

"You are honest and sensible too," said the old man. "So I will reward you with this moneybag. Open it each morning, and you will find a coin. But only open it once a day."

"Thank you," said the young man, pleased yet rather puzzled. He was lowered back to Earth and rushed to show his wife the moneybag.

At the first glimmer of dawn, the couple felt in the moneybag and sure enough there was a shiny coin. "Let's save it," suggested the wife. "We could buy ourselves something nice."

They set off for the forest as usual and returned with two bundles of wood. The next morning, they found another coin in the moneybag, put it aside, then headed into the forest. Day after day, the same thing happened and, coin after coin, the couple saved up a small fortune.

"We're rich!" announced the husband one morning. "Why do we keep going into the forest? Let's build ourselves a bigger, better house."

The wife agreed and they began to plan their new home. But the husband's plans became increasingly ambitious. "If only we had more money," he sighed.

Without telling his wife, he opened the moneybag a second time that day and found a second coin. He opened it a third time and found a third coin. He opened it a fourth time and found... nothing.

From then on, the moneybag was always empty. Soon all the couple's savings were gone. There was nothing they could do, but return to their old life, going into the forest each day for two bundles of firewood.

∾ 257 ∾

The Man & the Woods

Deep in the woods, the trees rustled their branches and whispered softly together. "Someone is coming," they murmured.

It was a man, walking into the heart of the forest. In his hand he held a smooth blade made from polished metal. The trees grew still and waited.

"Trees," the man called, "I need your help. Do you have a small branch for me to use as I please?"

The trees leaned together to confer privately. "What shall we do?" asked a maple.

"Why does he want a branch?" a slim holly said.

"And what is he holding?" demanded a tall pine. Then a massive oak joined in. "Let us give him what he asks," advised the oak. "It is only a little branch, after all. We can spare it."

The man heard him and smiled secretly to himself. When the

~ 374 ~

trees gave him the branch, he bowed to them. Then, he fitted the top of the branch into a hole in the polished metal blade he carried.

Too late, the trees saw that the blade was a hatchet, and the branch they had given was its handle. The man whistled as he set to work, chopping down the huge oak tree.

"I should not have been so rash," the oak tree moaned. "I have given my enemy the one thing he needed to destroy me."

∾ 258 ∾
Shoes

Two brothers we are,
Great burdens we bear,
On which we are bitterly pressed.
The truth is to say,
We are full all the day,
And empty when we go to rest.

∾ 259 ∾

The Clever Fox

Simon and Susan had an old dog and an old cat. Susan loved them both. Simon didn't...

"Why should we keep our cat any longer?" said Simon, one day. "She never catches mice. I'm going to get rid of her."

"Oh don't do that!" cried Susan. "I'm sure she could still catch mice."

"Pah!" said Simon. "The mice could dance all over her and she'd never catch a single one. Next time I see her, I'll drown her."

Susan was very unhappy about this – as was the cat, who had been listening from behind the stove. When Simon went off for work, the cat mewed and looked so pathetic, Susan picked her up and popped her out of the door. "Fly for your life, my poor beast. Get as far as you can before your master returns."

"Well," said Simon, when he returned home to find the cat gone, "now we must think what to do with the dog. He's deaf, he's blind and he barks at nothing."

"He's not as useless as that," cried Susan.

"Don't be foolish," said Simon. "Our house could be full of thieves and he'd never discover them. When I next see him, I'll finish him off."

Susan was very unhappy about this – as was the dog, who had been lying on the floor, listening to every word. As soon as Simon had gone back to work, he stood up and howled so touchingly that Susan opened the door and said, "Fly for your life, you poor beast, before your master gets home."

The dog ran away as fast as his old legs could carry him, and soon came upon the cat in the woods. They sat down under a holly tree and poured out their troubles.

"What are you two grumbling about?" asked a passing fox.

When he'd heard their woes, he tutted and sighed.

"A sorry tale," he said. "But that is the way of the world. Luckily for you, old cat and old dog, you have met a very clever fox. If you promise to help me when I need it, would you like me to help you?"

The dog and the cat agreed. "We don't want to end our days out here in the woods," they said. "We are too old. Our bones creak. We feel the cold. We want to go home."

"Then show me the way," said the clever fox. "And remember, do exactly as I say."

The dog and the cat set off for home, the fox following on behind. Every now and then he would pounce on a mouse, then carry it between his claws.

When they arrived at the house, the clever fox turned to the cat. "Go inside and lay these mice down before your master," he said.

The cat did exactly that.

"Oh!" called Susan. "Here is our old cat back again, and see how many mice she has caught."

Then the fox turned to the dog. "Your master has made some sausages and stored them in the shed outside. Tonight, go into the courtyard and bark as loudly as you can."

"Oh!" Susan cried out, later that night. "Our dog must have come back. I can hear him barking. Please go out and see what's happened. Some thieves may be stealing our sausages."

"Nonsense!" snapped Simon.

But the next morning, the dog was there and the sausages were gone.

"I don't understand it," said Simon. "I never thought the dog was so good at hearing."

"You thought you knew best," said Susan, "but from now on you must listen to me."

Simon did just that, and all four lived happily together for the rest of their lives. As for the fox, he was happy too, for he had run off with the sausages.

∾ 260 ∾
The War of the Wolf
& the Fox

The clever fox was in trouble. The wolf had declared war on him.

"Meet me here tomorrow in the woods," said the wolf. "I will come with my army – the bear and wild boar. Then we shall fight!"

The fox agreed; he had no choice if he were to hold his head high, but he knew he could never win the battle alone. So that night he slunk through the woods to the house of his friends, the old cat and dog.

"Once I helped you," he said. "Now, will you agree to help me?"

The dog and the cat agreed at once. "Even if we are killed," they said, "it is better to die bravely on the field of battle, than to perish without glory at home." And they shook paws and made their bargain.

The next morning, they set out together to face the enemy.

The wolf, the bear and the wild boar arrived first. After waiting some time for the others, the bear said, "I'll climb up into the oak tree, and see if the fox is coming."

The first time he looked, he said, "I can see nothing." The second time he looked, he said, "I can see nothing." But the third time he said, "I see a mighty army in the distance. And one of the warriors has a huge spear!"

The bear, you see, did not have very good eyesight. The mighty army was a bush. The huge spear was the cat's tail, poking up in the air.

"But they are very far away," finished the bear.

"Well in that case," said the wild boar. "Let's have a nap."

So the bear curled up in the fork of the tree, and fell asleep. The wolf lay beneath him and the boar buried himself in some straw, with only an ear to be seen.

When the dog, the cat and the fox arrived, the dog saw the wild boar's ear. Thinking it was a rabbit, he leaped on it. The wild boar shot off in fright and disappeared into the woods. The cat was even more startled and scrambled up the tree... right into the bear's face. With a mighty growl, the bear jumped out of the tree, landed on the wolf and squashed him flat. Then the bear lumbered away himself.

"Perfect," grinned the fox. "I'm even cleverer than I realized. With your help, I won – and I didn't have to do a thing!"

∽ 261 ∽
The Rugged Rock

Round and round the rugged rock,
The ragged rascal ran.
How many R's are there in that?
Now tell me if you can.

None. (There are no 'R's in the word that.)

Weathers

This is the weather the cuckoo likes,
And so do I;
When showers betumble the chestnut spikes,
And nestlings fly:
And the little brown nightingale bills his best,
And they sit outside at 'The Travellers' Rest',
And maids come forth sprig-muslin drest,
And citizens dream of the south and west,
And so do I.

This is the weather the shepherd shuns,
And so do I;
When beeches drip in browns and duns,
And thresh, and ply;
And hill-hid tides throb, throe on throe,
And meadow rivulets overflow,
And drops on gate-bars hang in a row,
And rooks in families homeward go,
And so do I.

Thomas Hardy

\infty 263 \infty

Sinbad: Voyage Five

My life in Baghdad was luxurious, but I longed for another adventure. Even though I'd faced death on four voyages, I was drawn back to the sea.

This time I bought my own ship and invited merchants from different countries to join me. After many days at sea, we discovered an unknown island and decided to explore.

The island appeared deserted, apart from a massive, smooth object. I recognized it to be the egg of a formidable bird, known as a roc. To my dismay, the merchants began throwing stones at the egg, trying to crack it open.

"Stop!" I cried. "The parents are sure to be near."

Sure enough, an adult roc flew into view.

"RUN!" I cried, heading for the ship and casting off. I thought we'd managed to escape unharmed, but then an ominous shadow fell over us. I looked up and saw the roc directly above, releasing a large boulder from its claws.

With a sickening crash, the ship was dashed to pieces. I clung to the mast and must have passed out.

The next thing I knew, I was on a different beach, being pelted by coconuts. I leaped to my feet.

"Here, put the coconuts in this bag," a stranger called to me. "And you'll need those," he added, pointing to a pile of stones.

The man and his friends were throwing stone after stone at some monkeys high up in the palms. The angry monkeys retaliated by throwing back coconuts, which was exactly what the men wanted.

I eagerly joined in the sport, throwing stones and catching coconuts. Soon I'd filled five bags, much to the men's delight. For my help, they offered to arrange my journey home. They also gave me a sack of pearls which were very common on their island but would be priceless in my city.

Exhausted and relieved, I thanked the men and set sail for Baghdad. I thought I was done with adventuring... but that is not the end of my story.

A Smuggler's Song

If you wake at midnight, and hear a horse's feet,
  Don't go drawing back the blind,
    or looking in the street,
Them that asks no questions isn't told a lie.
Watch the wall, my darling,
  while the Gentlemen go by!
      Five and twenty ponies,
      Trotting through the dark –
      Brandy for the Parson,
      'Baccy for the Clerk;
      Laces for a lady, letters for a spy,
And watch the wall, my darling,
  while the Gentlemen go by!

Running round the woodlump if you chance to find
Little barrels, roped and tarred, all full of brandy-wine,
Don't you shout to come and look,
  nor take 'em for your play.

Put the brushwood back again –
  and they'll be gone next day!

If you see the stable-door setting open wide;
If you see a tired horse lying down inside;
If your mother mends a coat cut about and tore;
If the lining's wet and warm – don't you ask no more!

If you meet King George's men,
  dressed in blue and red,
You be careful what you say,
  and mindful what is said.
If they call you "pretty maid"
  and chuck you 'neath the chin,
Don't you tell where no one is,
  nor yet where no one's been!

Knocks and footsteps round the house –
  whistles after dark –

You've no call for running out
   till the house-dogs bark.
Trusty's here, and *Pincher's* here,
   and see how dumb they lie –
They don't fret to follow when the Gentlemen go by!

If you do as you've been told, likely there's a chance,
You'll be give a dainty doll, all the way from France,
With a cap of Valenciennes, and a velvet hood –
A present from the Gentlemen, along o' being good!
      Five and twenty ponies,
      Trotting through the dark –
      Brandy for the Parson,
      'Baccy for the Clerk;
Them that asks no questions isn't told a lie –
Watch the wall, my darling,
   while the Gentlemen go by!

                    Rudyard Kipling

∞ 265 ∞

The Moonrakers

On a moonlit night, in a quiet English town, a band of smugglers was busy wheeling barrels past the town pond when word reached them that the customs officers were on the prowl...

"Push the barrels into the pond, quick!" ordered the chief smuggler.

Splash followed splash, and the barrels sank to the bottom of the pond. But it was a bright night and the barrels were clearly visible under the water.

A sudden clatter of hooves announced the arrival of the customs men.

"Pass me that rake!" the chief smuggler cried.

"What's going on here?" called a burly man in uniform. "You all look highly suspicious."

The chief smuggler began raking the pond, sending ripples over the reflection of the moon and obscuring the view of the barrels below.

"We're raking the moon for cheese, of course," he said calmly. "Would you like some, sir?"

"What a fool!" the burly man thought. "This gang couldn't smuggle a flea." He turned his horse around and led his fellow officers onto the next town.

The smugglers fell over themselves laughing. "Raking the moon for cheese!" they repeated. "You're a genius, Chief!" And to this day, the people from that town are known as Moonrakers.

∞ 266 ∞
I See the Moon

I see the moon,
And the moon sees me;
God bless the moon,
And God bless me.

∾ 267 ∾
The Owl

When cats run home and light is come,
And dew is cold upon the ground,
And the far-off stream is dumb,
And the whirring sail goes round,
And the whirring sail goes round;
Alone and warming his five wits.
The white owl in the belfry sits.

When merry milkmaids click the latch,
And rarely smells the new-mown hay,
And the cock hath sung beneath the thatch
Twice or thrice his roundelay,
Twice or thrice his roundelay;
Alone and warming his five wits,
The white owl in his belfry sits.

Alfred Tennyson

Candlelight

One chilly day, Nasreddin Hodja was challenged by his friends. If he could stay outside all night without a coat or a fire, they would cook him a fine meal.

"But if you cheat or give up, then you must cook for us," they instructed.

"Very well," said the Hodja, "I'll give it a try."

It was a clear night and the temperature quickly plummeted below freezing. It wasn't long before the Hodja was shivering and his fingers had turned numb. He was about to admit defeat and go inside when he saw the glow of a candle in a distant window. He imagined the warmth of the fire and somehow this sustained him through the long night.

"How long did you last?" asked his friends the next morning.

"All night," replied the Hodja, proudly. "The sight of a single candle was enough to keep me going."

"Then you cheated!" his friends declared. "You were warmed by the candle's flame!"

They didn't want to lose their bet – they wanted the Hodja to cook for them. The Hodja tried to argue his case but in the end he had to give in and invite them to dinner.

When his guests arrived there was no sign of food.

"It's cooking," the Hodja explained.

An hour went by of friendly chatter, but still no sign of a meal.

"It's cooking," was all the Hodja would say.

This time his guests went into the kitchen to see for themselves. They saw a large cauldron of ingredients standing over the small flame of a single candle.

"Nasreddin!" they called. "You'll never cook anything over a candle."

"Is that so?" replied the Hodja, mischievously. "But this candle warmed me all night from a distant window. Surely if it can do that then it can cook the ingredients in a pot directly above it?"

∽ 269 ∽
Fire Water

Have you ever wondered why monkeys live in trees? Well, it all began a long time ago...

Naresh, a gorilla who was king of the jungle, couldn't decide who should marry his daughter. Then, one day, he came across a barrel of water. At least, it looked like water. When Naresh took a little sip, it tasted like fire. It gave the king an idea.

"Whoever drinks this whole barrel may marry my daughter," he announced.

It wasn't long before a host of animals had lined up to take the challenge.

The elephant was first. He stuck his trunk into the barrel and sucked up a big mouthful. "Yeuch!" he cried, spraying out the fire water in disgust. "No one could drink this stuff."

The hippo was next. He took an even bigger

~ 394 ~

mouthful than the elephant. "Urrgh, horrible!" he moaned. Then he ran off to the river, coughing and spluttering, to wash out his mouth.

The leopard strolled up confidently. "A little fire water doesn't bother me," he purred. But he did no better than the others. "Yuck!" he complained. "I'd rather drink a bison's bath water."

Finally, a tiny monkey named Telinga scampered forward. "I can drink the whole barrel, no problem," he boasted to Naresh. "But may I drink a little at a time, with rests in between?"

The king agreed.

Telinga took a gulp of fire water, then ran off into the bushes. A second later, he emerged and took another sip. Once again, he ran off to the bushes and popped out a moment afterwards. This went on until the barrel was dry.

"Congratulations!" boomed Naresh. "Now you can marry my daughter."

"Ha ha!" whooped Telinga. "I'm going to live the

life of a prince."

Just then, a giraffe came along. "What are all those monkeys doing behind the bushes?" he asked.

Everyone followed the giraffe's stare. There, behind the bushes, sat a whole tribe of monkeys who looked just like Telinga.

"We've been tricked," roared the other animals. "Telinga took turns with his friends." And they chased the monkeys, who scrambled up the nearest tree to escape.

And that's why, ever since, monkeys have lived high up in the trees – where it's safer!

∞ 270 ∞

Twelve pears hanging high,
Twelve knights riding by,
Each knight took a pear
And yet left eleven there.

This is a very old riddle and no one knows the answer. Perhaps the knights took the same pear. Or perhaps one of the knights was named 'Eachknight' and he was the only one to take a pear. What do you think?

The Boastful Crow

A sooty black crow stood alone on a sandy beach, his beady black eyes on the lookout for food. It wasn't long before he heard a HONK-HONK and a whirring of wings. The next moment, a flock of geese blotted out the sun as they noisily flapped down from the sky.

The crow watched them with his beak stuck haughtily in the air. "How clumsy you are!" he told them, as they crashed down beside him. "I've been watching you and laughing. All you do is go flap-flap-flap. Can you glide? Can you do somersaults in the air? Pah! I don't think so!"

The largest of the geese waddled up to the crow until they were beak to beak. "Let's have a flying competition," he declared.

"Yes!" squawked the crow. "I'll show you what flying really is."

The crow set off right away, with all the geese looking on. He soared straight into the air, flying up and up and up. "I'll show 'em!" he thought. He flew in circles, swooped down like an arrow, then shot up again.

He did a loop-the-loop and a twirly-whirly and finished with a tail-spin dive. "Caw!" he called, triumphantly, landing with an artful flourish of fluttering wings. "Beat that!"

"I will!" said the goose. He launched himself into the air and began flying over the sea. The crow flew after him.

"Just as I thought," called the crow. "All you do is flap-flap-flap."

On and on they flew, until water stretched out on all sides. After a little while, the crow stopped taunting the goose. It was all he could do to keep up with him. His aching wings begged for rest and he looked with fear at the endless water below.

The goose smiled to himself. "Why do you keep touching the water?" he asked. "Is it another of your flying tricks?"

"No!" cried the crow, all pride gone. "I can't...

last... much longer. If you don't help me, I'll drown!"

"Do you promise never to boast again?"

"I promise!" gasped the crow and flopped, exhausted, onto the goose's back.

The goose beat his powerful wings and together they turned back to the shore.

"Ah!" sighed the crow. "Slow and steady. No fancy tricks. Just flap-flap-flap! What a *perfect* way to fly."

∽ 272 ∽

$\mathcal{A}$ frog he would a-wooing go,
Heigh ho! says Rowley,
A frog he would a-wooing go,
Whether his mother would let him or no.
With a rowley, powley, gammon and spinach,
Heigh ho! says Anthony Rowley.

∽ 273 ∽
The Fieldmouse

Where the acorn tumbles down,
Where the ash tree sheds its berry,
With your fur so soft and brown,
With your eye so round and merry,
Scarcely moving the long grass,
Fieldmouse, I can see you pass.

Little thing, in what dark den,
Lie you all the winter sleeping
Till warm weather comes again?
Then once more I see you peeping
Round about the tall tree roots,
Nibbling at their fallen fruits.

Fieldmouse, fieldmouse, do not go,
Where the farmer stacks his treasure;
Find the nut that falls below,
Eat the acorn at your pleasure.
But you must not steal the grain
He has stacked with so much pain.

Make your hole where mosses spring,
Underneath the tall oak's shadow,
Pretty, quiet, harmless thing,
Play about the sunny meadow.
Keep away from corn and house,
None will harm you, little mouse.

Cecil Frances Alexander

Hurt No Living Thing

Hurt no living thing:
Ladybird, nor butterfly,
Nor moth with dusty wing,
Nor cricket chirping cheerily,
Nor grasshopper so light of leap,
Nor dancing gnat, nor beetle fat,
Nor harmless worms that creep.

Christina Rossetti

❧ 275 ❧

The Bat & the Weasels

High among the dark canopy of the forest, lived Bat. He rarely left his branch, for the forest floor was full of danger. Only in the dead of night would animals catch the briefest sight of him – a speeding shadow, swooping past.

One blustery day, Bat was snoozing upside down on his branch, when a gust of wind swooshed through the trees. As the branch shook, Bat's claws came free and he fell towards the forest floor... Thud.

Bat woke with a start. Feeling a little groggy, he looked around at the unfamiliar surroundings and saw a threatening shape looming above.

"It's my lucky day," said a voice. "A tasty bird has fallen right in front of me."

Bat blinked. He could see a long furry head, sharp teeth and glinting eyes. A weasel! "Please let me go, Weasel," he begged. "I don't belong down here. I belong in the trees."

"Oh I know you do, *Bird*," snarled the weasel. "Birds are the enemy of all weasels."

Bat thought quickly. "I'm no bird!" he insisted. "Look I have no feathers. Can't you see I am in fact... a mouse?"

"Hmmm," pondered the weasel. "It's true you don't have any feathers. All right, Mouse, I'll let you go, but next time you might not be so lucky."

Relieved, Bat hastily fluttered back to his roost.

The following day, his belly full from the night's hunt, Bat fell into a deep sleep. The next thing he knew, he awoke with a start on the forest floor. "Not again," muttered Bat.

"Not again what?" snarled a voice from behind.

Bat spun around, to come face-to-face with a furry, pointed snout – another weasel! "Oh pardon me, Weasel," Bat said quickly, remembering his encounter the day before. "I am simply a... a mouse fallen out of a tree – and certainly not a bird."

"A mouse!" cried the weasel furiously. "The only creature I detest more than a bird is a little ferreting mouse." And the weasel bared sharp, glinting teeth.

"Wait!" yelled Bat. "I'm a bat. Look I have black wings for flying," he added frantically, spreading them for the weasel to see. "And no tail."

For a second, the weasel eyed him suspiciously. "A bat? I suppose that makes sense – I've certainly never heard of a flying mouse. You can go then."

And Bat fled, thankful for his lucky escape.

∞ 276 ∞

Twinkle, twinkle little bat,
How I wonder what you're at.
Up above the world so high
Like a tea-tray in the sky.

Lewis Carroll

∾ 277 ∾

The Squirrel

Whisky, frisky,
Hippity hop!
Up he goes
To the tree top!
Whirly, twirly,
Round and round,
Down he comes
To the ground.
Furly, curly,
What a tail!
Tall as a feather,
Broad as a sail!
Where's his supper?
In the shell;
Snappy, cracky!
Out it fell!
Stir the fire,
Put on the pot,
Here's his supper
Hissing hot!

Humpty Dumpty's Song

In winter, when the fields are white,
I sing this song for your delight:
In spring, when woods are getting green,
I'll try and tell you what I mean:
In summer, when the days are long,
Perhaps you'll understand the song:
In autumn, when the leaves are brown,
Take pen and ink, and write it down.
I sent a message to the fish:
I told them, "This is what I wish."
The little fishes of the sea,
They sent an answer back to me.
The little fishes' answer was
"We cannot do it, Sir, because–"
I sent to them again to say,
"It will be better to obey."
The fishes answered, with a grin,
"Why, what a temper you are in!"
I told them once, I told them twice:

They would not listen to advice.

I took a kettle large and new,

Fit for the deed I had to do.

My heart went hop, my heart went thump:

I filled the kettle at the pump.

Then someone came to me and said,

"The little fishes are in bed."

I said to him, I said it plain,

"Then you must wake them up again."

I said it very loud and clear:

I went and shouted in his ear.

But he was very stiff and proud:

He said, "You needn't shout so loud!"

And he was very proud and stiff:

He said, "I'd go and wake them, if–"

I took a corkscrew from the shelf.

I went to wake them up myself.

And when I found the door was locked,

I pulled and pushed and kicked and knocked.

And when I found the door was shut,

I tried to turn the handle, but–

Lewis Carroll

This is how Lewis Carroll ended the poem.

Grimly Grange

"Look outside!" cried Darcy Snoot excitedly. His fellow ghosts peered out of the window. A TV crew had arrived, and the cameramen were busy setting up their cameras.

"It's the Spook Hunters," gasped Lady Frilly. "They visit haunted houses looking for ghosts."

"We shall be stars!" declared Roger Ruffle.

"We must look our best for the television," said Percy Puff, flicking the dust from his cuffs.

The ghosts spent the next hour powdering their wigs and painting their faces. "Perfect!" they agreed at last.

As the filming began, the proud spooks floated into position around the house.

"Welcome to Grimly Grange," announced Penny Probe, the presenter. "This deserted mansion is said to be haunted. Tonight we'll find out if that's true."

As she spoke, Darcy whizzed down the banister behind her.

But by the time he reached the bottom, Penny had already moved on. Darcy shot through an open window and got tangled in a prickly hedge.

"No spooks in the hall," said Derek De'ath, the show's expert.

The TV crew moved on to the Great Hall, where Roger and Percy were waiting to swoop down from the chimney.

"The soot's gone up my nose," whispered Roger. "I think I'm going to s..s..sn, atishoooo!"

Roger and Percy tumbled down into the fireplace, buried from head to toe in a huge pile of soot.

"No ghosts here either," sighed Derek. "Just a chimney in need of sweeping."

In the ballroom, Lady Frilly was adjusting her wig, when it snagged on the chandelier.

"Agh!" she wailed, grabbing her bald head. "I can't be seen on screen like this."

She dashed behind the curtain and hid in fear, as Penny and Derek poked around.

"Another spookless spot," sniffed Derek.

When the coast was clear, Lady Frilly met up with her fellow ghosts in the Hall of Mirrors.

"We look a fright!" she moaned, patting her head.

"Thank goodness there are no TV cameras in here," agreed a soot-covered Percy.

"Ghosts!" came a shout.

The spooks turned in horror to see Penny, Derek and the TV crew racing towards them.

"I've decided I don't want to be a TV star," whined Roger.

"Me neither," cried Darcy.

With one last wail of shame, the four ghosts vanished into the cold night air.

❦ 280 ❧

The Little Donkey

Once upon a time, a king and a queen were expecting their first child. The day of the birth came and the palace buzzed with excitement, but alas, the child turned out to be a donkey.

"Oh no," wailed the queen.

"It doesn't matter," said the king. "He is our son and we will love him."

So the king and queen lavished their love on their donkey child and his furry ears grew beautifully long and straight.

One day, the donkey asked his parents for a lute. Now you may think a donkey playing a lute ridiculous. His parents certainly did at first. But like them you'd have been amazed at how gently his great hooves could pluck the small strings.

The donkey took his lute down to the riverbank and was happily playing a tune when he chanced to spy his reflection in the river.

The poor thing was so ashamed by his furry appearance, he decided to leave home at once. He wandered for days, with only his lute for company, until he arrived at a castle. Hungry and tired, the donkey slumped by the castle gate and began to play.

One of the guards heard the music and raced to tell the king. "Your Majesty," he panted, "there's an extraordinary musician at the gate."

"Well show him in," ordered the king. "He can join us for dinner."

The servants were informed and an extra place was laid at the table. Imagine everyone's shock when the musician turned out to be a donkey. But he was a very polite donkey, with excellent table manners, charming conversation and exquisite lute playing.

"Stay as long as you like," offered the king.

So he did. And that's how the donkey got to know the king's daughter. He loved her more than anything in the world and she adored him too, but how could a donkey ever marry a princess? The king noticed something was bothering his lute player.

"Little donkey," he called, "you look as sour as a bottle of vinegar. What on earth's the matter?"

The donkey refused to say, but by the way he was moping around, it was easy to guess.

"Little donkey," called the king the next day. "I have chosen a husband for my daughter."

The donkey's head drooped lower.

"He is charming and polite," the king went on, "and he plays the lute to perfection."

The donkey's ears pricked up, he stamped his hooves in delight, then he rushed to tell the princess the news. They had a magnificent wedding and the donkey's parents came to join the celebrations.

But when at last the donkey stood alone in front of his wife, he felt ashamed again.

He needn't have worried. One kiss from the princess and he transformed into a handsome young prince. They might even have lived happily ever after.

The Table & the Chair

Said the Table to the Chair,
"You can hardly be aware
How I suffer from the heat,
And from chilblains on my feet!
If we took a little walk,
We might have a little talk!
Pray let us take the air!"
Said the Table to the Chair.

∾

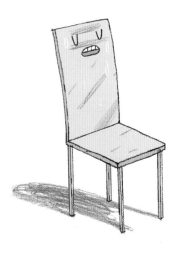

Said the Chair unto the Table,
"Now you *know* we are not able!
How foolishly you talk,
When you know we *cannot* walk!"
Said the Table with a sigh,
"It can do no harm to try;
I've as many legs as you,
Why can't we walk on two?"

So they both went slowly down,
And walked about the town
With a cheerful bumpy sound,
As they toddled round and round.
And everybody cried,
As they hastened to their side,
"See! the Table and the Chair
Have come out to take the air!"

&

But in going down an alley,
To a castle in the valley,
They completely lost their way,
And wandered all the day,
Till, to see them safely back,
They paid a Ducky-quack,
And a Beetle, and a Mouse,
Who took them to their house.
Then they whispered to each other,
"O delightful little brother!"

"What a lovely walk we've taken!
Let us dine on Beans and Bacon!"
So the Ducky and the leetle
Browny-Mousy and the Beetle
Dined, and danced upon their heads
Till they toddled to their beds.

Edward Lear

∾ 282 ∾
The Old Man of St. Bees

There was an old man of St. Bees,
Who was stung in the arm by a wasp;
When they asked, "Does it hurt?"
He replied, "No, it doesn't,
But I thought all the while 'twas a hornet!"

W. S. Gilbert

∾ 283 ∾

There was an Old Man of Peru,
Who watched his wife making a stew;
But once by mistake,
In a stove she did bake
That unfortunate Man of Peru.

∾ 284 ∾

There was an Old Person of Dutton,
Whose head was as small as a button,
So, to make it look big,
He purchased a wig,
And rapidly rushed about Dutton.

∾ 285 ∾

There was a Young Lady of Portugal,
Whose ideas were excessively nautical;
She climbed up a tree
To examine the sea,
But declared she would never leave Portugal.

all by Edward Lear

The Witch's Horse

"Where is that dratted thing?" cried Wilma the witch. She'd been hunting for her broomstick for two hours, with no luck.

"It's no use," she sighed, at last. "I'll just have to find another way of getting to the Annual Witches' Convention." She rummaged in her bag of tricks and pulled out a magic rope. "Now all I need is someone to tie this around," she thought with a grin.

She ran to the nearest road and hid behind a tree. A man strolled by, followed by his wife, who was struggling with their heavy shopping bags.

"Try to keep up, Cora!" barked the man.

"She'll do," thought the witch and threw her rope over Cora's shoulders. In a flash, the woman turned into a large white horse.

When the man looked back to tell his wife to hurry up, all he saw were some abandoned bags, and a horse and rider disappearing over the horizon.

"How annoying," he thought. "Now I'll have to carry the bags myself."

At last, Wilma arrived at the Convention and was caught up in a whirl of spelling lessons and cauldron brewing classes. There was even a daring broomstick acrobatic display to finish.

As the day came to an end, Wilma jumped on her horse and cantered home. She'd nearly reached her house, when she spotted the man she'd seen earlier.

"Take my horse," she said with a smile. "I don't need her any more."

"That's very kind," said the man, leaping up and riding off. But, back home, when he took off the rope from his new horse... FLASH! She turned into his wife. Well, almost – Cora still had horseshoes stuck to her hands.

From then on, whenever Cora and her husband went shopping, *he* had to carry the heavy bags. And that suited Cora just fine.

Choosing Their Names

Our old cat has kittens three –
What do you think their names should be?

One is tabby, with emerald eyes,
And a tail that's long and slender,
And into a temper she quickly flies
If you ever by chance offend her.
I think we shall call her this –
I think we shall call her that;
Now, don't you fancy "Pepperpot"
A nice name for a cat?

One is black, with a frill of white,
And her feet are all white fur, too;
If you stroke her she carries her tail upright,
And quickly begins to purr, too,
I think we shall call her this –
I think we shall call her that;
Now, don't you fancy "Sootikin"
A nice name for a cat?

One is a tortoiseshell, yellow and black,
With a lot of white about him;
If you tease him, at once he sets up his back;
He's a quarrelsome Tom, ne'er doubt him!
I think we shall call him this –
I think we shall call him that;
Now, don't you fancy "Scratchaway"
A nice name for a cat?

Our old cat has kittens three,
And I fancy these their names will be:
Pepperpot – Sootikin – Scratchaway – there!
Were there ever kittens with these to compare?
And we call the old mother – now, what do you think?
Tabitha Longclaws Tidleywink.

Thomas Hood

∽ 288 ∽
Robin Hood & the Three Squires

One cold autumn morning, Robin Hood ventured into the town of Nottingham. The streets were quieter than usual and Robin could clearly hear a woman weeping. He tracked her down and asked what was wrong.

"Three squires are being hanged today," she wailed, "and they're my sons."

"Hanged?" asked Robin. "Why, what have they done? Burned down a village?"

"Nothing of the sort," said the woman crossly. "They each killed one of the Sheriff's deer and now the Sheriff wants revenge."

"Well you've told the right person," said Robin, and he headed to the hangman's scaffold. On the way, he persuaded an old man to sell him his hat and cloak. And only just in time, for around the next corner stood the Sheriff himself.

"I hear you're in need of a hangman," Robin said to the Sheriff, in his new disguise.

"Indeed I am," the Sheriff replied. "Step this way old man."

They reached the scaffold and Robin leaped onto it. Three squires stood behind three nooses, with guards on either side. But Robin didn't reach for a noose, he reached for his horn. Three short blasts brought his men charging into the square. They easily fought off the Sheriff's men.

"Robin Hood!" screamed the Sheriff, as Robin threw off his cloak.

"None other," replied Robin. "And if I ever play at hangman again, watch out for your own neck!"

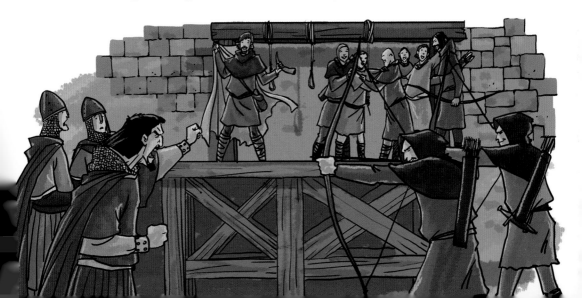

The Magic Words

A shepherd boy named Patrick was walking home from a hard day in the fields, when he noticed something bright and shiny on the ground. It was a tiny silver flute.

A fairy fluttered up. "You've found my flute," she cried. "Could I have it back please?"

"Of course," replied Patrick, handing it over.

"As a reward, here are some magic berries," said the fairy. "When you eat one, it will give you exactly the right words to say."

Patrick thanked her and went on into town. There he saw a poster:

WANTED ~
A HUSBAND FOR PRINCESS PRUNELLA.
SELECTION CEREMONY TODAY AT 6 O'CLOCK.

Patrick glanced at the town hall clock. It was nearly six. He'd never been inside the palace before, so he decided to go in and watch the ceremony.

A row of knights was lined up in the throne

room, before the king and his daughter.

One by one, the knights tried to impress them.

"I'm Sir Fit," said the first knight, leaping up. "I can fight longer and harder than anyone else."

"So what?" sighed the princess.

"I'm Sir Prize," said the next. "I've won more tournaments than any knight in the kingdom."

The princess just yawned.

"I'm Sir Loin," said the third knight. "I can eat more in one sitting than any other knight."

"Big deal," sniffed the princess.

Each knight boasted about his skills, but not one of them interested Princess Prunella.

"What about you?" said the king at last, pointing at Patrick.

"Me?" croaked the shepherd boy, turning bright red. "I only came to watch, I mean, I... er... um..."

Patrick didn't know what to say. Then he remembered the magic berries. Quickly, he popped one in his mouth and instantly the words came to him.

"Did you hear about the knight who was as tall as a barn? He's the longest knight of the year."

The princess giggled. Patrick ate another berry.

"What do you call a man with a dragon on his head?" he asked. "Bernie!"

Princess Prunella burst our laughing. "At last!" she gasped. "A man who will make me happy."

"Congratulations, young man," said the king. "You may marry my daughter."

So Patrick and Prunella were married, and they lived very, very happily ever after.

∾ 290 ∾

Yankee Doodle came to town,
Riding on a pony;
He stuck a feather in his cap
And called it macaroni.

∞ 291 ∞

There was an Old Lady whose folly
Induced her to sit in a holly;
Whereupon, by a thorn
Her dress being torn,
She quickly became melancholy.

∞ 292 ∞

There was an Old Man who said, "Well!
Will *nobody* answer this bell?
I have pulled day and night,
Till my hair has grown white,
But nobody answers this bell!"

∞ 293 ∞

There was an Old Man of Dundee,
Who frequented the top of a tree;
When disturbed by the crows,
He abruptly arose,
And exclaimed, "I'll return to Dundee."

all by Edward Lear

Brer Rabbit Gets his Comeuppance

One sunny day, Brer Rabbit was bouncing along – lippety-loppity, lippety-loppity – when he saw Tortoise basking in the sun.

"Look at me!" cried Brer Rabbit, boasting as usual. "I'm the fastest rabbit in the world."

Tortoise wasn't having any of that. *No sir!* "I could beat you in a race," he scoffed. "Meet me tomorrow morning right here. I'll wear a white feather so you can see me in the tall grass. We'll run all the way to that hill and then over three more."

"You're on," said Brer Rabbit.

Tortoise shuffled off to meet his family. "I'm racing Brer Rabbit," he said, "and I need to win. It's high time that boasty trickster was tricked himself. I'm going to give each of you a white feather. Then I want you to stand all along the racetrack – at the top of each hill and at the bottom of each valley. All you have to do is show yourself when Brer Rabbit comes by. Little Brother, you take up the starting point."

The next morning, Brer Rabbit stood alongside Tortoise's brother at the start, completely unaware.

"Ready, get set, GO!" cried an excited fox, and they were off. Brer Rabbit sped away. Plod, plod, plod, went Tortoise's brother.

But as Brer Rabbit came bounding up the first hill, he saw Tortoise trudging along ahead of him. "I thought I'd shot past him," thought Brer Rabbit. He put on a massive burst of speed. "Ha! Take that!"

He reached the bottom of the hill full of glee... but there was Tortoise ahead of him again, his white feather plain to see.

"How can that be?" wondered Brer Rabbit. "He must have crawled past me." He sped past Tortoise once more, but there he was again... at the top of each hill, at the bottom of each valley.

At last, the finish line was in view. "He'll never catch up with me now!" cried Brer Rabbit. Then, "Nooooo!" as Tortoise appeared right by the finishing line. He slowly lifted his foot and was... THE WINNER!

Brer Rabbit flew by in a flash of fur, but it was too late. He had lost the race.

"Three cheers for Tortoise!" cried the crowd.

Brer Rabbit collapsed, exhausted, on the grass. "I still think you're slow-moving," he told Tortoise between panting breaths. "But now I know you're quick-witted too. If only I could work out how you won that race."

Tortoise just smiled. For once, someone had outsmarted Brer Rabbit.

∾ 295 ∾
Algy & the Bear

Algy met a bear,
A bear met Algy.
The bear was bulgy,
The bulge was Algy.

∾ 296 ∾

Solomon Grundy
Born on Monday,
Christened on Tuesday,
Married on Wednesday,
Took ill on Thursday,
Worse on Friday,
Died on Saturday,
Buried on Sunday.
This is the end
Of Solomon Grundy.

∾ 297 ∾

The Lion & the Mouse

As a lion lay snoozing in the shade of a tree, he felt a soft tickle on one whisker. A little mouse was brushing past his nose.

Lazily, the lion reached out a paw, grabbed the mouse and opened his mouth, ready to eat her in one bite.

"Wait!" squeaked the mouse boldly. "If you let me go, one day I'll help you in return."

The lion roared with laughter. "How could a tiny mouse like you ever help a mighty lion like me?" he chuckled. But secretly, he was impressed by the mouse's courage, so he let her go.

Later that day, as the lion stalked proudly along, he was caught in a hunter's net. He struggled with all his might, but that only made the ropes tighter. The lion roared again, this time with terror.

The little mouse heard his cries, and ran to see what had happened. At once, she set to work. Using her sharp teeth, she chewed through the ropes one

by one, nibbling and gnawing for hours until the
lion was free.

"How can I ever thank you?"
the lion asked, full of gratitude.

"No need to thank me,"
the mouse replied. "It was
your kindness in freeing me
that saved your life. But next time, remember,"
she added as she scampered away, "no one is too
small to be helpful."

∽ 298 ∽

There was an old woman of Leeds
Who spent all her time in good deeds;
She worked for the poor
Till her fingers were sore,
This pious old woman of Leeds.

∾ 299 ∾
Sinbad: Voyage Six

After barely a year of luxury in Baghdad, I was desperate to escape, and once again I found myself heading for the coast...

I joined a ship and breathed a sigh of happiness when the shore finally disappeared from view, but the captain was not so content.

"A twirler!" he cried, barely masking his fear.

Only then did I notice the ship turning, slowly at first, then faster and faster. We were caught in a vicious whirlpool and it was pulling us under.

My next memory is of a rocky, desolate beach with a mountain towering above. A handful of sailors had reached the shore with me, but we had nothing to eat. In vain, we scoured the island for food but found only rocks and a stream.

One by one, the other sailors died of hunger, leaving only me. I gazed at my gaunt reflection in the stream... and realized that the stream bed was glittering with rubies and emeralds.

I hastily collected as many as I could, then stopped myself. I needed an escape plan from this barren island, not pockets full of jewels. It was then that I noticed the stream didn't lead into the sea but turned into a dark tunnel in the rock.

"That tunnel must lead somewhere," I thought. "And anywhere is better than here." So I made a raft from driftwood and propelled myself into the tunnel. With a sudden WHOOSH the water carried me off.

I lost all sense of time. Days could have gone by before finally I emerged in a beautiful valley.

Some kindly fishermen took me to their king. He was astounded by my story and gave me all the food and rest I needed to recover. When I offered him jewels in return he flatly refused.

"You might need them for your journey," he advised, and arranged a barge to take me home.

But if you've been following my adventures so far, you'll guess that this isn't the end of my story...

Jabberwocky

'Twas brillig, and the slithy toves
Did gyre and gimble in the wabe;
All mimsy were the borogoves,
And the mome raths outgrabe.

"Beware the Jabberwock, my son!
The jaws that bite, the claws that catch!
Beware the Jubjub bird, and shun
The frumious Bandersnatch!"

He took his vorpal sword in hand:
Long time the manxome foe he sought –
So rested he by the Tumtum tree,
And stood awhile in thought.

And as in uffish thought he stood,
The Jabberwock, with eyes of flame,
Came whiffling through the tulgey wood,
And burbled as it came!

One, two! One, two! And through and through
The vorpal blade went snicker-snack!
He left it dead, and with its head
He went galumphing back.

"And hast thou slain the Jabberwock?
Come to my arms, my beamish boy!
O frabjous day! Callooh! Callay!"
He chortled in his joy.

'Twas brillig, and the slithy toves
Did gyre and gimble in the wabe;
All mimsy were the borogoves,
And the mome raths outgrabe.

Lewis Carroll

This poem comes from *Through the Looking Glass*, the sequel to *Alice's Adventures in Wonderland*. In the story, Humpty Dumpty explains some words: brillig – 4 o'clock; slithy – lithe and slimy; a tove – a cross between a badger, a lizard and a corkscrew; gyre – to go around and around; mimsy – flimsy and miserable; a borogove – a shabby bird; a rath – a sort of green pig; to outgrabe – to bellow, whistle and sneeze all at once.

∾ 301 ∾
Why the Sun & Moon Live in the Sky

Many years ago, the sun and water were great friends, and both lived on Earth together. Every day, the sun would visit the water, but the water never returned his visits.

"Why do you never come to my house?" the sun asked at last.

"It's not big enough," replied the water. "If you want me to visit, you'll have to build a huge house, larger even than your imagination. My people, you see, are numerous, and take up a lot of room."

"I'll build a huge house then," said the sun. And he went straight home to his wife, the moon, and told her what he had promised. The very next day he set to work, building a house. He used the tallest trees, the longest reeds, hay for thatch and hemp for binding. He worked hard until it was done.

"Now come and visit," he said to the water. "I

have a house large enough for you and all your people."

When the water arrived, he called out to the sun. "I am here! Is it safe for me to enter?"

"Yes, yes, come in my friend," said the sun.

"You are welcome!" added the moon.

The water began to flow in, bringing with him all the fish and other creatures of the ocean.

Very soon, the water was knee-deep. "Is it still safe for us to come in?" the water asked.

"Yes, yes," said the sun and moon together. "It's still safe. Keep coming."

When the water was head-high, he said to the sun, "Do you want more of my people to come?"

"Yes, yes," said the sun and moon.

Not knowing any better, the water flowed on, until the sun and the moon were teetering on the top of the roof.

"There's still more," said the water. "Shall we keep coming?"

Again, the sun and moon said, "Yes! Come in." And the water rushed in, more and more and more, overflowing from the top of the roof, so the sun and moon were forced to go up into the sky.

And there they have stayed, ever since.

∾ 302 ∾

She Walks in Beauty Like the Night

She walks in beauty, like the night
Of cloudless climes and starry skies;
And all that's best of dark and bright
Meet in her aspect and her eyes:
Thus mellowed to that tender light
Which heaven to gaudy day denies.

One shade the more, one ray the less,
Had half impaired the nameless grace
Which waves in every raven tress,
Or softly lightens o'er her face;

Where thoughts serenely sweet express
How pure, how dear their dwelling place.

And on that cheek, and o'er that brow,
So soft, so calm, yet eloquent,
The smiles that win, the tints that glow,
But tell of days in goodness spent,
A mind at peace with all below,
A heart whose love is innocent.

Lord Byron

∽ 303 ∽
An Egg

In marble halls as white as milk,
Lined with a skin as soft as silk,
Within a fountain crystal-clear,
A golden apple doth appear.
No doors there are to this stronghold,
Yet thieves break in and steal the gold.

Wynken, Blynken & Nod

Wynken, Blynken, and Nod one night
Sailed off in a wooden shoe,
Sailed on a river of crystal light,
Into a sea of dew.
"Where are you going, and what do you wish?"
The old man asked the three.
"We have come to fish for the herring-fish
That live in this beautiful sea;
Nets of silver and gold have we!"
Said Wynken, Blynken, and Nod.

The old moon laughed and sang a song,
As they rocked in the wooden shoe,
And the wind that sped them all night long
Ruffled the waves of dew.
The little stars were the herring-fish
That lived in the beautiful sea –

"Now cast your nets wherever you wish –
But never afraid are we;"
So cried the stars to the fishermen three:
Wynken, Blynken, and Nod.

All night long their nets they threw
To the stars in the twinkling foam;
Then down from the skies came the wooden shoe,
Bringing the fishermen home.
'Twas all so pretty a sail it seemed
As if it could not be,
And some folks thought 'twas a dream they dreamed
Of sailing that beautiful sea –
But I shall name you the fishermen three:
Wynken, Blynken, and Nod.

Wynken and Blynken are two little eyes,
And Nod is a little head,
And the wooden shoe that sailed the skies
Is a wee one's trundle-bed.
So shut your eyes while mother sings
Of wonderful sights that be,
And you shall see the beautiful things
As you rock in the misty sea,
Where the old shoe rocked the fishermen three:
Wynken, Blynken, and Nod.

Eugene Field

∾ 305 ∾
A Candle

Little Nancy Etticoat,
With a white petticoat,
And a red nose;
She has no feet or hands,
The longer she stands
The shorter she grows.

∞ 306 ∞

Daisy & the Dinosaur

Daisy sighed. She wasn't enjoying the school trip to Mugly's Museum at all. Her class had come to hear a talk by the famous explorer Professor Huntly. But, so far, he had been really boring.

Mrs. Mugly sighed too. This might have to be the very last event at her museum. Apart from the occasional school trip, hardly anyone visited these days. Soon she'd have to close the museum for good.

"...and finally," droned the professor, "I would like to present my latest find to the museum." He whipped a dusty sheet off a stand, to reveal an egg, encased in a slab of ice. "This egg was laid sixty million years ago by a Hadrosaur."

"Wow!" gasped Daisy. "A real dinosaur egg."

"I found it buried in ice at the North Pole," explained the professor.

"Atishoooo!" snorted Mrs. Mugly, just then. The dust from the sheet had gone up her nose. She bumped into her husband, who cannoned into the block of ice, knocking it from the stand.

The ice splintered into a hundred pieces and the egg bounced away, out of sight.

"My egg!" wailed the professor. A search was made of the entire lecture hall, but the precious egg was nowhere to be found.

It wasn't until lunchtime that Daisy discovered what had happened to the egg. She opened her bag to take out her packed lunch... and a baby Hadrosaur shot out, in a shower of egg shell.

The little dinosaur ran through the museum causing chaos. Exhibits went flying, and children ran screaming in all directions.

"It's wrecking my museum," Mrs. Mugly screeched to a guard. "Find it and lock it up!"

Daisy felt sorry for the baby dinosaur. "I won't let them put him in a cage. I must find him first."

She thought for a moment and realized where the

Hadrosaur might go...

Sure enough, there in the prehistoric display room, she found the little dinosaur snuggled up to a model of a mother Hadrosaur.

"Honk!" went the baby.

Mrs. Mugly stormed in with a guard. "There it is!" she shrieked. "Get it!"

"No!" cried Daisy, "Wait!"

"Honk!" cried the Hadrosaur. "Honk! Honk!"

Mrs. Mugly stopped and stared. "My, my," she said softly, "What a lovely, musical sound."

That gave Daisy an idea.

Instead of putting the Hadrosaur in a cage, Mrs. Mugly agreed to add a special concert hall to the museum for him.

Soon, visitors were lining up around the block, and the museum was saved – all thanks to Daisy and the amazing, honking Hadrosaur.

∾ 307 ∾

Jerry Hall,
He is so small,
A rat could eat him,
Hat and all.

∾ 308 ∾

Lucy Locket lost her pocket,
Kitty Fisher found it;
Not a penny was there in it,
Only ribbon round it.

∾ 309 ∾

There was a Young Lady of Ryde,
Whose shoe-strings were seldom untied.
She purchased some clogs,
And some small spotted dogs,
And frequently walked about Ryde.

Edward Lear

∾ 310 ∾
Clever Katy

K aty lived on top of a high hill with her great big husband, Bernie.

Bernie was always boasting about how strong he was, but he never did a stroke of work.

Every day, it was poor Katy who had to walk all the way to the bottom of the hill to get water from the well.

"Are you sure you're the strongest man in the land?" Katy asked her husband, one afternoon.

"Of course," replied Bernie, lazing in a chair.

"Well I just met a man down in the village who said *he's* the strongest," said Katy. "I told him about you, and he's on his way up."

"Oh no!" gulped Bernie. "Did he have a red beard?"

"Yes," said Katy. "Do you know him?"

"That's Big Mac," croaked Bernie. "He really is the strongest man in the land. And he hates anyone who says otherwise."

Katy smiled. She had an idea.

"You can hide in the baby's bed," she told her bemused husband, leading him to the nursery. "Hold this," she added, plonking a large rock on his chest.

At that moment, there came a loud knock at the front door.

"Where's this Bernie?" roared Big Mac. "I'll squash him flat. No one's stronger than me."

"Really?" said Katy, going outside and pointing to a huge log. "Bernie could drive a tree trunk like that into the ground with his bare hands."

"Ha!" laughed Big Mac. "That's easy."

He picked up the log and thrust it so far down that it disappeared, leaving a deep hole.

Katy dropped a pebble into the hole. After a while there was a splash. Katy smiled.

"Now where's Bernie?" boomed Big Mac, striding into the house, followed by Katy.

Big Mac barged into the nursery.

"Please don't wake Bernie Junior,"

Katy begged.

Big Mac looked at the squashed-up – and very muscled – figure. "If that's Bernie's son, Bernie must be enormous," he thought, nervously.

Hearing Big Mac come in had terrified Bernie. He gripped the rock so tightly, it crumbled to pieces.

"That does it," thought Big Mac, with a shiver. "I'm getting out of here, before his dad returns." The terrified giant thundered out of the house and back down the hill.

"Whew!" sighed Bernie, "How can I ever thank you, Katy?"

"Perhaps you can do your share of the chores?" suggested his wife, with a grin. "And you could start by getting some water from the new well that Big Mac was kind enough to make for us."

"Clever Katy," said Bernie proudly.

How Many Crows?

"It is widely supposed that you can answer any question asked of you, Birbal. Let me see if you are worthy of your reputation," Emperor Akbar announced one day to his chief advisor.

"As you please, sir," Birbal replied.

"How many crows have I in my kingdom?" the emperor demanded with a twinkle in his eye.

"Seven thousand, four hundred and thirty-eight," replied Birbal promptly.

"Come now, you mustn't lie to me," chided the emperor. "What if I have someone count them and there turn out to be more?"

"I cannot account for crows who are visiting from other kingdoms," said Birbal solemnly.

"And if there are fewer?" demanded the emperor.

"Nor can I account for those who are away visiting relatives," said Birbal, with a slight bow.

The emperor chuckled. "You really DO have an answer for everything," he said.

∞ 312 ∞

Magpie, magpie, flutter and flee,
Turn up your tail and good luck come to me.
One for sorrow, two for joy,
Three for a girl and four for a boy,
Five for silver, six for gold,
Seven for a secret never to be told.

∞ 313 ∞

It's raining, it's pouring, the old man is snoring.
He went to bed and bumped his head
And couldn't get up in the morning.

Little Trotty Wagtail

Little trotty wagtail, he went in the rain,
And twittering, tottering sideways
he ne'er got straight again.
He stooped to get a worm, and looked up to get a fly,
And then he flew away ere his feathers they were dry.

Little trotty wagtail, he waddled in the mud,
And left his little footmarks, trample where he would.
He waddled in the water-pudge, and waggle went his tail,
And chirrupt up his wings to dry upon the garden rail.

Little trotty wagtail, you nimble all about,
And in the dimpling water-pudge you waddle in and out;
Your home is nigh at hand, and in the warm pig-stye,
So, little Master Wagtail, I'll bid you a good-bye.

John Clare

∞ 315 ∞

Oh, that I were,
Where I would be.
Then I would be,
Where I am not.
But where I am,
There I must be.
And where I would be,
I can not.

∞ 316 ∞

The Poor Soul Sat Sighing

The poor soul sat sighing by a sycamore tree,
Sing all a green willow.
Her hand on her bosom, her head on her knee,
Sing willow, willow, willow.
The fresh streams ran by her, and murmured her moans,
Sing willow, willow, willow.
Her salt tears fell from her, and softened the stones,
Sing willow, willow, willow.

William Shakespeare

∾ 317 ∾
The Three Dogs

Once, there was a poor shepherd who set out to seek his fortune, taking his sheep with him. He had not gone far when he met a man with three dogs.

"Those look like fine sheep," said the man. "Will you trade them for my dogs?"

"I'm not sure, sir," said the shepherd politely. "My sheep can eat grass, but dogs want better food and I haven't the money to buy it."

"Oh no," laughed the man. "My dogs will feed you and make your fortune. This little one, named Salt, will fetch food whenever you wish. The middle-sized one, Pepper, will fight your enemies. And that big, strong one, Mustard, can bite through iron."

The shepherd looked at the smallest dog. "Fetch me some food," he whispered – and it dashed off, returning with a basket of buns. "It works!" he laughed, ruffling the dog's ears in delight.

He gave each dog a bun, munched another himself and went on his way in high spirits, the three dogs trotting faithfully at his heels.

A little way on, he saw a carriage with a crown on the side, and a young woman crying bitterly inside.

"What's the matter?" asked the shepherd kindly.

It was the coachman who replied. "It's a dragon," he said. "It wants to eat the princess here – and if it can't have her, it will burn the whole country."

The shepherd frowned. "It won't do either if I can stop it," he said boldly. "Come on, dogs!" And they followed the carriage to a desolate mountain.

Here the coachman stopped in fear, but the princess and the shepherd went on, until they heard a terrible *roooaaarrr!* A huge, scaly dragon was flying straight for them, flames flickering from its fanged jaws.

"Pepper," called the shepherd. "This is my enemy." The dog growled and leaped up, seizing the dragon by the throat. There was a short, fierce struggle and then the monster lay dead upon the ground. Fire devoured its body, until only its fangs were left. The shepherd picked them up and put them in his pocket.

"You saved my life!" cried the princess, smiling bashfully at her rescuer. "How can I reward you?"

"Your smile is reward enough," said the shepherd. "Now I'm off to see the world, but I'll come and find you as soon as I get back." And so they parted.

The cowardly coachman saw his chance. "I'll tell everyone I killed the dragon," he chuckled. "And if the princess won't promise to go along with my plan, I'll kill her now – and say the dragon did it."

The poor princess was forced to remain silent, while the coachman became a hero. He was given fine clothes and heaps of jewels. The king even offered him the hand of the princess in marriage.

In despair, the princess begged the king to put off the wedding. But after three years, he would delay no longer. Wedding garlands were hung around the town and people were gathering in the squares, when a shepherd with three dogs arrived.

"What's happening?" he asked. When he heard the princess was about to marry her rescuer, he frowned. "*I* killed the dragon!" he said.

The townsfolk didn't believe him. "Liar!" they yelled. "Throw him in jail."

But the shepherd wasn't afraid. As soon as the iron door of his cell banged shut, he whistled for his dogs. "Mustard, get me out of here!" And Mustard bit through the door as easily as butter.

"Salt, fetch me some food – from a royal table, if you please." Salt ran swiftly to the princess. She recognized the little dog and sent it back with a cake wrapped in a note: *Tell the king what you did and save me again!*

Minutes later, there was a commotion outside the palace. Then the shepherd burst in and strode over to the king and the princess, his three dogs snarling at the coachman.

"That man is an impostor," the shepherd declared. "I killed the dragon – look!" And he pulled out the fangs to prove it.

The king was furious. "Take that lying coachman away," he snapped. "And cancel the wedding!"

"Wait," said the shepherd. "The princess was about to marry her rescuer..." He turned to the princess. "Would you like to marry me?"

"Oh yes," she nodded, blushing with happiness.

So the coachman was jailed, and the princess and the shepherd lived happily ever after, with the three dogs by their fireside.

∞ 318 ∞

Higglety, pigglety, pop!
The dog has eaten the mop;
The pig's in a hurry,
The cat's in a flurry,
Higglety, pigglety, pop!

∽ 319 ∾

Scientific Meeting

A foreign scholar was passing through Nasreddin Hodja's home town. Everyone knew he was coming, but nobody could speak his language. They decided that the wise Hodja should be the man to greet him...

Since the scholar and the Hodja had no language in common, they each picked up a stick and drew in the sand.

First, the scholar drew a circle. Then the Hodja drew a line across the circle, dividing it in two. Next, the scholar drew another line, dividing it in four. He indicated three of the parts, then the fourth. The Hodja nodded and drew a swirling spiral through all four parts.

Finally, the scholar raised his hands, palms up, and wiggled his fingers. The Hodja responded by holding out his hands, palm down, and wiggling his fingers. Both men nodded and the meeting was over.

As the scholar continued on his journey, his men asked him what had gone on.

"I told the Hodja that the world is round," explained the scholar, "and he said the equator runs around it. I told him the Earth is three parts water, one part land and he said there are ocean currents and winds. I told him the sun evaporates the water and he said it then returns to the Earth as rain. That Nasreddin Hodja is a very wise man indeed."

Meanwhile the people from the Hodja's town wanted to know all about the scholar.

"There's nothing he likes more than a plate of Turkish baklava," explained the Hodja. "I said I'd happily share it with him. He told me the syrup is made with three parts sugar to one part honey. I reminded him to mix it well. He told me we should cook it over a fire and I suggested sprinkling chopped nuts on top. I wouldn't say he's very scholarly, but at least he has good taste."

∾ 320 ∾

There was an Old Man on a hill,
Who seldom, if ever, stood still;
He ran up and down
In his grandmother's gown,
Which adorned that Old Man on a hill.

∾ 321 ∾

There was an Old Person of Chile,
Whose conduct was painful and silly;
He sat on the stairs
Eating apples and pears,
That imprudent Old Person of Chile.

∾ 322 ∾

There was a Young Lady whose bonnet
Came untied when the birds sat upon it;
But she said, "I don't care!
All the birds in the air
Are welcome to sit on my bonnet!"

all by Edward Lear

∾ 323 ∾

There was an old woman tossed up in a basket,
Seventeen times as high as the moon;
Where she was going I couldn't but ask it,
For in her hand she carried a broom.

Old woman, old woman, old woman, quoth I,
Where are you going to up so high?
To brush the cobwebs off the sky!
May I go with you?
Aye, by-and-by.

∾ 324 ∾

Moonlit Apples

At the top of the house the apples are laid in rows,
And the skylight lets the moonlight in, and those
Apples are deep-sea apples of green. There goes
A cloud on the moon in the autumn night.

A mouse in the wainscot scratches, and scratches, and then
There is no sound at the top of the house of men
Or mice; and the cloud is blown, and the moon again
Dapples the apples with deep-sea light.

They are lying in rows there, under the gloomy beams;
On the sagging floor; they gather the silver streams
Out of the moon, those moonlit apples of dreams,
And quiet is the steep stair under.

In the corridors under there is nothing but sleep.
And stiller than ever on orchard boughs they keep
Tryst with the moon, and deep is the silence, deep
On moon-washed apples of wonder.

John Drinkwater

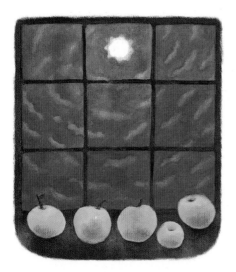

∽ 325 ∾

The Princess
& the Pea

"Will I ever find a real princess?" wondered Prince Henry, one cold, snowy night. He had hunted high and low across the land for a royal bride, without success.

"Be patient dear," said his mother, the queen. "I'm sure the right girl is out there somewhere."

At that very moment, there was a knock at the door. The king opened it, and a howling gale blew through the palace. There stood a pretty young girl, almost frozen to the spot.

"P...please," she stuttered, her teeth chattering with cold. "C...could I shelter here for the night?"

"Of course, Miss...?" said the king.

"Lily," replied the girl, "Princess Lily."

The prince couldn't believe it.

While the king took Lily to warm up by the fire, Henry turned to his mother.

"Do you think she could be a real princess?" he whispered excitedly.

"There's one way to find out," she replied.

Taking a pea from the royal kitchen, she went to the bedroom where Lily was to spend the night and placed the pea under the mattress. Then she told the maids to pile twenty more mattresses on top, followed by twenty feather quilts.

The next morning, Lily joined the royal family at the breakfast table.

"Did you sleep well, my dear?" asked the queen.

"Not a wink, I'm afraid Ma'am," Lily said, with a yawn. "There must have been something hard in the bed. I just couldn't get comfortable."

"Only a real princess would be so sensitive," cried the prince with delight. "Dear Princess Lily, will you marry me?"

Lily had fallen in love with the handsome prince.
"Yes," she replied, her cheeks blushing.

So Henry and Lily were married.
And if you ever visit the Royal Museum,
you'll find a special spot reserved for the
pea that brought them together.

The Sound of the Wind

The wind has such a rainy sound
Moaning through the town,
The sea has such a windy sound,
Will the ships go down?

The apples in the orchard
Tumble from their tree.
Oh will the ships go down, go down,
In the windy sea?

Christina Rossetti

Robin Hood's Golden Prize

"Will you lend me your robes?" Robin Hood asked Friar Tuck one afternoon.

"Why, what mischief are you planning?" said the Friar.

"I'm not sure yet," said Robin, with a grin. "But you never know who you might meet..."

Although the Friar's thick brown robes were a little short on Robin, they disguised him well enough and he strode out of the forest onto the road to Nottingham.

Before long, two monks came riding by, dressed in long white robes.

"My brothers!" called Robin. "Please help me. I have had nothing to eat or drink all day. Could you spare me a coin?"

"Alas we have nothing," the monks replied.

"Then please pray with me," said Robin. "The

Lord listens to those in need..."

The monks couldn't argue with this, so they dismounted their horses and knelt beside Robin.

"Dear Lord, please send us some money," they chanted together. Then the monks looked around and checked their pockets. "Nothing," they sighed.

"I know," said Robin, as if the idea had just come to him, "let's check *each other's* pockets." And reaching deep into the monks' robes he discovered no fewer than 500 gold coins.

"The Lord has blessed us today," said Robin. "And since you both prayed so hard, I'll give you 50 coins each."

Robin gathered up the rest of the money and walked home delighted with himself, leaving behind two very grumpy monks.

∞ 328 ∞

The man in the moon
Came down too soon,
And asked his way to Norwich;
He went by the south,
And burnt his mouth
With supping cold plum porridge.

∞ 329 ∞

There was an old man of Tobago,
Who lived on rice, gruel, and sago;
Till, much to his bliss,
His physician said this –
"To a leg, sir, of mutton you may go."

∞ 330 ∞

There was a little girl, who had a little curl,
Right in the middle of her forehead.
When she was good, she was very, very good,
But when she was bad, she was horrid.

Henry Wadsworth Longfellow

∾ 331 ∾

Lumpy Lenny

Lenny Louis had a problem – a big problem. Poor Lenny had a round, red lump on his nose. It had sprung up a week ago, and it seemed to get bigger every day. He had never felt so miserable.

"Stop grumbling and get it looked at," snapped his wife one day. "Go and see Presto the wizard."

So Lenny went to visit Presto in his cottage.

"Hmm," said the wizard when he saw the lump. "It's certainly a large one." He flicked through his book of magical cures. "Ah ha!" he cried at last. "Here we are – *Lumps and How To Lose Them*. Now, let me see... You must rub the lump with a stone, put the stone in a paper bag and then bury the bag near a crossroads at midnight."

"That seems easy enough," said Lenny.

"But be warned," added Presto. "Whoever opens the bag will catch the lump."

It all sounded rather strange to Lenny, but he was

desperate, so he followed the instructions exactly.

The next morning, Lenny was overjoyed. His lump had vanished in the night.

"Hoorah!" he cried, dancing down the street on his way to work. "Good old Presto's done it."

But when he returned home that evening, he got a shock.

"Look at my nose!" yelled Lenny's wife, as he stepped through the door.

Lenny stared. On the tip of his wife's nose was a big, red, round, lump!

"I heard that someone had buried a bag by the crossroads," she wailed. "I thought it must be treasure, so I dug it up. Presto has told me all about his cure for your lump – now I've got it."

"Never mind, dear," said Lenny, trying not to laugh. "I think it rather suits you."

~ 332 ~

I Had a Little Nut Tree

I had a little nut tree,
Nothing would it bear
But a silver nutmeg
And a golden pear;

The King of Spain's daughter
Came to visit me,
And all for the sake
Of my little nut tree.

∽ 333 ∽
A Walnut

As soft as silk, as white as milk,
As bitter as gall, a strong wall,
And a green coat covers all.

∽ 334 ∽
A Tree

In spring I look gay,
Decked in comely array.
In summer more clothing I wear.
When colder it grows,
I fling off my clothes,
And in winter quite naked appear.

❧ 335 ❧
The Lion & the Hare

Lion was hungry. He was hungry for some hare. He'd been spying on a large hare, frolicking in the fields, but whenever he crept closer the hare lolloped off.

"I'll find out where he lives," resolved Lion, "and give him a nasty surprise..."

Just then, a little mouse scurried by. Lion pinned her tail with his claw. "Tell me where Hare lives," he roared, "or I'll gobble you up."

"Past the hillock by the stream," said the terrified mouse. She didn't want to tell on a friend, but she didn't want to be eaten either.

Lion strode to the stream. When he found Hare wasn't at home, he decided to lie in wait. But hares are canny creatures, especially this one.

On his way home, Hare's ears pricked up: he could sense trouble. His sensitive nose twitched: he could smell trouble. He saw a large paw print – and knew exactly who that trouble was.

"Time for some fun,"
he thought to himself.
"Salaam, House," he called.

His greeting was met
with silence.

"That's strange," he said in
a loud voice. "My house always answers me, but not
today. Perhaps someone is inside…"

Instantly, a gruff voice replied, "Salaam, Hare!"

"Silly Lion!" chuckled Hare, lolloping away.
"Whoever heard of a house that could talk?"

"Wait!" groaned the hungry lion.

But Hare was waiting for no one, and Lion had to
go home with an empty, grumbling stomach.

∾ 336 ∾

Hey diddle diddle, the cat and the fiddle,
The cow jumped over the moon;
The little dog laughed to see such sport,
And the dish ran away with the spoon.

Johnny-head-in-the-air

As he trudged along to school,
It was always Johnny's rule
To be looking at the sky
And the clouds that floated by;
But what just before him lay,
In his way,
Johnny never thought about;
So that every one cried out,
"Look at little Johnny there,
Little Johnny Head-in-air!"

Running just in Johnny's way
Came a little dog one day;
Johnny's eyes were still astray
Up on high,
In the sky;
And he never heard them cry,
"Johnny, mind, the dog is nigh!"

Bump!

Dump!

Down they fell, with such a thump,

Dog and Johnny in a lump!

Once, with head as high as ever,

Johnny walked beside the river.

Johnny watched the swallows trying

Which was cleverest at flying.

Oh! what fun!

Johnny watched the bright round sun

Going in and coming out;

This was all he thought about.

So he strode on, only think!
To the river's very brink,
Where the bank was high and steep,
And the water very deep;
And the fishes, in a row,
Stared to see him coming so.

One step more! oh! sad to tell!
Headlong in poor Johnny fell.
And the fishes, in dismay,
Wagged their tails and swam away.

There lay Johnny on his face,
With his nice red writing-case;
But, as they were passing by,
Two strong men had heard him cry;
And, with sticks, these two strong men
Hooked poor Johnny out again.

Oh! you should have seen him shiver
When they pulled him from the river.
He was in a sorry plight!
Dripping wet, and such a fright!
Wet all over, everywhere,
Clothes, and arms, and face, and hair:
Johnny never will forget
What it is to be so wet.

And the fishes, one, two, three,
Are come back again, you see;
Up they came the moment after,
To enjoy the fun and laughter.
Each popped out his little head,
And, to tease poor Johnny, said,
"Silly little Johnny, look,
You have lost your writing-book!"

Heinrich Hoffmann

❧ 338 ❧
Robin Hood & the King's Disguise

The Sheriff had been making life miserable for the people of Nottingham. While King Richard was away fighting a long and bloody war, the Sheriff was forcing the poor to pay cripplingly high taxes – and using their money to make himself more powerful.

Robin Hood and his men constantly tried to stop the Sheriff, but they faced danger at every turn.

"Do you think the king will ever come home?" asked Little John one day. "Or will we always be outlaws in the forest?"

"I heard he's died in battle," said Will Scarlet.

"I heard he's being held prisoner in the middle of a desert," said Alan a Dale.

"Those are just lies spread by the Sheriff's men," Robin replied. "The king will return, but until he does, we have work to do."

In fact, unknown to the outlaws – and to the

Sheriff – King Richard *had* just returned. He was shocked to hear how the Sheriff had been treating his people... and he was eager to meet Robin Hood.

He and a few knights disguised themselves in hooded cloaks, then rode into the forest.

"Stop right there," said a voice from the trees. Robin Hood swung down on a vine and stood before them. "Who are you and where are you going?"

"Who are you to ask such questions?" the king responded.

"I am Robin Hood the outlaw, and I am protecting the people of England until King Richard returns."

"And how do you do that?" asked the king.

"I take money from the rich to give to the poor," said Robin.

"And do the rich get anything in return?" queried the king, as he took out a purse of gold coins.

"A feast!" Robin replied.

He led the cloaked horsemen to his hideout, where the merry men had prepared a magnificent meal. Roasted venison, partridge and goose were all served on wooden platters, washed down with homemade ale.

"To the king!" toasted Robin.

"To the king!" chimed the king and his knights.

Robin looked suspicious. "Why would you toast our noble king?" he demanded.

"Is he not a good leader?" asked the king.

"The best in the world. But you are servants of that scoundrel Sheriff. You are plundering our country while the king is away."

"No, we are sent by the king, and I give you my word that he will reward you for your loyalty."

"Only the king himself can promise that," said Robin warily.

"You are right," said King Richard, sweeping off his hood to reveal his crown. "Kneel down, Robin Hood," he commanded. "You are no longer an outlaw, you are one of my knights."

"Thank you, Your Majesty," Robin replied, humbly. "I will serve you well. But may I still live in the forest? I rather like it here..."

∾ 339 ∽

Jeremiah

Jeremiah, blow the fire,
Puff, puff, puff!
First you blow it gently,
Then you blow it rough.

∽ 340 ∾
Witches' Chant

Round about the cauldron go:
In the poisoned entrails throw.
Toad, that under cold stone
Days and nights has thirty-one
Sweated venom sleeping got,
Boil thou first in the charmèd pot.
Double, double toil and trouble;
Fire burn and cauldron bubble.

Fillet of a fenny snake,
In the cauldron boil and bake;
Eye of newt and toe of frog,
Wool of bat and tongue of dog,
Adder's fork and blindworm's sting,
Lizard's leg and owlet's wing.
For a charm of powerful trouble,
Like a hell-broth boil and bubble.
Double, double toil and trouble;
Fire burn and cauldron bubble.

Scale of dragon, tooth of wolf,
Witch's mummy, maw and gulf
Of the ravenous salt-sea shark,
Root of hemlock digged in the dark.
Add thereto a tiger's chaudron,
For the ingredients of our cauldron.
Double, double toil and trouble;
Fire burn and cauldron bubble.

William Shakespeare

∞ 341 ∞

Sinbad: Voyage Seven

After six life-threatening adventures I decided it was time to stay on dry land.

"After all," I thought, "soon I'll be too old to travel." Then I panicked. "Oh no! Soon I'll be too old to travel. I'd better go on one last journey."

So I sat calmly on the deck of a ship, heading out into the Arabian Sea. I'd seen storms and whales and shipwrecks and whirlpools and giants. What else could go wrong, I thought, rashly. That's when a giant squid reached its tentacles overboard and dragged the entire ship under the waves.

Somehow I managed to struggle to the surface. I saw a barrel and clung on tightly. "Now I just wait until I reach a shore," I thought.

Sure enough, the barrel eventually washed up on a beach. I explored inland in search of food and drink and discovered a rushing river.

"Ah ha," thought I, "this is where I build a raft and sail off through a dark tunnel to find some friendly people."

So I made a raft out of driftwood and climbed aboard. Only, this river didn't lead me into a tunnel. It rushed faster and faster towards an immense waterfall. There was no way to stop the raft and soon I was plummeting down and down until I suddenly stopped in mid-air. I'd been caught in a huge net.

"Funny sort of fish," an old man observed.

I thanked him for saving my life and he took me home for some food and dry clothes. It was there that I met his beautiful daughter, Emira, and fell in love. I realized I never need travel again. At last, my story was at an end.

"Will you marry me?" I asked her, one evening.

"Oh yes please," said Emira, her eyes sparkling. "We could sail around the world together. I've always wanted an adventure..."

You Are Old,
Father William

"You are old, father William," the young man said,
"And your hair has become very white;
And yet you incessantly stand on your head –
Do you think, at your age, it is right?"

"In my youth," father William replied to his son,
"I feared it might injure the brain;
But now that I'm perfectly sure I have none,
Why, I do it again and again."

"You are old," said the youth, "as I mentioned before,
And have grown most uncommonly fat;
Yet you turned a back-somersault in at the door.
Pray what is the reason for that?"

"In my youth," said the sage, as he shook his grey locks,
"I kept all my limbs very supple
By the use of this ointment – one shilling the box.
Allow me to sell you a couple?"

"You are old," said the youth, "and your jaws are too weak
For anything tougher than suet;
Yet you finished the goose, with the bones and the beak
Pray, how did you manage to do it?"

"In my youth," said his father, "I took to the law,
And argued each case with my wife;
And the muscular strength, which it gave to my jaw,
Has lasted the rest of my life."

"You are old," said the youth, "one would hardly suppose
That your eye was as steady as ever;
Yet you balanced an eel on the end of your nose.
What made you so awfully clever?"

"I have answered three questions, and that is enough,"
Said his father; "don't give yourself airs!
Do you think I can listen all day to such stuff?
Be off, or I'll kick you down stairs!"

Lewis Carroll

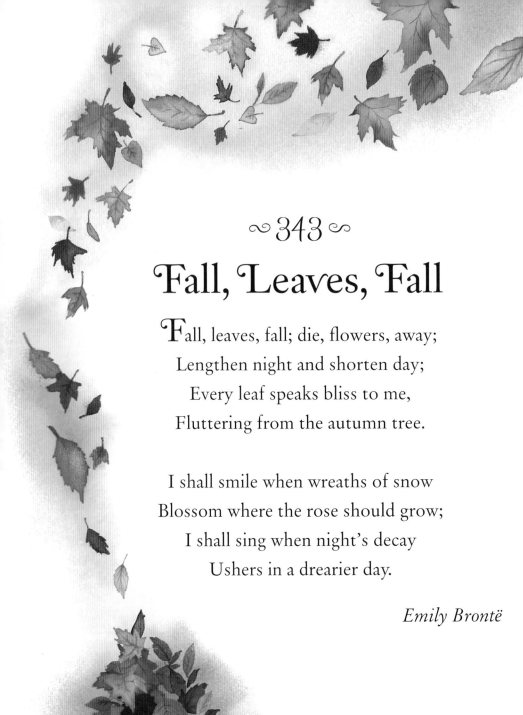

⌇ 343 ⌇

Fall, Leaves, Fall

Fall, leaves, fall; die, flowers, away;
Lengthen night and shorten day;
Every leaf speaks bliss to me,
Fluttering from the autumn tree.

I shall smile when wreaths of snow
Blossom where the rose should grow;
I shall sing when night's decay
Ushers in a drearier day.

Emily Brontë

∞ 344 ∞
The North Wind Doth Blow

The north wind doth blow and we shall have snow,
And what will poor robin do then?
Poor thing.

He'll sit in a barn, and keep himself warm,
And hide his head under his wing.
Poor thing.

∞ 345 ∞
A Robin

I'm called by the name of a man,
Yet I'm little as a mouse.
When winter comes I love to be,
With my red breast near the house.

∾ 346 ∾
The Snow Child

Long ago, in Russia, there lived an old couple who longed for a child. So, one starlit winter evening, they built a child out of snow – a pretty little girl, with dainty curls and a dimpled smile, all white and frozen crisp.

"Dear little one," sighed the woman, kissing the girl's snowy cheek. "I wish you were real." As she spoke, there was a sound like icicles tinkling and the snow moved. The snow child was laughing!

"I *am* real, Mother," she cried, stretching out her frosty arms for a hug. "See?"

"You're as cold as ice," exclaimed the startled woman. "Come in by the fire and have some hot porridge to warm you up."

The girl shook her head. "I must stay in the cold and eat only ice, or I will melt."

So the old woman filled a bowl with crushed ice, and the little snow girl ate it up and licked the spoon.

And when it grew dark, the old man made her a bed of soft snow under the stars.

The three of them lived happily through the winter. But as spring approached, the couple began to be afraid. Would their new daughter melt like the snow? Already green shoots poked through the blanket of white and it was getting hard to find fresh ice for her bowl.

One clear, starry night, as they put her to bed, there was a blaze of light overhead.

"A shooting star," cried the old man. "Quick, make a wish! Wish for what you want most in the world. On a night like this, who knows..." And all three closed their eyes and wished.

The next morning, the couple woke to dazzling sunshine and the drip, drip, drip of melting snow... They rushed outside. "Oh no!" The girl's snowy bed was a puddle of water.

A tinkling laugh rang out behind them. They spun around and saw their little girl – and she wasn't a snow child any more. Dark curls tumbled down

her back, her cheeks glowed pink and her lips were
as red as blood.

The old couple flung their arms around
her. "Our wish came true!"
they sighed happily.
"Mine too,"
whispered the girl.
"Mine too."

∾ 347 ∾
The Cold Old House

I know a house, and a cold old house,
A cold old house by the sea.
If I were a mouse in that cold old house
What a cold, cold mouse I'd be!

∾ 348 ∾

There was an Old Man of the Wrekin,
Whose shoes made a horrible creaking;
But they said, "Tell us whether
Your shoes are of leather,
Or of what, you Old Man of the Wrekin?"

∾ 349 ∾

There was an Old Man who supposed
That the street door was partially closed;
But some very large rats
Ate his coats and his hats,
While that futile Old Gentleman dozed.

∾ 350 ∾

There was an Old Person of Basing,
Whose presence of mind was amazing;
He purchased a steed,
Which he rode at full speed,
And escaped from the people of Basing.

all by Edward Lear

∾ 351 ∾

The Bear Son

In a land far away to the north, where the ground is thick with snow, a little old woman lived by the shores of a frozen sea.

For company, she had a polar bear cub, given to her by a hunter who had slain its mother. She called him little nanoq, and each night she went to sleep with the bear cub beside her, curled up in a snow-white ball.

At first, the cub played with the children in the village, and the old woman would say, "Remember, little nanoq, you must put your claws away." And he did. But after a while, he grew too strong to play with the children, so he wrestled and tussled with the men instead, and they rode on his back. The bear grew stronger and stronger.

That winter, the men looked at the bear and said, "We call him little nanoq, but he is as big as an iceberg. Let us take him with us when we go hunting. He may help us catch seals."

When she heard this, the old woman wove little nanoq a collar. "Now everyone will know you are mine," she said, "and that you are not to be harmed."

That day, with the bear's help, the men caught many seals, and he went out with them each day after that, hunting on the ice in winter, creeping up on the seals in summer as they slept.

And when the bear returned, he and the old woman would share his catch. They would sit together in the door of her hut, and the old woman would point to the shining stars. "There is the Great Bear," she said. "Like you, he fell into the hands of men. And when he died, he became wonderfully bright, and rose up as stars in the sky."

But then a new band of hunters came from beyond the mountains. They had heard of the bear who must not be killed, and the chief hunter said, "Of all the animals we hunt, the nanoq is the most prized. And this is the greatest nanoq of them all. If I ever see that bear, I will kill it."

When the old woman heard this, she wept, for she knew what she had to do. "You cannot stay here, little nanoq, even though you are like my own son. If you stay among men you will die."

And the bear thrust its muzzle into the palm of her hand, its black eyes sad.

The old woman waited until the frost melted in the sun, and the sky was clear of clouds. Then she said, "It is time for you to leave. Travel north, across the sea of ice. There you will find your own kind."

As the bear turned to go, the old woman dipped her hand in oil and smeared it in soot. Then she stroked her hand along its side, leaving a broad black line. The bear looked at her one last time, and walked away across the sea of ice.

Spring turned to summer. The ground was no longer white, but bright with flowers. Geese flew overhead. Each time hunters passed through the village, the old woman asked, "Have you seen a great white bear, with a broad black streak on its side?"

But the hunters always shook their heads, and the old woman sighed.

Then, at last, as the waters began to freeze again, hunters came from the far north, with tales of a great white bear, as big as an iceberg, with a broad black streak on its side.

"So he is alive," said the old woman. And in the long winter evenings, she looked up at the stars, at the Great Bear in the sky. And she thought of her bear, living far away, and smiled.

∞ 352 ∞

Cross-patch,
Draw the latch,
Sit by the fire and spin;
Take a cup,
And drink it up,
Then call your good friends in.

∽ 353 ∾

Ice Dragon

One chilly winter evening, George and Jane were out walking when they noticed a strange glow in the sky.

"It must be the Northern Lights," said Jane.

"Let's see if we can find them," suggested George.

So they turned North. As they walked, it grew colder and colder. Before long, they were crunching through thick snow. They even saw a polar bear.

A little later, they came to a road paved with ice and lined with frosty trees. Moonbeams and stars were strung along the trees to light the way, and a sign pointed: THIS WAY TO THE NORTH POLE.

"Come on," cried George. They went skidding and sliding down the road, faster and faster... until suddenly it ended and they tumbled into a soft snowy heap. Above them towered a column of ice, surrounded by strangely glowing fires.

"That must be the North Pole," breathed Jane.

"And the Northern Lights," added George.

There was something else around the Pole, too – something made of glassy ice, with an icy blue heart.

"It's a dragon!" exclaimed Jane. "Made of ice."

Just then, a flock of snow geese flapped overhead. The wind from their wings made the strange fires flicker and go out. Without the fires, the air grew colder and colder. CRACK! Woken by the sudden chill, the ice dragon broke away from the ice.

"It's heading for the road," said George. "If we're quick, we can hitch a lift."

So they crawled up the dragon's tail onto its back. Soon, they were flying back up the icy road, faster and faster, until... bump! They landed right back in their own garden, where a bonfire was blazing merrily – and the ice dragon melted away.

"What an adventure," sighed Jane, stumbling to her feet. Then she yawned. "It's been a long night."

"Come on, let's go in," said George. "I think it's time for bed."

∞ 354 ∞

Snow in the Suburbs

Every branch big with it,
Bent every twig with it;
Every fork like a white web-foot;
Every street and pavement mute:
Some flakes have lost their way,
   and grope back upward, when
Meeting those meandering down
   they turn and descend again.
The palings are glued together like a wall,
And there is no waft of wind with the fleecy fall.

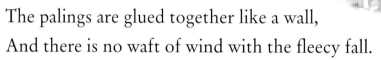

A sparrow enters the tree,
Whereon immediately
A snow-lump thrice his own slight size
Descends on him and showers his head and eyes,
And overturns him,
And near inurns him,
And lights on a nether twig, when its brush
Starts off a volley of other lodging lumps with a rush.

The steps are a blanched slope,
Up which, with feeble hope,
A black cat comes, wide-eyed and thin;
And we take him in.

Thomas Hardy

∽ 355 ∽

Jeremiah Obadiah

Jeremiah Obadiah puff, puff, puff,
When he gives his messages,
He snuffs, snuffs, snuffs,
When he goes to school by day,
He roars, roars, roars,
When he goes to bed at night,
He snores, snores, snores,
When he goes to Christmas treat,
He eats plum-duff,
Jeremiah Obadiah, puff, puff, puff.

∽ 356 ∾

The Hazelnut Child

Once there was a couple with no children. They prayed for one every night, even if it were no bigger than a hazelnut. At last, their prayers were answered. They were given a child exactly the same size as a hazelnut, and he never grew an inch.

The couple loved the child and cared for him, and he was both clever and wise. One day, when the

hazelnut child was fifteen years old, and sitting in an eggshell on the table beside his mother and father, he turned to them and said, "I am going to set out into the world, and as soon as I have

become rich, I shall come back to you."

The parents laughed at their little son's words. They did not believe him for a moment. But that evening, the hazelnut child crept onto the roof, where two storks had built their nest. He climbed on the back of the father stork, then he crept among its soft downy feathers and fell asleep.

The next morning, the storks flew south for winter. The hazelnut child flew through the air on the stork's back until he came to a far-off land, baked dry by the heat of the sun. When the people saw the hazelnut child, they were astonished and took him with the stork to their king.

The king was delighted and kept the hazelnut child with him always. He grew so fond of the little boy that he gave him a diamond almost as big as the boy himself.

"Now I can return home at last," thought the hazelnut child, and he fastened the diamond under the stork's neck with a ribbon. When it was time for the stork to make its northern flight, he climbed onto its soft downy feathers once more, and away they went. They flew over mountains. They flew over seas and oceans until, at last, they came to the hazelnut child's village.

He undid the ribbon from
around the stork's neck so
the diamond tumbled to the
ground. Then the hazelnut child went after it,
dragging it down the path to his parents' house.

"I'm back," he called. "And look at the treasure
I've brought."

"Our hazelnut child! You've returned!" cried his
parents, overjoyed to see him.

And so the hazelnut child and his parents lived
for the rest of their days in wealth and happiness.

∞ 357 ∞

Flour of England, fruit of Spain,
Met together in a shower of rain;
Put in a bag, tied round with a string;
If you'll tell me this riddle,
I'll give you a ring.

This riddle was popular with carol singers in the 19th century.
The answer is Christmas pudding.

∞ 358 ∞

The White Queen's Poem

First, the fish must be caught.
That is easy: a baby, I think, could have caught it.
Next, the fish must be bought.
That is easy: a penny, I think, would have bought it.

Now cook me the fish!
That is easy and will not take more than a minute.
Let it lie in a dish!
That is easy because it already is in it.

Bring it here! Let me sup!
It is easy to set such a dish on the table.
Take the dish-cover up!
Ah, that is so hard that I fear I'm unable!

For it holds it like glue –
Holds the lid to the dish, while it lies in the middle:
Which is easiest to do,
Un-dish-cover the fish, or dishcover the riddle?

Lewis Carroll

The answer is an oyster.

The Tinder Box

A poor soldier was on his way back from a war, wondering how he would survive on the few coins in his pocket, when he met a witch.

"I can make you rich," she offered. "Just climb into that hollow tree. Underneath is a cave with a chest full of silver."

"Great!" cried the soldier. "Do you want a share?"

The witch shook her head. "I never touch silver," she said. "All I want is my grandmother's tinder box. It's down there somewhere." She handed the soldier an apron. "The chest is guarded by a fierce dog, but put the dog on this and he won't hurt you."

The soldier climbed down the tree into the cave – and there was the treasure chest, complete with guard dog. Gently, he lifted the dog onto the apron, before cramming his bag full of silver. He was about to head back up, when he remembered the tinder box. After scrambling around in the dark for a while, he

Tinder boxes were used for starting fires before matches were invented. Each box contained a flintstone, a piece of steel and some tinder (cloth or straw). Hitting the steel with the flint made sparks. The sparks set light to the tinder. The tinder could be used to light firewood or candles.

found a little brass box and clambered back up the tree. But, as he jumped out, a coin fell from his bag and hit the witch.

"Agh! Not silver!" she screamed, exploding in a cloud of smoke.

The soldier felt terrible, but there was nothing he could do. So he headed to the nearest town and found an inn. That night, he went to bed without feeling hungry for the first time in months. The next day, he bought some clothes, and then began sharing his good fortune. Within a month, the money was all gone.

Sitting in his dark, cold attic, he remembered the tinder box once again. "I wonder why the witch wanted this?" he thought, striking it. At once, the dog from the cave appeared.

"What is your command?" it barked.

The soldier gasped. "Can you give me anything at all? Because, if you don't mind, I need more money."

Minutes later, the dog returned with a bag stuffed with gold. The soldier was even richer than before. Soon, he was living in a grand house in the very middle of town.

One afternoon, the king and queen rode by in a gleaming carriage. The townspeople ignored them.

"Why is no one cheering?" the soldier asked.

"We don't like them," a maid replied. "They keep the princess locked up so no one can see her."

"Poor thing," thought the soldier. "*I'd* like to see her. Just for a moment." That evening, he took out the tinder box and summoned the dog. Eager to obey, the dog brought the sleeping princess to the soldier's house. The soldier fell in love at once.

When the princess awoke the next morning, she told her parents of a strange dream she'd had about a visit to a handsome soldier.

The king and queen were horrified. "What if it wasn't a dream," they asked each other. So, when the princess was asleep, the queen tied a tiny bag of flour to her nightdress, and cut a hole in the bag.

The next morning, they followed the flour trail from their castle to the soldier's house.

"No one may see the princess!" roared the king at the soldier. "You'll be executed at dawn tomorrow."

Just before sunrise, the soldier saw his maid in the street outside his prison cell. "Please would you bring me my tinder box?" he asked.

She hurried home for the box and passed it to him through the cell bars.

At dawn, the soldier was led outside. The crowds begged for mercy.

"Silence!" bellowed the king.

The executioner stepped forward... and the soldier opened the tinder box and made a spark.

"Punish the king and queen!" he commanded the dog, the second it appeared.

With a spine-tingling growl, the dog chased them from the kingdom. The soldier rescued the princess and married her that afternoon. The new king and queen ruled wisely and well. Everyone adored them and they met cheering crowds wherever they went.

∽ 360 ∽
Speak of the North

Speak of the North! A lonely moor
Silent and dark and tractless swells,
The waves of some wild streamlet pour
Hurriedly through its ferny dells.

Profoundly still the twilight air,
Lifeless the landscape; so we deem
Till like a phantom gliding near
A stag bends down to drink the stream.

And far away a mountain zone,
A cold, white waste of snow-drifts lies,
And one star, large and soft and lone,
Silently lights the unclouded skies.

Charlotte Brontë

∾ 361 ∾
The Wind

When the wind is in the east,
It's neither good for man nor beast.
When the wind is in the north,
The skilful fisher goes not forth.
When the wind is in the south,
It blows the bait in fishes' mouths.
When the wind is in the west,
Then it's at the very best.

∾ 362 ∾
Winter

Cold and raw the north wind doth blow,
Bleak in the morning early.
All the hills are covered with snow,
And winter's now come fairly.

∽ 363 ∽

Holly Leaf

Highty tighty, paradighty,
Clothed all in green,
The king could not read it,
No more could the queen.
They sent for the wise men,
From out of the East,
Who said it had horns,
But was not a beast.

∽ 364 ∽

Christmas is coming, the geese are getting fat.
Please to put a penny in the old man's hat.
If you haven't got a penny, a ha'penny will do.
If you haven't got a ha'penny, then God bless you!

∽ 365 ∽

Snow White & Rose Red

Deep in the forest, in a little cottage covered with climbing ivy, lived two sisters named Snow White and Rose Red. One snowy night, as they sat by the fire, there was a heavy knock at their door.

"Who can it be?" wondered Snow White, drawing back the bolt. "Oh!" Outside stood a huge, black bear. She glanced anxiously at her sister.

"I won't hurt you," growled the bear. "Please, I just want to warm myself at your fire."

"Come in," said Rose Red bravely.

The bear shook the snow from his coat and lay down quietly by the hearth. He seemed so gentle, the sisters lost all fear. They stroked his thick black fur and tickled his tummy, and all three were soon the best of friends.

In the morning, the bear left – but he came back again that evening, and for many evenings after. But as the days grew warmer, he began to look sad.

"What's the matter, Bear?" asked Snow White.

"I must leave you for a while," he answered. "I am hunting for a wicked dwarf. In winter, he hides away underground. When the ground thaws, he will be back to make more mischief – unless I stop him."

The next day, they said their goodbyes. As the bear padded away, a bramble thorn caught a tuft of his fur. Snow White thought she glimpsed something golden beneath. But before she could say anything, he was gone.

A few days later, the sisters were gathering firewood when they spotted a little man hopping up and down, his long beard snarled in a prickly bush.

"Hurry up," he snapped. "Get me out of here."

Snow White and Rose Red did their best, but they couldn't untangle the beard. In desperation, Snow White pulled out her scissors... *snippety-snip.*

"How dare you cut my beard!" howled the man. He stomped off, dragging a heavy sack with him.

The next day, the sisters were out by the river

when they saw the little man again. He was jumping around, trying to free his beard from a fishing line – while a huge fish tugged on the other end. The fish was so strong, the man was almost in the water.

"Hurry up," he yelled. "Get this off me."

Again, Snow White and Rose Red tried to free the beard, but it was no use. So Snow White pulled out her scissors... *snippety-snip.*

"Fools," shrieked the little man. "You cut it again!" And he stomped away, still dragging his sack.

Some days later, the sisters were walking to the village when they saw the little man for a third time. Just then, an eagle swooped down and lifted him and his sack into the air. Snow White and Rose Red grabbed his feet, pulling until the eagle let go and they tumbled into the dust.

"Clumsy oafs," grumbled the little man, getting to his feet. He yanked his sack so hard, it split. The sisters gasped. Bright jewels poured out, sparkling in the sunshine. "What are you looking at?" he snarled.

He pulled out a knife and took a step towards them.

There was a growl behind him. A great black bear was heading straight at him. The little man turned pale. "Stop," he pleaded. "I didn't steal your treasure, it was these girls." But the bear didn't pause. With a terrible roar, it lifted a huge paw... *pow!* The wicked dwarf – for it was he – lay lifeless on the ground.

Snow White and Rose Red started to run away.

"Please don't go!" came a familiar voice.

"Bear?" whispered Snow White, turning back.

But the bear was no longer there. In his place stood a handsome, black-haired prince wearing a golden crown. "That wicked dwarf turned me into a bear and stole my treasure," he told them. "Now he is dead, the spell is broken. Thank you for your help," he added, a little shyly. "I hope we can still be friends now I'm human." Snow White and Rose Red nodded.

"Of course!" they said together.

And in fact, they became more than friends. In time, Snow White and the Bear Prince fell in love and married, then Rose Red married the prince's brother, and they all lived happily ever after.

∽ 366 ∽
Thirty Days Hath September

Thirty days hath September,
April, June, and November;
All the rest have thirty-one,
Excepting February alone,
And that has twenty-eight days clear
And twenty-nine in each leap year.

With 365 stories and rhymes, you have a story or rhyme for every day of the year. This final rhyme is for leap years.

Index

Stories retold by

Susanna Davidson, Katie Daynes, Rosie Dickins, Sam Lake,
Anna Milbourne, Russell Punter, Will Severs and Abigail Wheatley

Illustrations by

Barry Ablett, Lorena Alvarez, Galia Bernstein, Stephen Cartwright,
Cynthia Decker, Francesca di Chiara, Linda Edwards, Mauro Evangelista,
Laure Fournier, Christyan Fox, Mike and Carl Gordon,
Daniel Howarth, Raffaella Ligi, Katie Lovell, Anna Luraschi,
Alan Marks, Rocío Martínez, Gustavo Mazali,
Paddy Mounter, Mike Phillips, Nick Price, Silvia Provantini,
Lisa Rackwitz, Laura Rigo, Angelo Ruta, David Semple, Cathy Shimmen,
Nicola Slater, Joe Todd Stanton, Kristina Swarner, Christa Unzner,
Amandine Wanert, Richard Watson, Phillip Webb and Norman Young

Edited by Lesley Sims
Designed by Sam Chandler and Caroline Day
Additional designs by Josephine Thompson
Digital imaging by Nick Wakeford